The Gathering

The Tavern where evil gathers for a cold beer

F.R. RIVERS

authorHOUSE®

AuthorHouse™
1663 Liberty Drive
Bloomington, IN 47403
www.authorhouse.com
Phone: 1 (800) 839-8640

Published by AuthorHouse 08/30/2019

ISBN: 978-1-7283-2407-4 (sc)
ISBN: 978-1-7283-2405-0 (hc)
ISBN: 978-1-7283-2406-7 (e)

Library of Congress Control Number: 2019912258

This is a work of fiction. All of the characters, names, incidents, organizations, and dialogue
in this novel are either the products of the author's imagination or are used fictitiously.

Print information available on the last page.

This book is printed on acid-free paper.

CONTENTS

PROLOGUE

For well over three decades, I've held off revealing this information. I wrote down the very strange incidents which took place many years ago with the intent of sharing them... but only at the right time. I memorialized the events of that strange, stormy evening because I figured the awful visions and the memory of the terrible discoveries would surely fade in time. They have not. I can still recall these nefarious characters and their dreadful secrets as if I'd learned about them yesterday.

First, I have to be brutally honest with the reader of this tale of horror. If you are easily offended by rough language and crude and, oftentimes, graphic descriptions, you may want to put this book down and pick up a touchy feely replacement that may better suit your softer nature. This story is not for the faint of heart. Furthermore, it is important that you know that when I wrote this accounting of an evening which opened my eyes to the darker side of the human spirit, it was well before the age of the political correctness craze that now permeates our society.

I could, with my daughter in-law's help and the few months remaining before the grim reaper comes for me, edit out the rough spots and make it more socially acceptable. However, as I lay here with a clear mind and little time left to live, I just don't give a damn if feelings are hurt. Perhaps this attitude makes for a better story. Perhaps not.

Stage four lung cancer. Shortly after hearing my diagnosis, I recalled my father's last piece of advice before he passed away so many years ago:

"Son, when your time is near an end, you'll find your last days pleasantly liberating". He added, "You don't feel the need to pussyfoot around people's feelings."

Another pearl of wisdom from my father was, "If you find yourself in a conflict and wanting to say something in the heat of the moment, just say what's on your damn mind." Chuckling, "It will be the best thing you ever regret saying".

As he drew closer to the end of his life, he told me on more than one occasion "You can please some of the people all the time, you can please all of the people some of the time, but you can't please all of the people all of the time".

I had always considered that a profound statement by my father. However, I soon learned that he'd taken it from an Abraham Lincoln speech. My father just portrayed it as his own. I'm sure he knew it, but like he said, he didn't feel the need to pussyfoot around about the source of his supposed brilliance. I find it more than just a little amusing that Abraham Lincoln apparently didn't give a shit either, because he took the quote from a famous poet named John Lydgate.

It is at this stage of my life that I find myself in complete agreement with my father, and I've carried this new attitude with me since my diagnosis. I'm guessing this might explain why my friends no longer stop by... or maybe they're all dead.

Since the day the Oncologist illuminated my fate, my perspectives on life have changed dramatically as my father had so ably forecasted. Although I don't want to die —who does— I find this particular period of my life as bleak as it is peaceful... and fantastically liberating. But most of all, I have a clarity of mind I don't think I've ever experienced. I have contemplated, for some time, how to explain the 'clarity of mind' statement, but honestly, I think it's beyond me. Trust me... or not. I won't lose sleep over that. Ahh, there is that liberating feeling I mentioned.

After being diagnosed, I thought I'd look to God to ease my pain, but, alas, that has not been the case. The tranquility I've found is in my family and my cantankerous way of saying whatever I want, wherever I want, whenever I want. That is true power. It can also label you a mean old asshole, but I digress.

As you know, this newly found clarity came soon after my diagnosis of stage four lung cancer several weeks ago. How on earth could I have this form of cancer when I've never smoked a day in my life? It turns out that just hanging out with smokers can do the trick. Lucky me.

Once I passed the whole "It's not fair stage" as well as a few other "stages," I soon figured out that it takes imminent death or old age to obtain this glorious feeling of clarity. Have you ever contemplated why old people just say what they want? It's because they either got my father's advice or learned to let go of tiptoeing around thorny everyday issues on their own. It's the reason they ask all those Goddamn nosey questions that are none of their business, such as, "When are you gonna get married?" "When are you going to meet a nice girl?", "When are we going to be grandparents?", "Why did you break up with your last girlfriend?" "Are you gay?" "When are you going to get a real job?" They ask these questions because they've reached clarity of mind, which, in the end, liberates them to say what they want. It could also be senility, but I'm gonna go with my "clarity" theory; it sounds much more provocative, and it's my book. Again, quite liberating, don't you think?

I am sure you've heard the expression "Life is for the living." Well, in my humble opinion — and after many hours contemplating this poorly thought out expression while lying in my deathbed and filling my bedpan — I gotta say with all the emphasis possible, "Bullshit". It's my honest to God belief that "Life is for the dying". As I lay in my bed night after night, I've often pondered, do prisoners on death row, in the course of eating their last meal preceding their date with the chair or needle, savor every bite? As they take each bite, do they feel as if they've never truly enjoyed food before? Does it make them think of their mother's cooking?

How about a soldier that clings to life despite being cut in half by some man-made death machine? I reminisce about that soldier's last dying moment in the field. Does he still harbor some resentment toward a friend or family member for a minor slight, or is he looking at his last sunset thinking it is the most beautiful sight he'd ever seen?

I believe that these people are experiencing the comparable clarity that I feel now, however, in a far more dramatic and extreme scenario. It is my conclusion on this thought that at no other point in your life, will you feel more alive than when you are near death. If that does not make sense to you now, don't worry; it will.

It is now some thirty years after my first evening at The Last Call, and once my heart stops beating, this book will be released to the public for your perusal, assuming a publisher deems it worthy. This story will either be of great interest... or not. Won't matter to me. I'll be dead. Ahh, there is that beautiful feeling of liberating clarity yet again. Are you sensing a pattern here?

As I mentioned before, my beautiful daughter in-law is helping me type the prologue and the epilogue since I am not able to sit up for longer than 10 minutes without losing my latest meal, which I've worked too hard to keep down. As I lie here dictating the opening to this story about an evening that occurred so long ago, my daughter in-law understands that she is not to change a single damn word. Also, to prove what a prick I am, she understands that I would haunt her for the rest of her life if she does not meet that requirement. I've caught her rolling her eyes, and we share a light laugh. I know she will do me proud. I am so proud of my son; he turned into a great young man and married a terrific young lady. I could not have picked a better woman for him if I had a million attempts. I know my rough language occasionally upsets her as it did with my late wife and I know she'd love to edit the hell out of this story, but she's a big girl. She can take it.

I'll conclude this prologue by doing what I first intended before my rant about "clarity" and all its spectacular attributes—I will prepare you as best I can for the gruesome tale to come.

First of all, there will be many visions involved in this book of events that did happen, and they occur in several different perspectives. These are not visions that occur like a town fair, wing-nut psychic would have when they try to tell you what will happen in your future. What makes these visions different, and extremely intense, is that they were visions of what had already happened many years ago. The perspectives will change frequently. Many of the vision timelines might seem disjointed, but that is how I saw them. I am sure the reader will make sense of the various forms of visions as I did, because, trust me, I am no rocket scientist. (If you've not figured that out by now, you might want to hold off forwarding your resume to NASA.)

The awful and quite often disturbing visions I experienced that terrible evening were amazingly intense. When I described this to my daughter in-law and struggled to come up with the most accurate term, she thought I should say HD quality visions. It is still not a perfect term for these visions; however, it's a lot closer than anything I've come up with.

These visions draw you in; you are powerless to look away, similar to the way a car wreck holds your attention. Some may be streamlined and others fragmented. They will also appear to be from different perspectives or vantage points. Lastly, the visions tell stories… and sometimes a story within a story. Another aspect to this evening's strange happenings is the ESP moments, but that will be discussed later.

There was a time I considered sending this bizarre story to a publisher as a tale of fiction; however, I thought it better to release the events of this terrible stormy night in their true form. Time will tell if I made the right decision.

CHAPTER 1

My Arrival

"If you don't know where you're going,
you'll end up someplace else."

— Yogi Berra

I don't know if I'll ever share the events of this evening, but if you are reading this story, my name is James Riordan, and, yes, most people call me Jim. I'm a married man living a normal life in the suburbs with a small but beautiful family. I work a nine a.m. to five p.m. job in the city, and the commute sucks; however, it's a small price to pay. My lovely wife and I have two handsome boys. The older one is rapidly approaching his teenage years, which means I'll be drinking less water and far more alcohol in the near future. My younger son is five and he's a handful. Also, we are the proud owners of a large pain in the ass dog named Ralphie. The dog pays dividends in the yard as he keeps me alert. If I'm not paying attention when I'm walking in the yard, I could seriously injure myself in one of the many holes that he digs— more holes than the entire western front of World War 1. It was all blissfully ordinary, which was absolutely fine by me.

The evening that I am about to share with you was a Friday night, February, 1986. Heavy gusts of snow whipped at forty miles per hour. To make matters worse, the road I was traveling on was wrapped heavily in a thick fog due to the unseasonably warm day preceding my trip. I'd just transported my then nine-year-old son and his three friends to a cub scout weekend sleepover over the Connecticut border in Rhode Island.

This snow storm — predicted to arrive much later that evening, allowing ample time to safely complete my commute— arrived a few hours early thanks to Mother Nature deciding to make things interesting. The temperature, which had been hovering in the upper forties most of the day, dropped dramatically upon our arrival at the camp, and within ten minutes, a heavy, wet snow, accompanied by fog, began to cover the roads. The trip home ordinarily would have been about an hour and ten minutes, but this was anything but ordinary. After an hour of very stressful driving, I had not made much headway in my trip home.

It seemed as though I'd been driving forever, and each terrible driver I encountered seemed to age me another year. How do people live in the northeast all their lives and still not know how to drive in inclement weather? I apologize in advance for my random tangents, I can certainly go on a rant with the best of 'em.

As my vehicle crested the top of a long hill, I noticed through the dense snow and fog an oddly blinking restaurant sign. The name seemed to read "The Last Call", which took me a couple moments to confirm as a couple of the letters were not fully lit. I was actually surprised that something was open in this kind of foul weather. It looked like one of those dreary local joints that inhabit every rural town. Though the building didn't appear overly welcoming—nor was it the type of place I would have stopped if I were just traveling through under normal conditions—I needed a break in the worst way.

I kicked common sense to the curb and pulled into the parking lot. The full assault of Mother Nature greeted me and—if I didn't know any better—I'd swear it was trying to push me back to my car. I stood at the unopened door for a few moments, quickly growing colder. A bead of snow melted on my neck and made its way down my back. It encouraged me to push the door open.

I entered the smoke-filled establishment containing a whopping four people sitting at the bar, plus the bartender. Not a word was spoken, and not a single patron looked in my direction. I glanced around the rundown bar. A juke-box playing very softly in the corner caught my attention. I had to concentrate to make out the song "Love Hangover" by Diana Ross. The

irony of that title and the tempo in a bar filled with worn out customers...
well, if I wasn't so tired, I would have chuckled.

There were no diners at the tables or booths, and judging by the layers
of dust, I don't think anyone had dined there in some time. That was all
right, I'd be happy with just a drink since I was not nearly hungry enough
to inquire about the menu...if one existed. The eventual looks I received
from these patrons and the bartender after my entry was somehow both
welcoming and forlorn. It was uncomfortable, that much was for sure. Sadly,
I would soon learn why.

Trying to relax from the hazardous driving conditions, I settled into
a stool at the bar, but my discomfort continued. A mirror ran the full
distance of the bar that could easily seat a dozen people with ample room.
My impression was that the bar was far too large for the building it's in.
The bottles, of all shapes, sizes, and colors were fully stocked on two tiered
display shelves just below and in front of the mirror with whatever you
could possibly think of. The display was odd since everyone in the bar was
drinking beer, and all the beers were in bottles, not a frosty cold mug in the
room. This was not a crowd that enjoyed a frosty mug or mixed drinks. I
blinked when the mirror behind the bar gave off small, intense flashes of
light. I looked around for the source of the reflections, but found nothing.

These bright red flashes — like distant lightning in your peripheral
vision — was confusing and jarring. A torrent of extremely-graphic,
explosively fast visions assaulted my mind. The visions involved many
different people, and everything I saw seemed disjointed; they didn't make
sense. I gripped the edge of the bar, shakily wiped my brow, and looked to
see if anyone noticed my discomfort. I thought, "It's just the stress from the
road. I'm tired, too, damn it. When the hell is the bartender going to take
my order?"

The bartender eventually got around to me. Slowly walking over, he
said, "Hiya, we have a two drink minimum. What do ya have?."

I ordered my beer, and he swiftly returned with the drink and welcomed
me to his establishment. I told him that I was just passing through, and
the driving was treacherous and extremely stressful. He said, "You gotta
be somewhere, you may as well be where you belong," and abruptly left to
resume his conversation with a crazy looking one-legged woman at the end
of the bar.

It was a strange thing to say, and I had no idea what he meant, but honestly, I didn't care. I was just thankful I was far enough from home for nobody to recognize me having a beer in such a dive.

As I sat with my untouched drink, my gaze moved to the large clock on the wall. It was six-thirty p.m. The time was made more obvious with the half hour chime sounding. I'd head home when I finished my second beer. As I sat and pondered the weather and the crappy driving conditions, I again glanced at the mirror. Yet another flash, followed vigorously by silent quick scenes of violence. The visions were as fast as they were brutal. They were like the old "*Howard Cosell Monday Night Football* hi-lites without the volume and the blood. Placing my face in both hands, trying to shield the flashing and the terrible scenes, I contemplated whether or not I was having an unknown, serious, medical mishap. It was then that I noticed, to my dismay, an old man walking toward me. I was in no mood for company.

CHAPTER 2

Ken

**"I wrote a song about dental floss but
did anyone's teeth get cleaner?"**

— Frank Zappa

The person approached very slowly. He was a strange looking man with small, shifty eyes who appeared to be in his late 60's or maybe his 70's. This gentleman was quite tall despite being severely stooped over; he had horribly scarred skin and thin scraggly hair pulled back into a pathetic looking "Old man" ponytail. This man looked like life had crapped on him and then, for good measure, crapped on him again. He introduced himself as Ken something. If he said his last name, I soon forgot. In addition to this man's state of disrepair, I immediately noticed that he was in drastic need of a visit to the dentist. From the angle I had of this gentleman, I could only see one tooth in his head. I considered, for just a brief moment (maybe you would have too, if you were in my place), "Does he have more teeth in back?" All I know is, based on what I could see, I didn't want to see anymore.

I would learn later that this man was just 55 years old at the time. Despite the fact I barely acknowledged his presence, he began telling me some jokes which required sound effects using his nearly toothless mouth. To this day, I don't know what was more horrifying: the toothless sound effects with the accompanying spray of spittle, or the life story I was about to witness. After his sad attempt at a comedic performance, he began to speak to me about some innocuous topic, but I wasn't listening (for many reasons which I won't state here because all of them make me look shallow). Even if I had wanted to listen, it would have been impossible, because I was about to see his life story in my head like a projector from hell. It was a projector that didn't have an off switch. What I did see is very difficult to describe.

In just the time it takes to slug down a cold beer on a hot day, I saw events in this man's life and I will do my best to share them with you. It began slowly, as if a friend whispered, "I need to tell you something," and you listen out of concern and the fact that everyone loves a secret.

The truly strange part of this upcoming scene, which I would discover later in the evening, was the fact that I was seeing lengthy portions of his life that would take hours to comprehend if seen in a movie, book, or by word of mouth. It was, however, taking just seconds. It was like I was absorbing his life story as fast as a sponge absorbs water. The only other thing I thought of was, maybe the bar was able to slow down time, but soon realized that theory was completely insane.

To this day, I can see these events in my head over and over as if I was replaying my VHS. I don't have to "Be kind and rewind." Just thinking of this toothless specimen brings back the vision, and I get to witness his story and his subsequent atrocities repeatedly. Also, in addition to the visions, I was surprised to be provided with instant information about this man's past. A lot of information that was not provided in the vision would be provided with instant knowledge and, for lack of a better term, I'll call this ESP Moments.

KEN'S EARLY YEARS...

When Ken was just a child, his mother (Debbie) was a passenger in a motor vehicle that was broadsided by a drunk driver operating a large moving truck. The truck and the vehicle in which Debbie was a passenger were both proceeding through an intersection, but the driver of the truck was far too inebriated to stop for the red light. Ken's mother was killed on impact; the driver of the truck walked away without so much as a scratch.

Ken's father, "Larry", was understandably devastated by this event but, appeared to be handling things as well as could be expected. He got the children to the wake and to the funeral without help from his side of the family. Larry's parents lived several states away but managed to attend the funeral. Larry's parents were not close to their children and abruptly departed following the funeral. Larry never did understand why his parents were so aloof, but he understood that it was their manner. His parents often claimed, "We raised our children without help; you raise yours."

Debbie's mother, "Lena", was a charming woman, in Larry's opinion, but Debbie's father, "Edward", struck him as peculiar and moody with a legendary temper that could erupt without a moment's notice. Larry had heard many whispers of molestation and even beatings that had happened when his wife and her siblings were children. Debbie and Larry had made great efforts to avoid having Lena and Edward watch the children, which was upsetting to Lena. She had been living her entire married life in denial about her husband's actions, but she managed to understand in her heart why they were not asked to care for the grandchildren.

It would only take a few days for the childhood of Ken and his siblings to spiral downward from loving to an outright nightmare.

A few days after the funeral, the children were dealt yet another devastating blow. It began innocuously, as Larry tucked in each child and answered their many questions about their mother, heaven, and death in general. Ken and his siblings, to this day, remember that evening with clarity: the tenderness their father exhibited and the sadness in his eyes. After the children were tucked in and asleep, he telephoned his mother in-law and asked if she would come over to their house and stay with the children while he went out to clear his head.

Once Lena arrived, she could tell that Larry was completely devastated but realized it was understandable since her son in-law now faced the daunting task of raising five young children on his own. He would have to do this without the woman he'd been in love with since they were in high school. Upon further reflection, Lena realized it was probably healthy for him to get out and have a good cry by himself; he'd been so strong so far. As Larry left, he gave her a hug and said thank you, and that simple small act had a finality to it that deeply unsettled her. Not wanting to wake the children, Larry closed the door softly behind him. He gave Lena a smile and a wave as he passed by the window, hopped in his car, and proceeded to drive his vehicle at well over 100 mph into a concrete barrier. There were no skid marks; he was not intoxicated; and he knew the area. It was correctly termed a suicide.

The children were quickly assigned by the state to Debbie's parents as there were no other relatives in the state, and Larry's parents expressed no interest. The children would quickly learn that grandpa Edward would rule their lives with an iron fist. Anything resembling normalcy was a thing of the past.

The children lived with their grandparents for 10 years, give or take. While their grandmother appeared, on the surface, to be a kind soul, Ken and Paul (Ken's twin) would grow to despise her as much as they had loved her. These conflicting emotions would trouble the children for their entire lives. As kind as Ken's grandmother was, she could not or would not defend her grandchildren from the physical and psychological abuse that her extremely volatile husband regularly inflicted on the entire family.

The more I focused, the faster the visions appeared, and I deliberated in my mind, "How is this happening? Have I been drugged?, Am I hallucinating? Was this some kind of fucked up Jedi mind trick?" I glanced down at the drink that I had been sitting next to and I had not taken so much as a sip of. Sitting at the bar, I took in the scene, looking at the rows of alcohol which were lined up in front of a very large, looming mirror. I again noticed the occasional flashes of red coming from the bottles, or were they coming from the mirror? I didn't know.

In order for you to really appreciate what's coming, I need to give you a bit more information on the family dynamic. The oldest children were Ken and Paul. They were twins, but not identical in any way imaginable. I know this even though I've never seen Paul, nor met him. I continued to listen, see, absorb or whatever the hell I was doing. I didn't want to "witness" this story in any capacity; however, I was helpless and powerless to pull away from the mind of this toothless horror show.

VENGEANCE IS A BITCH...

Now, onto my travels to "fucked-up-ville" we go, and it starts with the back-story ESP moment I had mentioned a moment ago. Ken and his siblings had been at the mercy of their abusive, deviant grandfather for what seemed like forever. Grandpa took to beating his grandsons for the smallest of transgressions and molested his young granddaughters whenever the mood struck, which usually followed a night of drinking.

There was not a big age gap between the children, as there were two sets of twins separated by only 3 years. There were no "older" siblings to protect them. The first set of twins were born sometime in the early 1930s, followed by Leota one year later, and finally the next set of twins (Jimmy and Ellen) two years following Leota. This made for easy pickings for their abusive grandfather. Although, I hadn't yet seen what Ken's siblings looked like, I was made aware by an ESP moment that Ken was the child that got short-changed in the looks department. At the same time, it was known to me that his brothers were good looking, and his sisters were very pretty. Ken always appreciated that, no matter what kind of argument he and his siblings would have, it was never mentioned that he was the homely one (by a long shot).

As the years passed, the children and the grandmother traveled further together into their unspoken nightmare under the thumb of grandpa. They developed a form of collective denial and figured, "If it was not discussed, maybe, just maybe, it was not happening." Sadly, it was happening, and happening a lot.

While Ken got along amicably with his brothers, he was devoted to his sisters. The closest connection was with his youngest sister, Ellen, as the two were truly kindred spirits and they enjoyed each other's company for hours at a time. Ken was 3 years older than Ellen, but the brother and sister bond was always very strong between them. The bond he shared with his twin was next to non-existent; they were as close as two distant cousins. The only thing they ever worked on together was the objective to keep grandpa away from the girls. Ken and Paul did their very best to shield their sisters from their drunken grandfather's roving hands and they were crushed when they failed.

Ken and Paul started referring to their grandfather as Mr. Molester, but never to his face.

As the years continued to pass by, Mr. Molester's assaults on Leota and Ellen progressed well into their teenage years, although maybe not as often. But with this type of behavior, once is too often. Grandma Lena occasionally tried to run interference for the girls; however, that would lead to her own beatings. She, no doubt, felt as hopeless as her young grandchildren.

As Ken entered his teenage years and entered high school, he was growing taller, developing a lanky build, but his body mass had not yet caught up to his height. However, he had massive fists and was aching to use them (especially on Mr. Molester). This desire to hit typically followed the occasions that he and his brother had fallen short in protecting one of their sisters. To the outside world, Ken was a courteous and polite young man, but the pressures at home were just too intense, and this intensity was growing every day.

It was just such an occasion (Mr. Molester had struck again that weekend) when, on a Monday afternoon, a fellow student made an untimely comment about his sisters. It was quite the innocuous insult and should not have warranted the response that Ken gave it. As juvenile as the comment was, akin to "Your sister wears combat boots", it was poorly timed, and Ken approached this student with eyes blazing, most of his teeth grinding (oral issues were beginning to manifest) and clenched fists.

Ken dared him to repeat his comment with a look of seething anger apparent in his eyes. The student immediately realized that he was in trouble and stuttered out a half-hearted apology to save face, hastily adding that he was only kidding. Everyone in that gathering of students knew the apology was too late, and the fear this student was displaying emboldened Ken.

The unfortunate student with dreadful timing had just turned to leave, and his buddies were reaching out to escort him away from trouble when Ken reached out and grabbed the young man's shoulder to turn him around...

The right cross with the massive fist delivered its payload on the bridge of this young man's nose, and the blood fired out in spurts. The victim's friends were as shocked as the victim was; for a moment, they were paralyzed in a stupor. While Ken's victim and friends remained frozen in surprise, Ken continued with his assault. Once the victim's friends snapped out of their shock, they tried to intervene to assist their friend. However, the unfortunate young man had already been struck in the face and stomach several times in rapid succession, and the only thing that kept him standing was the wall of lockers behind him. In their efforts to rescue the young man from a vicious beating, they tackled Ken to the floor. Ken managed to escape the clutches of the friends, and just as he was about to resume his assault, he was pulled backwards and slammed to the ground with brutal force. For a moment Ken thought he saw cartoon birdies flying around his head, but he soon realized, it was the massive gym teacher who also served as the football coach that had stopped him. As Ken pushed the birdies from his brain and resumed squirming under the teacher's grip, he was told quietly, but very firmly, "Do not move one more fucking muscle". As he laid there pinned down on his stomach with his face against the cold tile floor, he noticed his school mate still dazed, bleeding profusely, could only manage to stand with the assistance of his friends.

Ken was suspended for three weeks. He was surprised that it was not a longer suspension due to the injuries he inflicted. He would learn years later that it was primarily due to the intervention of his sisters. The sisters were deeply ashamed of their grandfather and, unjustifiably, themselves as well. Ken's sisters knew this was the source of their brother's anger issues. It was now their turn to protect their big brother. Leota and Ellen didn't elaborate to the police or the principal on the family matters leading to Ken's stress; however, they did assure them that it was substantial and a deeply personal family matter. They also asked the principal to consider Ken's history, which was devoid of fighting, as well as the fact that he had never even received a detention. The fact that the victim ended up with a broken nose, broken glasses, a fractured tooth, fractured cheekbone, and three broken ribs meant that Ken was extremely fortunate with his punishment. Part of the deal for that lenient punishment was that Ken would have to apologize to the student, apologize to the students that he struck while trying to resume the assault, and, lastly, pay for the glasses and medical treatment of his victim.

While his record of good behavior softened his punishment by the school, the police were not inclined to let Ken off. It was only because the parents of this victim had been very close high school friends to his deceased parents, and as upset as they were about the attack, they were not inclined to press charges. So, while Ken learned there would be no other repercussions, he was firmly told that he was on the police radar.

Shortly after his successful fight at school, Ken decided it was time to stand up to Grandpa the next time he took Leota or Ellen to his room. Ken had had enough.

It was a late Saturday evening, and, while Grandma was at a friend's house, the old man, once again, made his move. As Mr. Molester was heading to his room with Ellen in tow, Ken intercepted them at the door, standing tall with his back to the door. He hollered, with a somewhat shaky voice, that he was tired of his grandfather taking advantage of his sisters. trying to gather all the courage he could because his grandfather still scared him to death. He further stated that the old man should be ashamed of himself, and the behavior had to stop. Grandpa glared at Ken, no doubt sensing the fear in him. For just a moment, Grandpa seemed to relax as he put his hands on Ken's shoulders, and said in an apologetic way, "You know, you are" …

Explosively, Grandpa pulled Ken's upper body and head in a fast downward direction toward his right knee, resulting in a brutal collision. Ken was actually out on his feet, and his nose was spurting blood like a water cannon, and several teeth were knocked out. As Ken slowly regained his feet, bent over while trying to gather his senses, Grandpa, striking swiftly, grabbed Ken by the back of the shirt and proceeded to throw him head first into a wall. Grandpa then calmly proceeded to the bedroom with Ellen close behind. Just prior to closing the door, he completed his earlier partial statement with a wink, "beginning to piss me off". The ending of the thought was not soothing. It was said with abhorrence.

This fight, if you can call it that, was maybe just seconds long, but it was brutal in its effectiveness. Grandma Lena only crawled deeper into her denial. The boys now felt more hopeless than ever, and the daughters continued to feel unwarranted shame and despair. This was a colossal setback for the entire family, except Mr. Molester that is. The damage to Ken's teeth was massive. He would never try to repair them. For what reason, maybe a shrink could figure out. My non-professional opinion is that he was too ashamed of what happened to his sisters, and maybe his teeth were an appropriate punishment or a reminder of his grandfather's total authority. Maybe? Don't worry, I won't quit my day job.

Ken would spend time recovering and working hard to physically improve his strength. As crushing as that fight was, it galvanized him as well. He would not lose to Mr. Molester the next time they tangled. Even more importantly, he was determined to not let that "Old fuck" get the drop on him again. He decided, until the time for a rematch was right, he and his brother would just try to keep the girls active as much as possible in school clubs or dances.

Another violent storm would be brewing, and it would have permanent effects on the entire family.

The mirror is rapidly flashing scenes of violence in a chaotic manner. The bottles in front are reflecting light back onto the mirror and out toward the bar. It is difficult to comprehend what is happening. Then just as quickly, it is clear...

The fuse to the powder keg in their home finally exploded like an A-Bomb. Ken arrived home and found out his sister Ellen was in the bedroom with Mr. Molester. He had just gotten home from hanging out with a friend and he had let his guard down. He and his brother had scheduled their sisters to be at the community center and out of harm's way. He didn't know that Mr. Molester had come home early and requested Ellen's help with something in the bedroom. The term "help" was his code for his sick, incestuous desires. The first indication of trouble was when he saw his grandmother doing the dishes with trembling hands. She was unwilling to meet his gaze. He realized immediately what was happening and ran to the bedroom to save his sister from another attack. He kicked in the door, saw his grandfather's hands touching his sister in a place he had no right to touch her.

Ken attacked him in a rage that Mr. Molester would not be able to withstand this time. The conflict escalated quickly with Ken demanding that the "molesting fuck" get up and take his punishment for embarrassing himself, the family, the entire fucking town as well as the entire fucking male species. Mr. Molester rose slowly with caution, but still managing a shit eating grin. He soon met Ken's stare with cutting intensity. Mr. Molester informed him that, this time, someone was not going to leave this house alive, solidly poking Ken in the chest for emphasis. The firm chest poking was what lit the fuse. Ken fired a fist into Mr. Molester's face that may have been the killing blow all by itself; if not, the following deluge of shots would have done the deed. At one point, when Grandpa was basically out on his feet, Ken held him up with the left hand and continued to strike Mr. Molester so hard with his right fist that blood was spraying in every direction. It's hard to tell from my perspective how many punches were thrown while Ken pummeled his grandfather, but the old man was dead or near dead when the punches ceased. Even though Grandpa Molester possibly clung to life from this assault, Ken was nowhere near finished. If Grandpa still somehow clung to life, the countless kicks to the head and ribs with steel-toed boots certainly finished him off. Prior to each kick, Ken would say "This is for

Ellen", and then he'd continue to the next family member, and so on. It was the sound of his sister and grandmother's screaming that brought him back out of his blind rage.

The attack finally came to a conclusion with Ken saying to nobody in particular, "I guess you are correct again Mr. Molester. Someone is not leaving this house alive", finishing that statement with a solid kick to Mr. Molester's groin. There was no reaction.

As Ken walked to his room with his sister following closely behind, he instructed his grandmother to call the police in 10 minutes. Ken had Ellen sit down at his desk and he proceeded to his dresser. He opened his sock drawer, pushed some aside, and with trembling hands, removed a large wad of cash. Ken wanted to help her and their siblings financially because he had no idea how long he'd be in prison, or if he'd ever get out. Ellen stood up and hugged her big brother tightly; she wept on his shoulder for a couple minutes. It didn't take long for them to hear the sound of sirens drawing closer. His last thought before the police arrived was that Grandma sure as hell didn't wait 10 Goddamn minutes to make that call. As he was escorted out, he gave his sister one last smile and, for his Grandmother, an icy, hateful stare.

Ken would be sentenced to 12 years and would serve 6. Everyone involved with the investigation and prosecution understood the circumstances and considered him a nice young man that snapped with extreme family duress while trying to protect his sisters. It sure didn't hurt him to be charged as a minor when the prosecution could have tried to convict him as an adult as he was very close to age 18.

After serving his time and being released due to good model behavior, he was expected to do well back in the community. During his time in prison, he obtained a high school equivalency degree and impressively earned a B.A. degree in forest management. In addition to his degree, the prison counselor had a job lined up for Ken upon his early release.

Ken does not mention to anyone, especially his counselor, that as he was beating his grandfather to death, he truly enjoyed himself and felt great satisfaction with taking a life. In his heart, he felt as if it was the first objective he had ever set and he had met this objective in glowing fashion.

On the rare occasion that someone would ask why he killed his grandfather, Ken would state that the attack was to protect his family and make the world a safer place by disposing of the garbage. Judging by the actions of his grandfather, it is hard to argue this point. The extent to which he now desired to take the lives of others was not clear to me. Maybe you, the reader, will figure out an answer in the upcoming moments of Ken's life.

THERE GOES THE NEIGHBORHOOD...

Ken's first unprovoked murder was far less disjointed than the visions I had seen earlier upon my arrival, and I don't know the reason. Maybe because it was a murder that didn't involve revenge or the noble idea of protection? This event appeared to be completely random, and if I understand what I saw correctly, it was not anticipated nor premeditated, but an opportunity knocking on his door.

I would guess the time period to be the early 1960's, give or take a few years. This is mainly attributed to the music on the radio. Also, Ken still had a youthful appearance, and his lanky frame had developed and filled into a solidly developed and powerful man. His hair was dark, curly, and generally unkempt. He still suffered from the dental issues he'd had even before Mr. Molester caved in a bunch of his teeth. His skin, although free of acne, bore the plentiful evidence of scars. His eyes were, as usual, small and shifty, made more evident by large ears that protrude outward. He had a thin beard that didn't fill in very well. My guess is that the beard was Ken's attempt to camouflage his acne scars, or his poor dental condition, or both. It didn't. Judging by the visions of the family I've had up to this point, Ken was clearly the duckling in a family of swans. His best quality, aside from loyalty to his sisters, was the fact that he was an extremely hard worker. Loyalty was a trait he possessed in spades.

I notice the mirror is acting up again in the same manner as before — more scenes of violence with interference shining from the bottles, again. Soon, everything becomes clearly visible..

Ken's unexpected opportunity happened when he was driving home from work one night after a double shift. He saw a man on the road that appeared in Ken's mind to be of Hispanic descent. The man was on the side of the road walking away from his vehicle that had either run out of gas or broken down. Ken pulled over and asked the young man if he needed a lift.

The man was a large young fellow and didn't show any reluctance in entering the vehicle, doing so quickly and politely. It was discussed and soon agreed that they would travel to the next gas station a few miles down the road where the young man could call a tow truck from a pay phone. After some further small talk, this young man informed Ken that he'd not seen his family in many years, but was thinking of returning home to South Carolina. He had been out of work for several weeks and was quite homesick. He claimed to greatly miss his family whom he had not contacted for a long time and he especially missed his mother's cooking, as well as listening to the Redskins on the radio with his father. Ken, always quick to give a nickname, even if just in his own head, had already assigned him the name of Pancho. This was the first Spanish name that he was able to think of.

It was during their trip to the garage that Ken found himself squeezing the crowbar in his right hand between the seats and next to the emergency brake. Once the vehicle was between two street lights, and the cab of his vehicle almost black, he cocked the crow bar back and swiftly swung it as hard as he could toward his passenger's head. The bar struck his passenger cleanly on the bridge of the nose, and before the young man knew what was happening, he had been struck two more times with bone shattering results. The second strike made a strange sound, almost like glass breaking, as it struck the top of the young man's mouth. The third strike made a sickening sound like a rug being beaten with a long stick. The striking of this young man was exhilarating for Ken. Just after striking his passenger a third time and using his peripheral vision, Ken could not tell if the man was dead or alive. If his passenger so much as twitched, he'd wallop him again. To Ken's disappointment, there was no movement.

Ken pulled over in a dark, deserted rest-stop and briefly admired his handiwork. As he restarted his vehicle, he said to nobody in particular, "The fucker sure made a mess, I better pack a tarp next time". As Ken completed the short trip home, he chortled at the thought of getting pulled over and having to explain a dead guy in his passenger seat. However, he was not truly concerned, because the two officers on duty at this hour were sleeping in their cruiser several miles away. One of the positives (or negatives, depending on how you look at it), of living in a small town is that everyone knows what everyone else is doing. It is true from my observation that small town people are the most predictable people in the world.

As Ken drove into his long, dark driveway, he realized the body would have to be buried the next night as he would have to use his backhoe to dig the hole during the day. It certainly would raise suspicions from his nosey neighbors if he started the backhoe at this time of night. He would have to wait until tomorrow evening to move the body under the cover of darkness. Ken moved his vehicle close to the garage and rolled the body out of the passenger seat and onto a large blue tarp. He had always kept a tarp on his second garage bay floor just in case he had some work to do. For some reason, the second garage bay was kept immaculate; he hardly ever worked in that section, other than to store some seldom used tools.

As he admired his handiwork once more, he maneuvered his victim down onto the center of the tarp. To his amazement, he realized that Pancho was somehow still alive. Ken heard a faint gasping and whistling sound coming from his victim's face, although it was hard to tell exactly from where. This guy's face was a mess, and it was hard to tell where his nose ended and his mouth began. Ken looked carefully and saw that blood was bubbling and he heard a faint but steady gurgling sound coming from somewhere in or near his chest. Ken was extremely fatigued from his unplanned attack on this unknown man he'd nicknamed Pancho, so he procured his sledge hammer, took aim, and promptly finished the job with just one swing to the head. To Ken's extreme dismay, this made a large and gory mess on the spotless side of his garage. He didn't look forward to cleaning up the gore as Pancho's brains exploded outward. It made him think of when you step on one of those plastic ketchup packages from a fast food joint. After a short sigh, thinking of what a mess he'd made, beleaguered, he entered his house through the connecting door, took off his boots, walked to his bed, and fell immediately into a deep sleep.

The next day, he awoke with neither joy nor dread but curiosity... or anticipation might be the better word. Did last night really happen? If it didn't, the dream was surreal. He soon realized, when he saw the gruesome mess in his vehicle and in the garage, this was clearly not a dream.

Ken began his morning by driving his backhoe into his back acreage and dug a hole that was basically 4' by 4' as he thought a grave shaped hole would not be in his best interest. He didn't give a shit how uncomfortable this Spanish guy was in the afterlife. He grumbled, "If this fucker just went back to where he came from, he'd not be in this square hole". Upon completion, it ended up being about 10' deep, Ken felt it was better safe than sorry to dig it extra deep. He dumped the body after looking around to make sure nobody could see him. He was apprehensive about the timing, but he wanted the body out of his house. Further complicating matters, placing his victim in the hole was not an easy feat, as full rigor mortis had set in. He thought of the expression, "Placing a round peg into a square hole". Once his victim was crudely shoved into the hole, Ken covered it and proceeded to level the area. He stood for a moment and simply mumbled, "I hope God takes better care of you than I did".

Ken set about cleaning his garage and was happy when most of the mess was taken care of by the tarp he had placed down. The tarp had done its job, aside from the mess caused by the sledge hammer blow. On the other hand, the truck was going to require a lot of work. The cab of his truck was covered in blood spatter, from the roof to the floor mats. The passenger seat was beyond cleaning, so he decided to just remove the seat and replace it later. He could burn the seat during the bonfire at his brother Paul's Halloween party this coming October. He worked on the dash, doors, and windows for a few hours until he was satisfied that his work was complete. At that point, wanting to be extra safe and being the hard worker that he was, he cleaned everything again from top to bottom. As I said earlier, this man was many things, but lazy was not one of them, and it was his objective to never return to prison. At that point, he went inside, had a beer, and finally had the chance to reminisce on his recent chain of events.

THE LADIES' MAN...

The subsequent event that I was somehow witnessing must have been a while later' how long, I don't know. Ken's hair was a different style, and his house seemed to have a woman's touch. The house was neat, and there were flowers on the table. I'd estimate that Ken was in his mid- 30's, give or take a few years, and his lack of teeth gave him an appearance of being older than he was.

Just as this vision seemed to have a nice, comfortable feel to it, it took an abrupt turn. The mirror informed me in an instant that this attractive young lady was entering Ken's kitchen to begin making a nice Sunday lunch for the two of them.

The flashing returns. I'm guessing that Ken is up to something deadly...

As the young woman entered the kitchen preoccupied with what she was going to prepare, she didn't sense the danger she was in. The peril to this woman, however, was clear to me. The vision revealed the view of a whiskey bottle arching rapidly down toward her head from behind. It struck with a vicious "thump", and she dropped faster than Richard Nixon's political career. What didn't go without my notice was the blue tarp that she landed on. This event had obviously been planned, unlike the disposal of Pancho. Ken brought a chair over and lifted the unconscious body and placed it onto the chair with what I took as a loving manner. This was in direct conflict to the violent act that had just occurred. Ken checked her pulse and speedily tied her wrists and ankles to the chair with Ty-Raps which were the precursor to Zip ties. Once the young woman was secured, he patted her cheeks to wake her and called to her in a soothing voice. Once he realized she would not soon wake, he took the lit Marlboro cigarette he had been smoking and placed the burning end on her forehead. She awoke with confusion, pain, and, well, mostly fucking horror. Sadly for this young lady, her nightmare had not even begun. After she had been struck, Ken moved her to his basement, which he had turned into a makeshift torture chamber. I could not tell how long this woman was kept prisoner, but it was my impression that she had been kept and tortured for several days, maybe even weeks. I am sure however long it was, the stay felt eternal to her. Ken's random moments of kindness must have been baffling to her, as it would appear before, during, or after brutal sessions of sadistic torture and constant mind games that would end with him always professing his love for her. The torture included many different methods, but mostly involved fire and pliers. Ken would cauterize her wounds with the same iron that she had purchased to keep his church clothes pressed. Do you think she got the irony?

This woman, who had been living with Ken, was somehow just a brief chapter in his life; however, she undoubtedly had a large impact on Ken in her time with him. During this brief stay, she had made noticeable, positive changes in his appearance. It was clear to me that she had provided Ken with the first positive stability in his life. However, while it seemed to the outside world that he was flourishing, inside, he had been harboring a tremendous disdain for her. It was the similar vibe I sensed when the ESP moments told me about Ken's grandmother. I do not know why. I'm sure that, had he known the reason for his hatred of the young and fairly attractive woman in his life, it may have been made clear to myself in the visions, as well.

I will tell you what I know about her; however, it won't be much. This young woman, for whatever reason, remained nameless in the visions, aside from the not so endearing name Ken assigned to her: "the slut". This was likely due to his own sense of self-worth.

Ken's lady friend appeared to be 5-10 years younger than Ken, and the thing that struck me in the few glimpses I had of her were her big brown eyes and her slim curvy figure. I'm not sure of her height or weight, but if I had to guess, I'd say 5'6" and about 130 lbs. Her hair was light brown with below the shoulder length wavy curls. She had perfectly straight white teeth which greatly contrasted Ken's vanishing, crooked, yellow ones. Her lips were full and pouty, and she had the prettiest little freckle on the lower lip. They were lips that any man would want to kiss. This young lady was easily out of Ken's league; however, in all fairness, I would say Ruth Buzzy would be too pretty for him, as well.

As far as specifics about her life before Ken, she either didn't tell him about her earlier family life, or he just didn't give a shit. It appeared to be a brief time that ended almost as soon as it started, and he ended it in striking fashion (yep, that pun was intended). I can only hazard a guess as to how long she was in Ken's life. It was long enough to make an impression on Ken's appearance — an impression that wouldn't last as long as the one made by the bottle to her head. While his home had begun to show a woman's touch, I'd bet money that she was not there over six months.

Continuing on with this portion of the story and getting to its sickening conclusion, on this final day when Ken opened the door to the basement, and the light shone from behind him, he cast a very ominous shadow. He remained standing there for a couple minutes and finally walked down the stairs toward her with a jovial smile displaying his few jagged yellow teeth. His guest still tied to her large wooden chair in the basement, and as her eyes were desperately trying to adjust to the light, she was terrified to see Ken spread out a shiny new tarp beneath her. She had known Ken long enough to know that he always used a tarp when he was about to do something untidy. It was obvious to her, however, she had neither the will nor the strength to fight or to even talk her way out of this. He ripped the tape off her mouth and loudly exclaimed, "I'm fucking bored now, and all good things must come to an end". He put the gun to her head, pulled the trigger, and she heard a click. It was just a moment later that she realized the weapon was not loaded, or had simply not fired. This new mind game, whether intentional or not, actually caused her to urinate. Ken gave a near toothless chuckle, clapped mockingly three times, and said to her, "Wow, that was an unexpected surprise". It was at that point that he plunged a bowie knife into her throat and rotated it left and right. She painted his new blue tarp a deep shade of red in just a couple minutes.

The next morning was time to crank up the old backhoe, and, as he drove to the slut's new home, he thought, pretty soon his former lady friend would have a new friend and neighbor that will treat her better in the afterlife. Pancho would not betray her or leave her, and they would be eternal partners. Also, the best part of this situation that made Ken extremely happy was that Pancho would never get into her panties. He was in what I'd call a damn good mood.

I will digress a few moments before I get into Ken's next adventure because somehow I'm seeing something, but not in a vision. It is a very strange feeling. I know the appearance of Ken's house, both inside and out. I don't know why it's important, but just bear with me. The location of the room in which he finished off the slut is a mystery to me, but my best guess is that it was the basement. The mirror would not confirm, nor deny my supposition.

Anyway, Ken's house was located in the rural town of Killingly, Connecticut where the average lot size was five acres. Many of the houses sat far back on the property — I'd say about 40 or 50 yards from the road — and had roughly 3-4 acres of wooded land in the backyard. He had purchased the property several years earlier and performed most of the repairs himself. The house had been a fixer-upper and, due to the fact that it was in the middle of nowhere, he had gotten a great price and had long since paid it off. The house was not much to look at, but it was solid and ready to move into (not that he had much). It was an ugly color that he would refer to as pea soup green with white shutters. The house and shutters were in critical need of a painting; however, he had never had the desire to do so. It was a three bedroom ranch, one full size bath, large living room beautifully furnished with a TV, and a single, very well-worn recliner pock-marked with a plethora of cigarette burns as well as stains from spilled beverages. The living room also featured a massive fireplace that he would never use despite the ample acreage of trees in his yard. The chair he had procured for "the slut's" television viewing pleasure, and her torture sessions had been removed promptly after she met Mr. Bowie. Lastly, there were no pictures on the walls of the living room, nor a knick knack on display.

Ken's bedroom had a twin bed and a dresser that had long seen better days. There was one picture hanging noticeably crooked above his dresser that displayed his siblings at a Halloween party he'd gone to several years ago. It is unlikely the picture had been dusted in the entire time it had been hanging over his dresser. Also on the dresser, he'd keep his keys, wallet, pocket knife, and several rubbers that looked old enough to have been purchased by Mr. Molester. Other than the dusty photograph, bed, and dresser, the room was empty. Ken's closet had very few clothes — mostly flannel shirts and jeans. He had five pairs of shoes which consisted of a nice pair of sneakers, crappy beater sneakers, two pairs of boots, and one nice pair of black shoes for the occasional funeral or wedding. He had a nice suit for the same reason. The suit, dress shoes, and his iron would be the last physical items remaining in his house that connected him to the young lady that he had relocated to his backyard.

The kitchen was the largest room in the house, but painfully barren. It contained a small refrigerator for milk, eggs, and whatnot. He also had a very large chest freezer that contained a massive amount of Swanson TV dinners. He had a frying pan, a few pots, and some basic utensils to round out what he had in the kitchen. There was no kitchen table; he ate his meals in the dining room. The dining room appeared very large, as well, but that may have been due to the fact that it only contained a small card table and two plastic lawn chairs. The room looked as if it had been painted white but had yellowed in time from the years of cigarette exposure. He always kept two chairs at the table in case an occasional friend came over. However, the only visitors he's had lately were now laying dead in his backyard, and neither one of them would be joining him for a frozen dinner anytime soon. As with the rest of his home, aside from his bedroom, there were no pictures hanging or other furniture in this room. To say this room was "drab" would be a massive understatement.

The garage was attached to the left side of the house but set back a few feet. It was a two car garage that, for reasons even he didn't understand, was always immaculate on one-side. (If only he cared for his teeth in this manner). As mentioned earlier, Ken didn't store much of anything in that clean side other than some basic hand tools, yard equipment, and his chainsaw. He didn't even store his favorite toy in there (the back hoe). The back hoe was stored in the back of the house in a Jerry-rigged plastic tarp carport next to his patio. The patio had a very old cast-iron hibachi encrusted with many years of steak and hamburger grease, a sun-bleached red plastic chair that was very similar to his fine plastic dining room chairs. Ken had a small plastic table for his outside dining experiences, and it was covered in all manner of bird shit, spilled beer, and peanut shells. Lastly, on the corner of his makeshift patio, about five feet away, was a large flower pot that had never held a flower or plant. it served a far less noble purpose — it would serve as his urinal when he was too soused to walk the additional 20 feet to his bathroom.

The house looked like this before his lady friend arrived and again shortly thereafter, as it didn't take long for Ken to erase her footprint on his life as well as her very existence.

The driveway was a single car width at the road, and, as it drew closer to the house, it widened gradually enough for the two available garage spaces. The laser straight sidewalk leading to the house from the road was just concrete and didn't contain any decorative aspects at all. There was an oak tree about ten feet from the road to the left, and one to the right of the entryway sidewalk. The only chance you would've seen a flower on this property would be if it grew wild on its own.

HOLY SHIT, MR. MOLESTER IS A FUCKING ZOMBIE...

This next "adventure", or should I say "opportunity" for Ken was just as surprising as his chance meeting with Pancho. It began innocuously when someone knocked on his door obscenely early in the a.m. The thundering knock woke Ken from a sound sleep. He didn't want to answer, but whoever the fuck this was was damn persistent and really Goddamn loud. As he went down the hall towards the front door, he grabbed his handy home defense device (.44 magnum) which was hanging on a nail near the door. At this moment, as pissed off as he was, he didn't have sinister intentions. As he approached the door, he grew further agitated. He impulsively came to the conclusion that scaring this asshole with a weapon would teach this dream-interrupting interloper a lesson. How often do you have a hot dream about banging Marsha Brady's brains out in the kitchen with Alice serving hors d'oeuvres and beer with Jan loudly exclaiming, "Marsha, Marsha, Marsha, it's always Marsha!" This was really crappy timing, and whoever this asshole was, they certainly had it coming. Ken decided he'd scare the shit out of him. (He was not sure why, but he knew by the hard knocking, it was a man). As he got to the door, he looked through the peephole and noticed this rude asshole was very tall. He found his grip tightening on the weapon.

Ken opened the door reluctantly and, in short order, realized this man was a dead ringer for his grandfather. He thought to himself, "Great, another fucking pedophile on this planet!". Even his height was indistinguishable or close "e-fuckin-nuff", as Ken was prone to say. This was the moment that he realized that this "dream interloper" must be his molesting asshole grandfather back from the grave. This evil, "walking dead", Goddamn molester was gonna have to die again. From this point on, Ken, as was his custom, now referred to this man as "Zombie Molester".

Zombie Molester seemed overly apologetic and in a hurry explained that he had hit a deer with his car, which Ken now noticed was the piece of shit VW Fastback now parked in his driveway. He relaxed his grip on the gun, which Zombie Molester had just noticed. Ken immediately saw the man's concern and said, "Aw fuck, it ain't loaded; it's just for protection cuz there's so many crazies out here in the sticks". Thanks to whatever power was providing these visions or ESP moments, I knew otherwise. The gun was loaded. It was always loaded.

Since Ken had instantly decided, at that moment, that Zombie Molester was going to die, he had to act post haste. He asked his guest if he'd like to stay overnight in the garage because it was really late. Ken informed his guest that he had a cot which he could setup, and it would be comfortable enough. He apologized, but said that since he didn't know his guest; he felt uncomfortable inviting him into his house. Zombie Molester understood and appreciated the hospitality offered and even made a comment that, if Jesus could sleep in a manger, he could handle a night in a garage. Ken pretended to turn around to pick something up, rolling his eyes, and thought, "Mother fucker, this new Zombie Molester is a Jesus freak, I have all the luck".

Anyway, Ken asked Zombie Molester to move his vehicle, stating it was parked in his wife's spot, and she'd be returning from her 3rd shift job in the morning. At that point, Ken left to get his guest a pillow and blanket while Zombie Molester moved his vehicle. It was suggested he park under the tree on the side of the garage. It is apparent that Zombie Molester didn't realize that this parking location would conceal his vehicle from street traffic or nosy neighbors. However, maybe he did, as you'll learn in a little bit…

As the vehicle was being moved, Ken briskly set up the cot and he made sure that the blue tarp was centered under the cot. If Zombie Molester asked, he'd just say there are a lot of oil stains on the floor and he did not want his guest to fall or get oil on his shoes or socks should he wake during the night. Just as he had finished unfolding the cot and placing the pillow and blanket down, Zombie Molester entered through the typically unused side door. This both surprised and unnerved Ken; it could have been nervousness or anticipation — he didn't know.

Ken's guest had, in fact, noticed the tarp and asked if he was gonna get whacked mob style, soon followed by a nervous chuckle. Ken shared the laugh on the outside, but his instincts took another hit. He now had more than a smidge of doubt as to whether or not he should resume his plan, but not much. After pausing a moment and taking a breath, he just told Zombie Molester the "Just keeping him safe from oil stains" story he had thought of earlier.

Zombie Molester seemed to buy it.

Ken informed his guest that he knew a good auto-body guy in town, and they'd head over after his wife cooked them up a big country breakfast. He reflected on this imaginary wife of his and compared her to his departed lady friend whom he'd relocated to the back yard with Pancho. With a chuckle, he thought to himself, "I'd like a stronger woman, one that won't let a little bottle of booze go to her head". While he was making small talk with his uninvited guest, he continued to reflect on the young lady taking up residence in his backyard. Thinking, "She woulda been a keeper if she had a bit more real estate in the backyard. Maybe his future wife would meet his criteria." Ken was not a picky man.

I'm finding it strange. at this point in time. that I not only see these terrible visions, I'm also experiencing what I'd call ESP moments (knowing things but not seeing them). I also have the ability to hear thoughts. The evening just continued to become stranger by the minute.

After his moment of contemplation, Ken announced to his guest that he was exhausted and was going to bed for a few hours. Zombie Molester thanked him for his act of kindness and said, "It was a crappy day, but it could have been worse, I coulda been the deer". The two men shared a tired chuckle. As Ken walked through the door, he thought to himself, that deer had it lucky compared to this molesting zombie mother-fucker and he'd soon regret his return from the grave.

As Ken left the garage, he poured himself a shot to settle his nerves. He decided to locate his trusty three foot lead pipe for some hands on action with his grave-returning, dream-interloping guest. Due to the fact that it was very late, Ken figured that Zombie Molester would not take long to get to sleep. Ken waited for 30 minutes and then figured an additional fifteen more minutes would be safer still. When the time came around 3:00 a.m., Ken grabbed the heavy pipe and downed another shot for good luck.

The Flashing returns: the bottles deflect. It's the same as before. Scenes of violence come and go. then. as usual. the picture becomes clear. and the story unfolds...

The garage was dark, but there was enough moonlight coming through the windows to give him better vision than he had anticipated. He didn't want to stub his toe and yell "fuck" with a pipe in his hands. He slowly opened the door to the garage wide enough to slip inside. Ken was able to make out the cot, ruffled blanket, and the pillow. He raised the pipe and brought it down with all the strength he possessed. To his astonishment and even more so, his horror, he abruptly realized that Zombie Molester was not on the fucking cot. His mind was spinning, Where the fuck is he? The very second he finished the thought, he heard Zombie Molester behind him saying, "Jesus, what the hell do you think you're doing?". As Ken spun around to see where the voice came from, he was energetically struck with a solid fist to his mouth which would have hurt far more if he'd had a full set of teeth. Ken's first fleeting thought was, "Wow, the guy even hits like

Mr. Molester". Ken quickly recovered from the unanticipated blow and retaliated against Zombie Molester with the pipe to his right shin. Judging by the sound of the blow, it had to have hurt like a mother fucker. As it turned out, it was an extremely effective strike. Zombie Molester dropped to his left knee and grabbed his shin while swearing a blue streak featuring Jesus Christ himself. Ken now had the upper hand and he took advantage, just as he had with that poor young man in H.S. that had so long ago made the mistake of insulting his sister. Remembering an old Babe Ruth saying, "I swing like my life depends on it". Ken swung the heavy pipe at Zombie Molester's head with everything he had. The victim tried to block the swing, but only slightly deflected the trajectory of this lethal weapon. Ken struck the dream- interloper's right temple area with solid results and a sickening sound. Zombie Molester looked at Ken, or I guess I'd say he looked through him, because his eyes revealed an empty home. The brief eye contact was a mixture of pain and bewilderment followed by Zombie Molester finally collapsing onto his left side. Ken was now physically overcome and exhausted from this mixed cocktail of surprise, adrenaline, extreme sleep deprivation, and the hard punch he had taken to the mouth. Ken sat down against the door leading to his house to gather his thoughts, soon falling into a restless but deep sleep.

He awoke a few hours later with a start and immediately looked toward where he had left Zombie Molester, but he wasn't there. He panicked; in his head he screamed, "Where the fuck is this guy now?" Ken was thinking what a pain in the ass this guy was. He had the gall to wake him up during an epic dream and then won't even have the common courtesy to stay dead. The search for the inconvenient dead molester from the grave was very short as he was only a few feet away from where he had originally dropped. He had apparently tried to reach the backdoor by crawling when he finally succumbed to his extensive head injuries.

Now it was time for Ken to add to his backyard neighborhood. Pancho and the slut were going to get a new neighbor. Ken briefly contemplated why he named his now long departed girl friend "The slut", remembering that it took weeks to get into her panties. After some sordid reflection, he got back to the task at hand. He'd wait until evening when he could do his work under the cover of darkness. He would dig the hole today, but would move the body in the evening as he had done before. It was not out of the ordinary for him to use his back-hoe during the day so the noise would not raise any alarms. With a chuckle, he thought that his new underground neighbors would not keep him up at night with loud parties, nor would they interrupt his dreams of the Brady girls. He longed for their return, but if not the Bradys, maybe Annette Funicello could make an appearance, as we know by now, he ain't picky.

Ken did have some concerns about Zombie Molester's car, but that could wait until later. It was time to dig.

Later in the day, he did put some thought into the "car" situation, but not too much. He really wanted to get Zombie Molester in the fucking ground and then he'd feel much better. Ken briefly considered removing Zombie Molester's head - because that's how you kill zombies. However, he came to the logical conclusion that it would be a lot of work and acknowledged that zombies are not real. Maybe he's not fucking bat shit crazy after all.

As the day finally entered twilight, Ken began to wrap the body in the handy blue tarp. He then had an English style Fish "n" Chips Swanson Hungry Man TV dinner along with another shot to calm his jumbled nerves. As he ate, he pondered, "If I could only have three items in my life, they would be blue tarps, zip ties, and duct tape". Even he concluded that it was a strange fucking thought to have.

I have to reflect again, "How am I hearing what he's thinking?"

Upon finishing our random thoughts as well as his meal, he briefly considered possibly trading the duct tape for a fat ass wife that could cook, but promptly realized he'd be happier with the duct tape. His thoughts turned again to his using alcohol immediately following the hobby he'd taken to, and worrying that it could cause him to become sloppy. He took a deep breath and then went to the garage to pick up his victim and realized that this guy was one heavy son of a bitch. He opened the back garage door and dragged Zombie Molester by his boots to his new home, while briefly considering stamp collecting as a much better hobby to have. He took Zombie Molester just down the row from Pancho and most assuredly away from "The slut". Crazy or not, he was not going to let Zombie Molester anywhere near either one.

Under the cover of darkness, Ken managed to drag the body to the hole and dropped him in. The body fell on its head with the legs sticking up awkwardly. Ken sighed and thought to himself, "This guy is a real pain in the ass". He said a Catholic prayer for the dead which he was stunned that he remembered and even more stunned that he felt compelled to say aloud. It had been a long time since he'd uttered this prayer, but he remembered it like it was yesterday:

"Eternal rest grant unto him, O Lord,

and let perpetual light shine upon him.

May the souls of all the faithful departed, through the mercy of God, rest in peace."

Just before he pushed the dirt onto Zombie Molester's oddly positioned corpse, he briefly mulled over why he had said a prayer for him and not the others. Of the three he'd killed and buried, he liked the slut and Pancho far better than Zombie Molester. Maybe it was because they were far more cooperative. He finished with a direct order to his new victim, "Don't be fucking around with your neighbors. The slut is in charge of the neighborhood crime watch around here." He then belched with all the force of a trumpet and strolled back to the house.

Ken entered the kitchen and washed up again, took out a beer, popped off the cap and finished it with one massive slug. It was energetically followed up by yet another equally impressive belch. He then grabbed another beer, some nuts, and attempted to watch some reruns of "Leave it to Beaver". He was unable to stay awake to the first commercial, as killing and burying was exhaustive work. Ken's last thought before drifting off was, "God help the sum bitch if anyone interrupts a dream of him banging any of his favorites, Mrs. Cleaver, Marsha Brady, or Annette Funicello". "With my luck," he thought aloud, "I'll have an uninterrupted night's sleep with a nightmare of being molested by Grandpa Munster".

He awoke the next morning with the sun shining through the windows and a piss warm beer by his side. Against his better judgement, he drank it in one shot, briefly musing if Europeans might be onto something, but after he finished the warm beer, he decided they weren't. As for his evening's sleep, it was restful, but his favorite TV ladies failed to make an appearance in dreamland. On the positive side, Grandpa Munster didn't make it, either. Ken proceeded to his morning routine. He referred to this portion of his day as the "3S" (i.e. shower, shit, and shave). As Ken shaved, he mused upon what his "make believe" wife would think of his dreams.

He now needed to stop procrastinating and figure what to do with Zombie Molester's fucking car. As the day progressed it really began to weigh on him. He then had a very unsettling thought, "Where was the deer that Zombie Molester struck with his vehicle? Could that lead to him somehow? Was the deer nearby? Were there some tire tracks leading to his driveway?" He grabbed his walking stick, affectionately referred to as his wife beater, and went for a much needed stroll to scope out the area with the hopes of accomplishing this as discreetly as possible. As Ken approached the end of the driveway, he didn't see any tire tracks. He then recalled hearing some rain when he had woken up. It had sounded very light, but seemed to have washed away whatever damning evidence there may have been. He made a deep sigh of relief and continued on his walk, looking left and right, but didn't see a carcass. "So far, so good". He then chose to go right as that was the likely direction of travel because the highway entrance and exit ramps were in that direction. At about one hundred yards up, he did see some heavy but short skid marks. He deduced that Zombie Molester had hit the animal at a high rate of speed and probably failed to apply the brakes until the actual collision occurred.

As Ken was walking and discreetly scouting the area, a neighbor hollered out to him from his truck as he exited his driveway. "Hey, Ken, someone tagged a big damn buck, and the fucking thing died in my backyard... scared the shit out of my wife and kids with its death groans". He said this while laughing himself practically to tears.

Ken tried to appear to his neighbor as only vaguely interested, but inside he was greatly relieved. As he continued his walk, he put more thought into the vehicle situation. He realized that there was no police report, and Zombie Molester was not a local. Ken came up with an idea of how to dispose of the vehicle that was quick and he realized that fresh air was better than alcohol as a remedy to stressful situations any day of the week. Once Ken returned home, he put his plan into action. He drove his back hoe to his back acreage and found the long abandoned chicken coop with double doors on the side opposite the line of sight of his nosey neighbors. Ken finessed the badly weathered and damaged doors open with great effort and returned to get the car. He again looked toward his neighbor's house and noticed the dog was outside in his kennel run. and the two vehicles were not in the driveway. These neighbors couldn't park in the garage because they stored a ton of shit in there and they were also the same family that had the deer die miserably in their yard. He briefly thought, "Why do people need so much crap?" Returning from that trivial thought, he knew that the coast was clear to proceed with his plan to hide Zombie Molester's piece of shit car.

Upon entering the shed again, he was relieved that there were no recent signs of used rubbers, marijuana rolling papers, homemade bongs, roach clips, beer, or wine bottles in his shed. The local teenagers used his shed to get high, drunk, or fuck, and most likely all of the above, as drinking and smoking pot usually led to fucking when teenagers were involved. He grumbled quietly, "It's my shed and I never fucked anyone in there".

As he approached the car, Ken realized to his great dismay that he buried Zombie Molester with his keys. After several choice chastising words aimed at his own stupidity, he concluded that he would hotwire the car because it was too far to push, and the land slanted uphill toward the shed.

The vehicle was a light blue 1966 Volkswagen Fastback Type 3 which had seen its better days. But like all VW's, if taken care of, it would run forever. The vehicle was covered with various scratches, nicks, and minor dents as most 10 year old cars would be, however, the engine looked well maintained. It had extensive front-end damage, but that's to be expected when you hit a large deer. Considering the size of the beast that lay dead in his neighbor's yard, the damage looked pretty light. When thinking of his bad luck with the keys, he chuckled and said, "Hey, like the zombie said, I coulda been the deer." Ken returned to his task while whistling "hi ho, hi ho, it's off to work we go".

ZOMBIE MOLESTER COULD MOONLIGHT AS DON RICKLES

Ken opened the door and sat down behind the wheel. It was tight, and he was baffled as to how Zombie Molester ever fit inside this damn car. Recalling his mistake with the keys, he looked around just to see if there was anything valuable in the car before he disposed of it. He looked at the passenger seat which was covered in all manner of fast food wrappers and other assorted garbage. He noticed a small gym bag which contained a wallet with $3.00 inside. He briefly considered looking in the back seat, but realized it would be a waste of his time, concluding that most people keep their valuables close by and he already found the piddley amount of money.

Ken grimaced and mumbled, "This fucking asshole had more crap in this piece of shit car than money".

As Ken looked through the wallet and registration, he noticed the driver's license had expired two years earlier, and the registration had been expired for several years.

The name on the license was Rocco Ponziani, and the address was Brooklyn, N.Y. Ken knew immediately that the man he killed didn't match the photograph on the license. This molesting dream-interloper apparently dabbled in car theft, as well. The next thought Ken had was, "What became of this Rocco Ponziani?" Leisurely realizing he didn't give a shit, he concluded that the wop got whacked mob style by Zombie Molester.

The term "WOP" surprised Ken as it reminded him of grandpa molester and the colorful terms he'd use for Italian immigrants. Remembering the term WOP meant "working on pavement". He allowed himself an additional moment to reflect on other off-color labels Mr. Molester would use for anyone that was an immigrant. His off color terms for immigrants was not limited to Italians; he included everyone. If a person spoke with an accent or if their skin was a darker shade, he would more than likely find a derogatory term in his list of off handed attempt at humor. Ken found the expressions amusing, although he knew it was wrong. With a chuckle, he thought further, who was he to pass judgement on Grandpa Molester when he found himself frequently using the equivalent expressions?

Letting his memories of his grandfather continue, Ken did have some favorites that Mr. Molester had used. To share just a few, for the French, his material was related to their proud history of surrendering their nation to anyone that passed through, with nicknames such as, "rifle dropper", "surrender monkeys", "white flagger", and "blackfoot". Apparently, after looking into the term "blackfoot", I found it was derived from WW1 due to the French soldiers remaining in their trenches so long, that the mud eventually ate their boots, giving them muddy feet, hence the "blackfoot" name.

Mr. Molester also loved to insult the Irish. He would refer to them as "coal crackers", "drunks", "fire bush", "fire crotch", "potato heads" and "spud fuckers". For some reason, "spud fuckers" always got a laugh from Ken, and, on occasion he would use it himself. Most of these names had to do with the stereotype that the Irish had red hair (everywhere), consumed primarily potatoes, or the fact that they were treated similar to black people, albeit, for a much shorter period of time, unless you include the treatment from the English, but that's another story.

Blacks were easy for Mr. Molester. They were simply referred to as "spear chuckers". Grandpa Molester rarely used this term, but when he was deeply intoxicated and a black person had made the news for some accomplishment or another, he'd break out that term and a few others.

Lastly, for reasons known only to his grandfather, Mr. Molester really had it out for people of Asian heritage. Mr. Molester was extremely ignorant and could not tell the difference between Chinese, Japanese, Korean, Filipino and so on. So, not knowing any better, he lumped all members of the Asian race into the "Chinese" title. He had a boat load of names relating to their facial features that emphasized their eyes such as "bedtime", "coin slot" and "socket face". As for the food they ate, he would refer to them as "bug eaters" or "dog eaters". If he was just referring to an Asian person in general, his favorite term by far was "ching chong". Now I saved Ken's favorite one for last, and I am embarrassed to say it made me laugh. Mr. Molester had crossed paths with a person of Asian heritage, this person, whether gay or not, seemed to be dressed in an overtly feminine manner. As grandpa walked by him, he barked an order to the young man, "Out of my way chinkerbell!". I have no doubt that Mr. Molester would make Archie Bunker seem like a flaming liberal.

As I was trying to say before my tangent on Mr. Molester's viciously unkind terms for anyone different than him, Ken was now trying to recall how to hotwire a vehicle. He had done it a few times with an old friend during his teenaged years. His friend had been a grease monkey and knew everything about VW's. Ken proceeded to open the steering column and expose the wires. He remembered the solid colors were the supply wires, and the wires with a stripe were switch controls. He also recalled that the red was positive and the red wire with a stripe goes to the ignition coil. The brown wire is the ground wire. He didn't care about the brown wires because this car would not require headlights where it was going. So, he would connect solid black to solid red, touch red with white stripe to the solid red to crank the engine.

Ken was able to finally start the vehicle after some laborious work. It was not as easy as it is portrayed on television or in the movies. He drove the car along the overgrown path and proceeded to the shed. Upon arriving, he pulled in through the open double doors, centered the vehicle, and exited carefully. He grabbed his chainsaw from the backhoe and placed it in the corner. Being very careful, he pulled up some floorboards in the corners of the shed and then cut through the support beams carefully with his chainsaw. After some hard work, the car dropped as planned into the 5' crawl space. Again, he stopped to contemplate, "Why does a chicken coop need a crawl space," but in the end, he was glad for it. His work was far from perfect, but it would do. "Fucking good e-nuff", he mumbled to himself. Ken promptly returned to the backhoe and knocked down the outside portion of the shed. If anyone asked him why he did that, he'd just explain he was tired of the teenagers using his shed as a place to smoke their dope, get drunk, and have sex, adding "I'm worried that some stoned kid would make a fire and get hurt or worse". Ken could not fathom anyone having a problem with that line of thinking, and if they did, "Who the hell cares, it's my property".

TIME MARCHES ONWARD...

As the days turned to weeks then months, he stopped worrying that someone would inquire about Zombie Molester, the slut, or Pancho. Due to his good fortune and his scary close call with Zombie Molester, he'd put a stop to his murders, despite that he'd been tempted many times. That is a very rare behavior for a person that had killed 3 people (not including Grandpa) in a relatively short period of time.

Ken remembered the killings with fondness. He remembered the dates of the murders and recalled each one in vivid detail. He would end his recollections with, "It was fascinating to kill them and torturing the slut was a blast, but, I fear going to prison for life and getting butt-fucked far more". That is not a fun thought, thinking what grandpa might say, "A pain in the ass, unless you are a bumhole engineer, bum driller, cock jockey, ring raider or to put it simply, a faggot." Ken thought about his grandpa again, thinking, "I guess the man's colorful vocabulary was as talented as his fists, and aside from the beatings, my sisters being molested, and the fact that Mr. Molester was a complete asshole, he was not without some charms after all."

As Ken's story came to an uncertain conclusion, he walked away slowly in a gait that matched his life. The best way I can describe this observation is that he walked in a determined manner like he had something important to do; however, he would suddenly veer off in an odd direction before realizing his mistake and correcting his course.

CHAPTER 3

Wheels

"I suppose sooner or later in the life of everyone comes a
moment of trial. We all of us have our particular devil who
rides us and torments us, and we must give battle in the end."

— **Daphne du Maurier**

As I was pondering the visions and observations I had seen of the toothless marvel named Ken, a very thin, worn out woman with ghost white hair approached me in a wheelchair that looked as worn out as she did. The wheelchair had a pronounced wobble to it, like one of the wheels had been bent at some point and had never been properly repaired. I soon figured out the need for her wheelchair was due to an above the knee amputation which, I've recently learned, is called a transfemoral amputation. The passenger in this wheelchair introduced herself in a loud, boisterous voice as Leah Rose, swiftly followed by an awful cackling laugh as well as an accompanying coughing fit. I could tell she was proud of her name, maybe that's why I remembered it, plus she said it so loudly that it burned into my brain just from the sheer volume. It certainly was not due to her beauty (because that ship had sailed many years ago, if it ever sailed). I would soon learn that this woman was nicknamed "Wheels" by her bar cronies, and she seemed to enjoy the attention it gave her.

On several occasions, Wheels would loudly burst out and proclaim that she was the hottest woman in the bar. I soon noticed nobody stated the obvious: she was the only woman in the bar. Not only was her voice loud, but her laugh projected and reminded me of the laugh the Wicked Witch of the West had in "The Wizard of Oz", only far more piercing. As worn-out as she was, it was obvious that she had received plenty of attention from men in her youth owing to her frequent loud proclamations of male conquests and graphic descriptions of the acts performed with them. As if the loud, piercing voice, cackling laughter, and smoker's cough were not enough, every once in a while, when things would get quiet, she'd shout out something like "Everyone wanted to fuck me, cuz I was hot", or "My friend's husband used to do me doggie style, he'd even growl and bark". At that point, one or all of the customers would raise their beverage to her and proclaim a toast such as, "To Wheels, the best piece of ass in Connecticut", and they'd all take a drink. Not wanting to feel left out, I found myself joining in after the first couple of proclamations.

I now noticed this woman wheeling herself toward me, and she drew uncomfortably close, nearly rolling a wheel over my foot. She saw my concern when I looked down at my foot and she just said loudly, "Don't worry. I won't run over your precious tootsies". Again, I noticed the wobbling wheelchair. I don't know how it didn't drive her crazy. Anyway, her stump was covered with a light blue bar towel that was draped neatly over a black pair of polyester slacks.

Wheels saw me looking at her slacks and told me with a wink, "Like my pants? I get 'em half off". This drew a light chuckle from a few of the patrons in the bar. I'm thinking they heard the joke several times and laughed as a polite gesture to their friend.

I noticed soon after meeting Wheels that when she became excited, agitated or began talking about one of her long ago lovers (which was far too frequent), her stump would wave around on her wheelchair. The more excited Wheels became, the faster the stump would gyrate. It was disturbing, to say the least.

Wheels asked me if I understood what was happening with a grin and a slow, but steadily waving stump. I told her I seemed to be seeing strange and terrible things, but blamed the stressful driving caused by the snow storm. I also stated that time seemed to be moving slowly for some reason, the fact that I'd felt like I was there for several hours, but only minutes had passed was very peculiar. She assured me that it would make sense soon, although it may not seem that way. Leah Rose warned me that the flashes would commence again soon, with a feeling of dread, and with what had happened with Ken, I knew she was telling me the truth. Time would soon tell.

The old broken down woman in front of me was at first difficult to comprehend, because the woman featured in my corresponding vision was stunningly beautiful. The only reason I recognized her was because of the older pictures that I had seen on the wall as I had entered the bar. Those pictures showed Leah as her age progressed from the time she first started coming to The Last Call. I never would have recognized the woman in my vision as the woman sitting in front of me waving an amputated appendage as well as all her other well-worn charms.

This woman I was currently seeing in my vision was simply stunning. She reminded me of a woman that would have been painted on a WWII airplane. She was curvy with long, flowing, wavy red hair and green eyes that were bewitching, to say the least. Her skin was like alabaster, and her delicate features conformed beautifully to her overall attractiveness.

When I finally put the two together, it was hard to comprehend how this tragic looking woman sitting in front of me had gotten to such a state of disrepair. She was obviously well north of 70, completely broken down, and didn't project the inner beauty and intelligence that many women maintain when they reach their golden years. Her hair was white, sparse, and frizzy. Her skin was badly wrinkled, especially around the mouth. She had more than her share of facial scars. Her teeth were almost as bad as Ken's, although she still had most of hers. While much of this is a natural process of aging and should not count against her, it was the death of the inner beauty of her youth that stood out to me. It had long since rusted over, decayed, or died on the vine. It was most obvious in her eyes, as they were cloudy with cataracts. The right eye tended to wander off to the left sometimes when she became excited. Her hearing was shot, which was made more obvious because everything she said was exceedingly loud.

What complicated matters was the very different time period when these visions were taking place, which, if I had to guess, would be the 1940's.

Wheels would frequently interrupt a vision or conversation and announce to the room that I was getting a boner whether I was or was not. To my dismay, her accuracy rate was uncanny, although, I'm proud to say, was not 100%. The flashing would resume, and the vision would continue.

Her actions, as crude and sickening as they were, didn't bother me too much. To be honest, down deep, she had a funny side to her, and maybe some of the inner beauty she possessed would occasionally manifest itself as if proving her spirit was not totally vacant. Wheels would smile often with her deeply-yellowed, tobacco stained smirk and offer to give me a hand job for $5.00. To which I politely declined. Although, if the younger Leah Rose offered, I would have given her my car. Ok, sorry, I didn't need to share that, but I would. You want to know what really scares me though? Somehow she knows. How I know she knows? I don't know, but I know. Ok, that was fun, moving on...

I need to pause a moment as I feel a need to describe a strange aspect to the visions I've seen so far which differentiates them from dreams. The visions are very clear, far more clear than a dream because, with a dream, you soon forget what you had seen, except for the very few that remain in our memory for a lifetime. However, with these visions, they all have long lasting effects. It has been several weeks since my night at The Last Call and my putting this story to paper. While I can still see the visions, I don't understand why I had them or why they remain so vivid. It is not easy to write about something that you yourself don't understand, but I will give my very best effort.

The other amazing aspect to these visions, or I should call them additions to the visions, are the extra-sensory perception, or what I call ESP elements that merged with the visions. I struggled with how I would describe the ESP moments, so to begin, I'd like to tell you the definition, and then I can elaborate.

Extrasensory perception (ESP) is defined as the ability to perceive events and information by means other than the physical senses. My sentiment of a person claiming to have ESP, or some type of other-world ability, is they either have it, or they are trying to talk their way into your hard earned money. What makes this particular ESP difficult to grasp is that it is powered by (for lack of a better term) the flashing mirror. These ESP moments happen before, during, and after the visions, and they are not seen, they are just known. For example, I have a simple vision of an unknown man and an equally unknown beautiful woman in a sports car driving on a country road. You would think that would be the extent of my vision. But the mirror combines the visions with ESP moments that allow me to know many additional facts not seen in the vision. I would know that the woman is not his wife; they had just left a motel where they had sex. I would also know the positions they used, how many times they climaxed, and the lies they told their significant others. Again, I didn't see or hear these additional pieces of information, but I know it for a fact, like an instantaneous memo was sent to my brain. This may not be the best description, but it's the best I can do. I will attempt to differentiate the visions from the ESP moments as clearly as possible.

Now, with Wheels, her story began with a mixture of visions and ESP moments. From what I gathered, her mother was known to be a bit of a lush, albeit a highly functional one. She cared for Leah and worked full-time at the local grocery store as a manager. Leah had spent a lot of her early youth at that store and hanging out in her mother's small office. The office was always supplied with children's books and toys that made her time there enjoyable. Many of her mother's co-workers would visit Leah and keep her company when things in the store got slow. They would play pick-up-sticks or Tic-tac-toe with her, making sure that Leah always won, as grown-ups tend to do. These were fond memories for Leah, but sadly, life was about to take a steaming crap on her.

Leah was just a very young girl when her father passed away from a massive heart attack at the age of 34. He died at his place of employment, a local lumber yard, when a rope snapped, sending a load of lumber on top of him. The doctor on scene assured Leah's mother that her husband didn't suffer, as he most likely died immediately. Leah's memories of the funeral and the wake grew faint as the years slowly passed. However, she does recall fondly that many people liked him, and his memorial service was very well attended by family, friends and co-workers.

Leah's mother tried to keep things together after the death of her husband, but it became increasingly difficult with the family income being severely impacted. The modest nest egg they had saved prior to Leah's father's passing was promptly depleted, but somehow they persevered and managed to make ends meet.

Years later, the other shoe would drop when Leah was a senior in high school. She was out on a double date with her best friend and their respective dates. Leah remembers this night because she had had a splendid evening and had wanted to stay out later, but had promised her mother she'd be home on time. She arrived in time to be rewarded with the sight of an inferno raging and news from one of the firemen that her mother was observed through a window and could not be rescued. Her mother's cause of death was smoke inhalation.

Apparently, her mother had been home, and since her husband's death, had been feeling extremely depressed about her life. Leah's mother uncharacteristically decided to have a smoke to go with her after dinner martini. As she sat on the chair listening to the NBC Pepsodent Show starring Bob Hope on the radio, she soon dozed off, and in her drunken stupor, the cigarette smoldered on the armrest and it eventually lit the couch on fire. In a very short time, their small house was engulfed in flames, and Leah's life was now up in smoke.

Leah didn't have any grandparents that were alive; she didn't have cousins that she knew of, and she found herself completely alone. She had been hoping to attend the local college in the fall, but had already postponed those plans because her mother didn't have the money to help her with her education. Prior to her mother's death, it had been decided that Leah would live at home and work for a year or two to save money for college. However, her parents were now gone. Her home was gone, as well as family mementos and photographs. With profound sadness, she realized that every photograph of her mother and father was forever lost.

All Leah had now was a part-time job as a waitress in a diner with an old horn dog for a boss. Her boss would constantly struggle to comprehend that Leah's ass was not on the menu.

Leah did have a good friend whose family had no qualms with Leah staying with them for as long as it took for her to get on her feet. Realizing her options were minimal, she graciously accepted their offer and planned to stay until she had saved enough money. When the time was right, she would travel south and find her path in life, whatever and whenever that might be. Leah was young and optimistic and figured that her luck would soon turn for the better because it could not get any worse. Young Leah Rose was about to learn that real life doesn't work that way.

The holidays were rapidly approaching, and despite Leah's boss being a persistent lech, she remained hopeful that the other waitress' claims of generous bonuses were true. It was this hope that kept her from taking any action that might hinder his generosity.

On bad days, Leah obsessed if she should give her boss that blowjob he was always pestering her about. But would it be worth sacrificing her self-respect? She also obsessed if her boss were not the ugly, short, bald, greasy, little toad of a man, would she still be very quick to decline the offer? On many occasions, usually following an illicit proposition, she'd wince at that thought and push the repulsive idea out of her head.

In the past several months, Leah had gone from being a doted upon only child to a young adult currently mired in the life of a nomad. She stayed with her friend's family for several months, but there came a point where she felt she had worn out her welcome. She had managed to save enough money to rent a cheap apartment in an unsavory section of town. The family she had been living with insisted that she was welcome to remain; however, she felt it was time to forge her own path in life, for better or for worse. She was a young, incredibly beautiful woman that still had her head screwed on correctly.

The apartment Leah found was in poor condition and required work, but it was hers. The large one room apartment had enough room for a couch, twin size bed, dresser, vanity, small table for her radio, and a six foot wide closet. The apartment also had a small kitchenette. The one feature that the apartment didn't have was a bathroom. She had to share a communal bathroom with two other apartment dwellers on her floor.

On the first evening at her apartment, she had pleaded with her boyfriend to stay the night because she was nervous about being alone. It was obvious that he was not thrilled with the idea of sleeping in such a dump. Once he was informed he didn't have to sleep on the couch, he was ready, willing, and able to be there for her. Apparently, chivalry has a price.

At one point in the very early morning, Leah awoke to a strange sound, not an uncommon occurrence in a new home. However, there was also a strange tingling on her face and body. There was just a little bit of pre-dawn light in the room, and as she looked at her boyfriend to ask him about the sound and what she was feeling on her body, she saw to her horror that he was covered in scurrying cockroaches. Leah immediately deduced that was what was making her feel "funny" during the night. Once that realization hit home, Leah shot bolt upright in a panic and began to brush at her body frantically, which in turn woke up her boyfriend. In just a few moments after rubbing his eyes, he saw the problem and joined her in a tragically funny moment of brushing, hopping on the bed, and screaming profanities. The two of them dressed in a hurry and went to the diner for breakfast and to calm down after the surprise meeting with her freeloading roommates. It was hastily decided that, with the money she had saved and the additional hours she was getting at the diner, Leah would try her best to evict her new friends. That very day, she put some money into roach traps and every insecticide she could find.

As Christmas eve finally arrived and her shift ended, her constantly ass-grabbing boss was handing out the bonus envelopes to the staff. As he handed an envelope to Leah with a lecherous grin, a wink, and a sneaky quick firm squeeze of her ass, he asked that she open the envelope before leaving because there was a proposal he'd like her to consider. She excused herself for the ladies room and opened the envelope with dread. When she saw the check, she was thrilled. However, once she saw the hastily written note offering an additional $10.00 if she'd be willing to give him a blow job in his office later that evening, her elation turned to disgust. It was at that point, however, the thought of her millions of 6 legged roommates, caused her to reconsider and accept his offer. Leah was determined to evict those damn critters as fast as possible. She'd have to get rid of them on her own, as her boyfriend had made himself scarce since the cockroach incident. She honestly didn't mind, after witnessing his less than manly reaction to the critters had not made a positive impression on her. Leah speculated, "If I could patent my skills in driving boyfriends away and use it on the cockroaches, I'd be rich." Joking aside, she used the additional money from her boss to spray again and set additional traps. Leah would swiftly learn that you don't win against these critters. They didn't seem to care about the traps. They just kept on coming to Leah's apartment for a free meal and a peep show.

Leah Rose needed a new plan...

Leah thought of one of her regular customers. He was a heavyset man with amusing southern quips that would often sit in her section of the diner. He would always tell her about opportunities outside the waitressing profession. Leah would politely decline to listen to his pitch as she was warned by other staff that, although extremely charming, his proposals would likely be sexual in nature. Knowing this information, she kept her distance but remained very polite due to his generous tips.

It soon became apparent that the cockroaches were winning the war, and what she did to her boss was not only disgusting, but the money didn't even make a dent in the cockroach population. Leah had to consider one of two options, both of which required her to break her lease as a first step. Breaking a lease was going to be expensive, as she'd lose her first and last month down-payment. If successful with breaking the lease, her first option would be to hope and pray her friend's family would welcome her back. The second option was even less savory. She could listen to the gentleman's proposal at the diner. What could it hurt? She continued to think that things would get better. She remained wrong in her assumptions.

The customer was known around town as "Double F", which were his initials. This man's name was Freddy Flynn, hence, the "Double F" moniker. However, behind his back, those matching initials stood for "Fat Fuck". He was an obese man with an engaging smile and charm to spare, which was accentuated by his slight southern accent and the overuse of amusing southern expressions. In time, Leah would soon learn that behind his facade, this man had an explosive temper that could make a grown man piss himself. He had only revealed his charming southern hospitality in the diner, and it was well known what this man did for a living. Double F ran many enterprises. Some were legal, but mostly he catered to the shadier side of town. When he became angry or someone had crossed him, he would order a severe beat down on them. Double F would use a colorful expression for this anger, such as "Madder than a pack of wild dogs on a three legged cat". It was part of his dangerous persona: he'd make you laugh with one of his quips one second and cut your throat the next.

As Double F finished his dessert, he loudly exclaimed that he had to go on a diet because he **"had** more chins than a Chinese phonebook", drawing laughs from nearby tables. This man truly enjoyed being center stage and consumed attention like his favorite dessert, which was always a double portion of key lime pie with extra whipped cream. Leah took a moment of brevity to inquire if she might have a moment of his time to speak in private about his earlier proposals for opportunities outside the diner. She knew it was more likely than not that "fat fuck" was going to suggest a sexual favor of some sort involving his penis (if he could find it) and her body. Leah's assumptions would be proven correct, however, not in the manner she had been dreading for so long.

Double F's illicit proposal was that he had opportunities that might suit her and loudly claimed for all to hear "She was hotter than donut grease at a fat man convention". He expressed no doubt that she'd succeed like gangbusters. He promised that if she followed his orders, she'd make fast money and accomplish her goal of going back to school within several months to a year at the most. He further claimed that he had a soft spot for her and then chuckled and added, "Well not too soft". Double F claimed that he would only introduce her to well off clients. He told her to think about this offer over the weekend or longer if she needed to. He would see her next week in his booth at the diner, not his office on Main Street, because that place was "Cold enough to freeze the balls off a pool table".

The more endearing quips the man used, the more she took a liking to him, which was exactly how he operated. Leah would later realize his strategy was simple and highly effective. Keep people off balance because, if you need to whack them, they'll never see it coming. He was as smart, crafty, and dangerous as he was obese.

The vexatious decision didn't take the weekend for her to decide; it was just one more night with her millions of roommates, and she'd made up her mind. She figured that, since she had blocked out what she did for her boss this past Christmas, she could do the same in her new short term career until she earned enough money to move out of her overcrowded apartment. It was still her plan to go to school once she earned enough money. It was clear to her this latest unfortunate occupation would be temporary...

Leah was very excited to hear that Double F was going to give her an advance and set her up in a nice place which she could use to entertain her customers cockroach-free. Leah reluctantly explained to Double F that she had foolishly signed a lease with her current apartment owner and feared she would not be able to break the one year lease. Leah was told, "Don't worry your pretty little head. I'll take care of it". The very next day she received a call from her current apartment owner telling her it was ok for her to leave. He'd return her first and last month deposit by the end of her shift at the diner. When the money was delivered as promised by a man that was visibly nervous, she realized that Double F had taken care of her as promised. Leah felt that her luck was changing and was "Happier than a tornado in a trailer park" (thank you Double F).

Just getting away from the cockroaches was a victory in itself. While Leah waited for her new apartment to become available at the end of the week, Double F put her up in a very nice hotel. She was thrilled because, not only did she have her own bathroom, she had a very large tub in which to enjoy bubble baths. Although she was sad to leave the hotel when the week ended, she was excited to get into her new apartment. Double F gave her the weekend to get settled, and she was told that their business venture would begin with a meeting at his hotel on Monday. Leah was not sure what scared her more, the first meeting with Double F at his place or her new job responsibilities. But she dreamed of a better life and felt that this was her ticket (albeit an expensive one) out of the roach hotel and the crappy life she had found herself embroiled in.

As for the meeting with Double F, she was amazed at what a perfect gentleman he was, aside from the not so subtle ass squeeze as she left his room. As she turned to depart, he abruptly added, "Sugar, you're gonna make our friends busier than a one armed monkey with two peckers". She found the comment endearingly humorous. She laughed at his quip and ruminated, "How the hell does he come up with all these funny expressions?"

During this meeting, Double F had been very clear with Leah about the arrangement: she would entertain five nights a week, which would comprise either two clients per night (early and late), or an entire evening with just one gentleman. He informed Leah that he would try to set up entire evenings whenever possible, as most of his ladies found them preferable to the double sessions. The single evenings usually proceeded at a more relaxed pace. Double F further stated that the entire evening arrangement usually consisted of a date and/or a movie before proceeding to her apartment for an evening of hanky panky. The double nights would tend to be men that just had to get their rocks off. She was told that he'd take the money for four evenings, pay half her rent, and ask for the occasional hand job when his wife was out of town. He didn't mind if she chose to work at the diner as well as long as it didn't interfere with her evening job. Leah would keep the money for the fifth evening and tips from all the evenings. It was further agreed to (as if she had a choice) that all monetary transactions aside from tips would go through Double F. This initially gave her pause; however, he insisted that it would lead to assured payments, "Cuz nobody is gonna steal from me". *I have to admit my disappointment that his comment was not an amusing southern quip.* It didn't take her long to realize that he was honest and timely with her share. Double F emphasized to her that the real money that she could rake in would be the tips. Leah took that to heart and decided that, since she was going to be involved in this type of work, she would go the extra mile. After all, men were easy pickings for a young, beautiful woman, and as Double F constantly told her, "She was purtier than a mess of fried catfish".

Things began as well as could be expected for Leah when you consider the profession she was involved with. The first customer was a very nice, slim, older man in his 40's. He treated Leah like a lady and took her out to a fine restaurant followed by a couple hours of dancing. To her astonishment, his hands never wandered south of her hips, and he was an amazing dancer. After the dance, the gentleman took her to her new cockroach-free home, subtly handed her some cash for her tip, and gave her a light kiss on the cheek. Lastly, he told her he had an enjoyable evening and kindly took his leave. Leah wanted to thank him by name, but Double F had made it clear that she should never ask for a name if one was not provided by the John himself. She actually felt bad about taking this man's money as she had a really nice time; however, she would get over that guilt double-quick.

Leah would learn from experience, mannerisms, and instinct who would treat her well and who might be trouble. To Double F's credit, when she experienced a difficult client, that person would be refused future transactions. He didn't want his prize employee bruised up. which he'd claim would, "Make him mad enough to drown puppies". Also, on the rare occasion that she got roughed up, Double F would send her some flowers, give her some time off to heal, and the John would unexpectedly vanish.

Leah looked forward to her two nights off with great anticipation, and she liked to go dancing with the soldiers on leave at the local base. She developed many casual friendships and the occasional real date which lifted her self-esteem greatly. However, it became noticeable that intimacy on her off nights was becoming difficult for her. These nights off were her moments to feel as close to normal as possible, and a normal life was exactly what she aspired to possess. It was becoming very difficult to turn her emotions on and off like a switch.

After a few months into her new career, Double F approached Leah with a new business strategy. He thought it might be worth including women on the clientele list.

After a lengthy discussion and more than a little coercion, it was agreed that, on rare occasions, Double F would set Leah up with a female customer. He advised her that these women would most likely be married and they would wish to keep their longings well hidden. Double F also informed Leah that he had contacts with an underground club that catered to the primarily female homosexual crowd in the area. He felt that finding female clients for Leah would not be difficult. Double F had to convince Leah that this would save her from the occasional rough treatment that he tried to protect her from, and this new strategy would prolong her shelf life by increasing her single session evenings. She reluctantly agreed, with a caveat: she would try this, but only if she'd be allowed to change her mind. Freddy amicably agreed.

It would not take long to see the benefits, as her occasional visits to the emergency room were reduced, although not entirely, not in this kind of work. There were some women that had jealousy issues (oddly similar to men), but when a woman became abusive to her, the abuse primarily manifested itself verbally. It didn't take her long to realize that words could not leave bruises or break bones. She realized that entertaining the occasional female was not bad for business, and in time, she learned how to physically enjoy their company. One dynamic that Leah would find interesting in her female relationships was that even homosexual relationships among women seemed to be gender based. The couple, for the most part, possessed gender roles where one of the females maintained their feminine role, and the other developed more masculine behaviors.

The timeframe of a year or so that Double F had specified came and went, and we now find her two years into her new life with a sizeable savings as he had promised. Unfortunately, as luck would have it, when she should have retired from her career, it would not be in the cards. The life she was now living had taken a toll on her, and the money she had earned never seemed to be enough. What made matters worse for Leah was that several of her clients, both male and female, had introduced her to cocaine and heroin. Years later, Leah would often think that, had she remained clean, Double F would have been just about right with his one year projection.

Leah's piercing voice cut into this vision like a hot knife through butter, and I'm pulled from the depressing story to see her in the chair with her stump waving around in a frenzied manner. The rapid stump movements matches her voice, "Fucking dyke got me hooked on heroin. I coulda kicked coke, but the heroin fucked me up".

After a moment to clear my head, I am returned back into the vision.

It was about this time in her life that Leah stopped trying to get tips the way she had done in the past with good old fashioned hard work. She now went right for her client's wallets or their purses once the John had dozed off. It didn't take long to get caught, and Leah suffered a beating that was swift and brutal. Once, her John had reached for his wallet to give her a tip for their date, he saw that his wallet was empty. He exploded, "My wallet was sure as fuck was not empty when I got here". He lunged at her with frightening speed and he struck her in the face and stomach several times. When he was done using her as a punching bag, he broke her right forearm like it was a twig despite the fact that she had told him where the money was hidden. After he reclaimed his money, the John picked Leah up, pressed her up above his head like a weight lifter, and dropped her down through her glass coffee table. She vaguely remembered him picking her up again, and then the memory fades. I saw every strike in vivid color as well as the tears that flowed afterwards.

Leah woke a couple hours after the beating. It took quite some time to pull herself from the glass table and to remove the several glass fragments from her arms, shoulders and face. Once cleaned up, her quick assessment found several items missing: her pride, money from her purse, her secret rainy day fund, as well as her new radio.

In addition to the above debacle, I saw many acts of violence acted upon her over the course of her career, but I didn't get a comprehensive vision of these. What I experienced this time was similar to what had happened when I entered this fucking bar from hell. It was like a rapid- fire, sick, and graphic hi-lite reel. I saw hits, broken bones, and more blood than I'd ever witnessed before. This woman had been through the ringer, to say the least. What I did find a bit perplexing was that Leah didn't see that her stealing was the cause for this latest bad turn in her life. In her opinion, it was just bad luck. It was her hope that Freddy would see it the same way.

Once again, Leah's voice pulls me away from the vision, or hi-lite film I'd been viewing, and I hear her say, "My God, stop acting like you are so horrified. You saw some amazing sex, and judging by your boner, you rather enjoyed it".

I didn't know what was more maddening: the fact I wanted to take notes, or that this crazy, one- legged broad was so in tune with my erections.

Knowing she called me out and how embarrassed I was, I let myself slide back into the vision, which resumes shortly after the robbery and subsequent beating. Double F had told her to take some time to heal and he'd also told her to get her shit together immediately. What she was doing was incredibly dangerous and stupid, and he proclaimed that, "If her brains were dynamite, she couldn't blow her nose". He made it very clear to her that she was rapidly approaching mid-level status as one of his employees. If her new game plan was to entertain drunks and dock workers, then by all means, she should continue on her current path. He further stated that if this behavior with stealing and drug use continued, she'd be "As useful as a pogo stick in quicksand" to him. Just before he left her room, he turned with a small smile and informed Leah that she should not worry about this gentleman any longer, "It is nothing that hard liquor and a hammer can't fix". His assurance was a small consolation after being beaten up and called stupid, but she appreciated his efforts to build her back up. Leah was again amazed at his run of quips and the fact that, when she woke the next morning, it was to music being played on her radio. A note simply said, "Sorry I didn't have time to clean the blood from the radio. It got a bit messy when I took it back. Get well soon, Freddy".

It was at this juncture in her life when one of her semi-regular female clients heard of her latest beating. She arrived with some bandages and assisted Leah in her recovery. During that week, they talked a lot and shared their victories and setbacks in life. The woman was named Daphne. She was an unmarried woman living with three children, "One of them being her long time boyfriend", they shared a laugh. She claimed to love her current boyfriend, but only felt sexually fulfilled in the embrace of a woman. Daphne also shared that her boyfriend told her, point-blank, that he'd never marry her; he just liked knocking her up. They agreed he was Prince Charming.

Leah didn't feel sexually attracted to females, but she certainly didn't mind the occasional liaisons. Leah understood how sexual satisfaction could be reached with a female lover and became quite adept at pleasing them. As the weeks progressed, she healed her broken body and, in the meantime, she and Daphne shared several tender moments. Over the following several weeks, with Leah back to work, the two women continued their relationship, and Leah's feelings toward Daphne grew to a love that she could not have foreseen. Love or no love, Leah did insist that Daphne continue to pay for their time together. Aside from her healing time with Daphne, Leah never dated a woman without being paid.

Leah's world was about to turn to shit once again.

The Flashing returns, but I'd say the intensity diminished somewhat. The bottles deflected, matching the intensity of the flashes. The mirror is showing scenes of violence again, sometimes repeated scenes from different viewpoints. Soon, the picture reveals itself with graphic clarity...

It was a bitterly cold winter evening, Leah and Daphne were curled up together on the bed enjoying the afterglow of a very special evening and just entering a blissful slumber. Without warning, the doorway exploded inward, and Daphne's extremely large boyfriend burst into the bedroom so fast that the door bounced back and closed without hitting him. He had an expression of blind, psychotic rage. The crazed looking man momentarily looked at Leah and simply said, "Get the fuck out, now", and returned his icy, hateful stare to Daphne. This mountain of rage stood there a moment after warning Leah to take her leave. He resembled a lumberjack and was seething with intensity. In his massive right hand, he held tightly to a large claw hammer. It would be just seconds later that he would use this hammer and claw on Daphne. Between the entrance and the attack, Daphne attempted to calm this man quietly by calling him sweet names like "sugar" this and "pumpkin" that, all to no avail. During this brief, frozen moment in time, the angry man had not noticed or cared that Leah remained paralyzed in place by fear and had not left as instructed. He was totally zeroed in on his wayward lady.

Daphne's boyfriend was as fast as he was strong. After the short-lived moment of apparent contemplation, he lunged toward her and struck her head with the claw end of the hammer. It was done with such force that it became fully embedded a good 3" inside her skull. He had a hard time removing the claw from her head, which caused him to sink further into his bubbling rage. Leah was frozen in fear and afraid to view this carnage, so she was only seeing things in starts and stops. At one point, she noticed that Daphne was still alive and screaming while trying almost comically to assist her boyfriend in dislodging her head from the claw of the hammer. If it were not so horrifying, Leah would have laughed herself silly. Seconds later, this crazed man had his boot on the top of Daphne's head which was now awkwardly laying on top of the footboard for leverage. He was pulling and twisting the hammer with all his strength, the claw released from the skull with a popping sound (like a soda pop), bringing an explosive torrent of blood, brains, and shattered pieces of bones.

The great effort to remove the hammer claw didn't stem his rage; it kept intensifying, and this man continued striking Daphne with a hatred that looked like he was a living bomb going off. It was impossible to tell what particular strike was the death blow, because she was still in a defensive position even after the claw end of the hammer finally came loose. Leah could not recall the amount of blows inflicted during this vicious attack (nor could I), but when he was done annihilating her, Daphne's upper torso and head were totally destroyed. The bedroom walls, floors, and furniture were covered with hair, blood, bone fragments, brain matter, and some other fluid I'd never be able to identify. Finally, this man spent, crumpled in complete exhaustion laying on Daphne's destroyed remains. He was murmuring, over and over again, "Why did you have to be a dyke?" After a few minutes, he finally climbed off of what had been the mother of his children and sat on the chair next to Leah's blood covered vanity. As he sat down with his chest covered in blood, the two of them were speechless for several minutes, or maybe seconds — it was hard to tell. He then quietly said, "Sorry about the mess. Mind if I smoke?" Leah didn't respond, and he lit his cigarette. In the distance, they could hear a siren.

After what seemed like forever, but was just a minute or two, Daphne's boyfriend again broke the silence, saying "Get dressed, we'll be having visitors soon". It was at that moment when Leah realized she is standing in front of this man completely naked.

Leah, for just a second during her confused state, considered this invading man handsome in a rugged sort of way. She pushed that thought vigorously aside and contemplated what the fuck was wrong with her? She may not have been "in love" with Daphne, but she did love her, and this man left her completely pulverized. How could she consider this man handsome? He was a monster.

Just as Daphne's boyfriend began to come to terms with what he'd just done, he glanced down at the floor toward where he had dropped the hammer. He was just figuring out that the hammer was not where he dropped it and had a perplexed look as the hammer came down on his head, and as they say in tennis: game, set, match.

Leah felt ashamed at her inaction of trying to defend Daphne during the attack. She reasoned that the assault came from nowhere and seemed to be over as fast as it began. Leah also believed that any attempt to stop that maniac would have resulted in her being killed as well. She soon came to a conclusion: shame was far preferable than death.

What really irked Leah the most was that, during the attack, as Daphne begged for her life, all she could think of was how annoying Daphne was with her over usage of the words "sweety" and "pumpkin". Every sentence began with one of those two words, and, as annoying as it was, she was going to miss her special friend.

Now, for an unknown reason, the portion of the story where Daphne's boyfriend had just realized his hammer was missing takes a different dynamic from what I had previously described. This was different perspective than anything I had experienced with Ken's stories. It is partially a replay of the same moment; however, what I had seen before was like a view from an unknown third party in the corner of the room. This time, it is like seeing the same scenario through Leah's eyes and continues from there to its stunning conclusion.

So, here we go again with version two...

The idea came to Leah as Daphne's boyfriend had slumped into the chair in complete exhaustion. She could not understand how a man filled with rage one moment could be quietly weeping the next. She saw his chest heaving in utter sorrow and took a moment to ponder how strange men were. Taking another look around the gore covered room, she was stunned at how much blood and even pieces of what might be brain or bone fragments were sprayed all over her room. It was at this decisive moment, while her uninvited guest was still looking down, sobbing, breathing very hard, and muttering incoherently, that Leah made a decision. She picked up the hammer, lifted it as high as she could over the head of the slouched and exhausted killer sitting on her chair. Leah brought the hammer down just once with a ferocity she had not known existed in her. *Like many things in life, once was enough.*

When she had finished, she sat down and, in just a few minutes had to get up to answer the door, for the police had arrived. The enormity of the past several minutes, which abruptly plummeted from pleasure to murder, left her a wreck, both physically and emotionally. But now, having to deal with the police seemed a minor inconvenience. Just one thing was on her mind now — how pissed off "Fat Fuck" was going to be.

The two older police officers responding to the call were completely taken aback, and understandably so. They had been expecting some kind of basic lovers quarrel, and instead found a bloodfest that may have been hosted by Al Capone himself.

The floor, walls, and ceiling were freshly painted crimson with textured effects of bone and brain matter. There were two dead bodies accompanied by a naked woman meekly standing and weeping while holding a large claw hammer dripping with blood and bone.

The two officers rapidly decided that an ambulance was required to treat the apparent victim who didn't appear, at first glance injured; however, she was badly shaken. Also, homicide detectives would be needed, and, once the initial investigation was complete, they would contact a coroner to remove the annihilated bodies.

Leah soon found herself in the back of an ambulance with officers asking a plethora of questions. To say she was unresponsive would be an understatement. She barely blinked. The officers correctly assumed that she was in deep shock from the grisly scene she had witnessed. After a few minutes of unproductive questioning, the ambulance personnel strongly suggested that the detectives interview the young lady after the doctor completed his examination. After some debate, Leah was finally transported to the hospital to be checked for injuries and possible concussion.

Leah's next memory was waking up in the hospital. Despite all the trauma of the previous night, she felt pretty good physically and clear-headed. She laid there hoping the past evening was a fucking nightmare, but soon realized, "Nightmares sure as hell don't bring you to the hospital". The previous evening had really happened. At that realization, a white-haired man with very light skin and extremely thick glasses (she remembered the term for his appearance was albino) entered her room and introduced himself as Homicide Detective Uliasz. The detective wanted to know if she felt well enough to provide a statement. Leah agreed, but asked for a glass of water or juice as she was extremely thirsty. Detective Uliasz requested some water from the nurse, which was soon delivered. Leah slowly drank the beverage in order to take a moment or two to get her story straight. The Detective instinctively knew what she was up to and tried to resume the interview, but without success. If there was ever a woman that knew how to stall an interview, Leah Rose was her. Detective Uliasz knew at once that he'd met a savvy, streetwise woman who had been around the block more than once. After several minutes, she finished her beverage and began providing her statement in a steady but very slow manner. She answered questions with a mix of truth, and some editorial changes, with the sole objective of saving her ass. Though she had not had much time to devise a story, her description and responses were the product of a person more than capable of thinking on their feet. It certainly didn't hurt that she was still a very beautiful woman, and she knew how to play a man for a dupe. If he proved a challenge, showing some cleavage would seal the deal, even with the seasoned Detective Uliasz.

Leah claimed that she and Daphne had been intimate before Daphne's crazy boyfriend arrived. She described the relationship in a way which was overly descriptive. It was Leah's hope that the detective's focus would shift to the picture she'd projected, not the case at hand. Toward the end of her statement, Leah leaned forward to expose her cleavage, and for good measure, she re-positioned herself in her chair, folding her long legs in a very slow seductive manner. Once she knew he was focused on whatever naughty vision he had in his head, she asked with a sexy smile if he was becoming uncomfortable in his briefs. The detective. who prided himself as a master at interrogations. found himself feeling like a mouse being played with by a feisty sexy street cat. It made him uncomfortable, and not just in his briefs. She smiled at him. She knew she had her mouse.

Yet again, Wheels barges into the vision like a bull in a china shop and proclaims, "Hey everyone, Jim has another boner!" This was followed by the worst bout of cackling and coughing I'd ever heard. If the others shared her laugh, I didn't notice.

I do my best to return to the vision like a shot for obvious reasons. I'm thankful to return as Leah continues giving her statement to the now befuddled detective. The detective finally snaps out of his befuddled state and asks Leah to remain on point. He clearly orders her to skip the foreplay

55

and get to the point where the boyfriend enters the room. Leah claims that, earlier in the evening, she and Daphne had been curled up on her bed still awake but very close to dozing off. Explosively and without warning, Daphne's crazy-fucking-boyfriend explodes into the room. He lunged toward the bed with frightening speed and began to smash Daphne with the hammer repeatedly, blood spraying in every direction. She didn't feel the need to describe the entire episode with the claw end of the hammer being almost impossibly lodged in Daphne's head. She just stated that at the end of his attack he dropped the hammer from complete exhaustion. Realizing that her opportunity to defend her friend had long passed, but now feared for her own safety as he had earlier threatened her as well. She grabbed the hammer to strike him from the front, but he turned his head defensively at the last second, and instead, the bone shattering blow appears to be from the back. Detective Uliasz didn't believe this story, but he lacked the evidence to counter it.

Also, due to the fact that Leah's rap sheet only involved a couple solicitation charges and that a vast majority of the bloody prints were connected to the intruder, the detectives didn't feel they had enough to arrest Leah at that point. Upon further investigation, the detectives would soon discover that the hammer had the gentleman's name and company he worked for engraved on the murder weapon. Despite the fact that the room looked like the results of a gang massacre, "The likes of which would have made Al Capone lose his lunch", she was soon cleared of any wrongdoing, and the case was closed. It was recorded in the report that the death of the estranged boyfriend was due to the occupant's claim of self-defense.

This was the first murder by Ms. Leah Rose. It would not be her last.

Double F was as pissed off as Leah had anticipated. Upon his arrival at Leah's apartment, he exploded, "I'm as mad as a mule chewing on bumblebees", which would have made her laugh if not for her terror. He was full of venom while spewing insults mixed with questions at her. "How are you going to entertain in a fucking bloody mess? Who is going to clean the fucking apartment?" Leah thought for sure he was going to kill her, but he never laid a hand on her and, as he left, he loudly exclaimed that the apartment "Smells like the shithouse door of a shrimp boat". The door was slammed with such force that a picture was dislodged from the wall, smashing to the floor.

Leah was greatly shaken from the murder that she got away with and the ongoing aftershocks from Double F. The act had been spontaneous, and the opportunity had actually smashed her door in. The opportunity delivered motivation and the weapon as well. The only cost was a person she cared deeply for. It was widely believed in the neighborhood that she had acted in self-defense; however, there were some that questioned just how innocent she was, most notably Double F and Detective Uliasz.

Aside from the initial police investigation, the serious repercussions were not from the law; it was indeed Double F as she had feared. A few days didn't ease his anger. He remained absolutely pissed off and basically cut her off from their business partnership. Leah was soon ordered out of the very nice apartment that she had grown to love. It was less than a week after the incident that he ordered a moving truck to her apartment. The furniture was removed, and he told her in no uncertain terms to "Get the fuck out". Just before he stormed out the last time, he hollered that "You're as useful as a trap door in a canoe", and "Since you don't use your head, you may as well have two asses". I had to admit, this guy's gift of gab was relentless.

Leah, due to poor life changes, had just a bit more money than when her life with Double F began. She would bring her meager belongings to the local women's shelter and hope for the best.

Amazingly, for someone that had been through so much shit, she was still in her mid 20's and still had a youthful appearance and a very shapely figure. She maintained her figure by still dancing frequently; however, she was beginning to look older than she was. Leah's lifestyle was beginning to take a toll on her appearance.

Leah had managed to obtain a few secret contacts from people she had entertained while in the employ of Double F. She was careful to contact the men that treated her in a gentle manner and those that tipped well. She was cautious to keep her contacts with these Johns a secret, as she didn't want to piss off Double F **any more** than she already had. If he got wind of her seeing his clients, the shit would hit the fan. Leah was well aware of the type of trouble Double F could bring to her door.

In order to stay at the shelter, Leah had to get a legitimate job, at least part-time. She took a job as a waitress at a local diner, since that was the only thing she knew how to do (other than the job she excelled at on her back).

In the next year or two, she began taking chances with some shadier clients to supplement her waitress job. Not having Double F screen contacts, make arrangements, and handle money transfers would again expose her to the occasional beating. Also, not having a secure location to entertain her guests led to riskier clientele in far riskier locales.

Leah, fully realizing her 30's were rapidly approaching, made a promise to herself to get her act together. In a few more years, she'd hope to recoup money to attain her long overdue goals. The drug hobby she had maintained was not helping her get off her back and go to school. It was still her hope to one day obtain a job that didn't involve her head slamming into the headboard. Also, Leah still dreamed of meeting a nice man and getting married, but she didn't put any effort into finding such a man. It was akin to dreaming of winning the lottery without purchasing a ticket. She continued going to the town community center to dance with soldiers from the base. She really enjoyed her time with them despite the occasional groping or squeezing. She liked the guys, and most of them behaved well. As long as she didn't date them or take them as a client, she felt she'd be ok.

The first and last time that she broke her rule was a brutal misjudgment. The older, dark-haired man was handsome and appeared to be very nice. His name was Tony. Leah had not met him before, and when he claimed to be on temporary assignment for the government, she broke her rule because she thought he might be a spy. "What could be more exciting than that?" she mused. Also, the fact that he had a long scar on his right cheek greatly added to the attraction she felt for him (sadly, I'm made aware by the freaky powers to be in this place that she's very attracted by scars on men). Leah whispered in his ear that she'd be happy to take their dance to her room for a "fee", and he quickly agreed. Leah was pleased that he was willing to pay, because she would have gladly entertained him on the house. He helped her with her coat, escorted her to his car where they took the short trip to her place. Once they arrived, he asked her to remain seated while he opened the car door for her, held her arm as they approached the front door of her latest apartment, portraying himself successfully as the perfect gentleman.

As Leah opened the door, reached inside to flip on the lights, and turned to tell her gentleman friend to keep quiet, she was promptly met with her gentleman caller's fist. Leah was struck so hard by the punch that it nearly knocked her unconscious. She reeled backwards with her brain spinning, yet somehow still recognized the taste of blood in her mouth. Before she could fully regain her senses, Tony gripped her blouse from the front with one hand just under her chin and dragged her to the couch where she was thrown and landed as if she were a rag doll. Her exciting, scarred, super-spy ripped off her skirt and violated her. In her confused state, she came to a startling realization, "Men with two radically different sides to them have always been her undoing".

However long this ordeal lasted, she eventually found herself flying naked on her couch in a state of shock and confusion as well as a world of pain. Leah soon realized that her kindly gentleman was deep asleep behind her with his arm draped over her waist. Could she slip off the couch undetected? She waited a few minutes for him to stir and heard him breathing deeply. As she thought about her situation, she realized that this might be her only chance to get away from this crazy asshole. Her anger created the clarity and boldness she needed. Leah very slowly rolled off the couch and thought, "If he wakes up, I'll say I need the ladies room". She hoped to God he'd believe her. She knew in her heart that he would not, which is why she had to succeed in her escape. Once she was free from his embrace, she held her breath a second presuming he was still deep asleep. She breathed again when she was safely off the couch and out of arm's reach.

Leah tiptoed to the bathroom and looked at her face in the mirror. It was a mess with blood everywhere, and her right canine tooth was shattered. After a few minutes of hurried cleaning, she was surprised to realize that her nose might not be broken, and aside from the damaged tooth, the rest remained intact, although they hurt like hell. The bloody mess in her mouth had been from the teeth being smashed into the inside of her mouth, courtesy of the mysterious super-spy. Leah also realized how much pain she had between her legs, and hoped to God this asshole didn't impregnate her. But time would tell, and it was more important at this time to think about the present, not what might happen nine months from now.

As Leah regained her composure, she immediately decided that this fucker was not going to hurt her again, or any other woman for that matter. While glancing again at the sleeping monster on her couch, she considered how she should proceed with this matter. Leah first thought of getting a knife; however, that would ring alarm bells when the police investigated this incident. She knew damn well the detectives that investigated her the last time still strongly suspected her for the crime. No, she knew that whatever she was going to use to kill this cockroach had to be from the room they were both in. It could not be a traditional weapon such as a knife, as that would look highly suspicious. She had to improvise by using an everyday item to make it appear as if she grabbed it during a struggle to defend herself. Many possible plans ran through her head in a short time. She deliberated if Detective Uliasz would buy the duplicate self-defense story again. The detective must know what she did for work, and being in dangerous situations would not be out of the ordinary. Looking at her guest again and seeing him stir troubled her. She had to make a decision immediately. Turning toward the mirror again, studying her face and the blood, she knew, "How could they not believe me again, given the way I look?"

It was time to put her plan into motion, for better or worse. Leah decided to not staunch her further blood flow. It was not time for vanity; she had to look like the victim that she was. Not seeing any other options with a fucking psycho just feet away, she looked one last time to see if the asshole was still asleep. She spotted the lamp with a heavy brass base near the couch on the end table. She knew the lamp weighed a ton because she had to carry the thing up to her apartment when the elevator was out of order. She recalled thinking she was going to die from exhaustion carrying that thing. Leah picked up the lamp as gently and quietly as she could, then placed it down on the floor to adjust her grip about a third of the way up the lamp, like a baseball batter choking up. Once her grip felt secure, she lifted the lamp up above her head and let it come down as hard as she could, using gravity to assist her. The wide, heavy base hit his left temple area with a dull and strange sounding thump. For a brief, terrifying moment, she thought she had missed, because immediately upon being struck, the monster named Tony jolted up off the couch. Leah prepared to take another swing because she knew this man's retribution would be fatal. As she reared back to take a swing, she sensed disorientation in his eyes. Just as soon as he had jumped up, he suddenly leaned forward, almost as if he were preparing to throw a bowling ball down an alley. He stumbled forward and ran tumbling head first right into a wall. She looked at him for some signs of life, but she didn't observe any.

Soon after Leah's guest took a header into the wall, her neighbor (another former prostitute) was soon banging on her door. Leah let her in and the woman saw a man's crumpled body on the floor, leaning awkwardly, his bloody face against the wall. There was an awkward silence, and Leah said matter of factly, "He's dead". Another neighbor was soon looking through the open door and impulsively ran down the hall to use the telephone to contact the police. The first neighbor tried to calm Leah down, because, judging by the bruises and blood on Leah's face, it was obvious that the asshole lying in a puddle of blood had this coming.

The police, upon arriving, took note that Ms. Rose had been soundly beaten. Also, upon further investigation, the police had discovered that the apparent victim had been involved in a previous self-defense homicide. The detectives questioned her at length, and it first appeared that they would not dismiss this case as soon as the first case. While it would be a gross understatement to say they didn't believe her, the investigation involving a **John and a hooker** didn't warrant a lengthy amount of time. Another factor taken into consideration was that the FBI soon informed them that the murder victim was a career felon who was wanted in their state as well as five others. The man Leah knew simply as "Tony" was, in fact, Anthony "The Knife" Albini and he had a rap sheet ranging from extortion to conspiracy to commit murder and just about everything in between. "The Knife" had spent 18 of his past 20 years in prison, and the scar on his face that Leah so admired was from a shiv attack while he was incarcerated for armed robbery, not the glamorous wound he suffered while defending his nation as a super-spy.

The police and the Homicide Detectives chalked it up to a dangerous neighborhood, and that the woman was a willing participant in a dangerous career who happened to cross paths with a very dangerous person. To the great chagrin of Detective Uliasz, the detectives didn't investigate Leah further. She was now on the police radar screen in two towns.

I didn't see anything in the mirror having to do with her travels to the hospital. Maybe she blacked out and there are not any memories for her to have or to share? Again, I'm not a shrink or an expert in magic mirrors. Judging by the brutal nature of the sexual attack and her physical injuries, it does not surprise me that she would block out a night like that to a great extent.

At the hospital, they treated and documented Leah's injuries that were far worse than what the officers had opined. Leah was treated for a severe concussion, two stitches above her left eye, extensive swelling to her jaw, shattered right canine tooth, bruises on her thighs, hips, back, as well as a severely sprained wrist. The report also stated that a rape had more than likely occurred. Lastly, it was noted that she was missing patches of hair caused from her attacker grabbing and dragging her by the head. The treatment suggested was basically time and ice.

As Leah laid in her bed at the hospital feeling very sorry for herself, she was told of a visitor who had been patiently waiting in the lobby hoping to have a brief chat. Leah didn't feel like hosting a visitor because she felt like shit and probably looked worse. It also occurred to Leah that the visitor might be a religious nut wanting to offer her his "Holy staff of salvation", or some other nonsense. She asked the nurse to kindly inform the person to come back later; she just was not up for a visit and hoped they'd understand. She added the last three words to be polite, because, honestly, she didn't give a damn if they understood or not.

The nurse returned a few minutes later looking a bit annoyed at being delegated as a messenger and said, "I think it would be to your benefit to have a short conversation with this woman. I do not get the impression that this person has religious motivations." A tired and frustrated Leah relented and thought it might be faster to just let this persistent, unknown pain in the ass visit and say their piece to get it over with. She just wanted to get some much needed sleep.

As the older woman entered, Leah immediately knew who this stout and stern looking person was. Everyone knew her as "Jess", and if you crossed her, she would live up to her other less pleasant alias: The Jackal. The origin of her alias was never known, and nobody had ever dared asking her. It was believed that if you called her by that name to her face, you'd find yourself missing the next day.

The Jackal's specialty was overseeing the call-girls that were getting past their expiration date (if you know what I mean). Soon realizing who her guest was, it struck Leah that she was now in the minor leagues of her career with nothing to show for it. She was now in her early 30's and looked even older. This visitor spoke to her in a kind manner and was surprisingly consoling. She strongly suggested to Leah that she needed protection from the animals that had been working her over. With a smile that was meant to be comforting, but came across as intimidating, she said, "I'd be happy to discuss future employment, if and when you're ready".

The jackal further promised that, as long as Leah played by the rules, she would be treated very well. It was only if she was screwed with that things would get ugly. The woman gave Leah a card and wished her a speedy recovery, stating, "You would be smart to join my family". As The Jackal turned to leave, she looked back at Leah one last time and, matter of factly, told her, "With only a few more years on your back, you should use them wisely."

As Leah drowsily pondered her guest's offer and her current state of life, her mind turned, and she began to think about the two men she had murdered. As she dozed off, she reflected, "Those two fuckers had it coming, and I'd do it again if I had the chance". With that thought turning in her head, she fell fast asleep.

Leah awoke the next morning with a splitting headache and a newly formed ambition that she would stop taking shit from men in her life. She'd had enough. Her plan to grab the bull by the balls and deliver her own world of justice greatly lifted her spirits. She concluded that men were easy targets. They had fucked up her life for the last time.

LEAH GETS THE BALL ROLLING

It was at this point in time that Leah's life went off the rails, or to be more precise, her moral compass went seriously askew. She was tired, fed up, and determined to dish out some punishment to the people that screwed up her life. That means men were in her crosshairs, but in a different way than before. As determined as she was, Leah obviously didn't want to go to prison and vowed to be careful. However, at the time, the risk of prison didn't deter her. She'd faced her demons many times over and came out stronger each time. Nothing scared this older, hardened Leah, but would her new found fortitude last long enough to put her plans into action?

The Flashing returns with dramatically increased intensity, the bottles deflecting equally. The vision takes on a different twist: in between bloody scenes, it reveals intermixed close-ups of a giggling

Leah Rose. These scenes of violence would last just a moment, then, as usual, the deflecting would cease and the vision would become clear...

It was a few months after Leah's epiphany of pay back that she took advantage of her latest John and set her plans in motion. He was a wispy, small man with very active hands that were constantly on her ass, or his bottle of beer, or frequently both. Leah had met him at a bar, and he was already three-sheets-to-the-wind and could barely walk. Leah feigned remorse for the intoxicated patron and mentioned to the bartender that she was going to help him outside and hail a cab. The bartender simply uttered that he'd better pay his fucking tab first; otherwise, she could throw him in the gutter for all he cared.

Leah searched the man's coat, looking for his wallet in order to pay for the several drinks he had consumed. Once she found the wallet, she discovered he had absolutely nothing in it. The license listed his name as Danny O'Malley and she was amazed that drunken piece of shit was only 37 years old and his height was listed as 5'6". He looked far older and he must have been delusional if he thought his height was 5'6". Leah grudgingly paid his tab, because bartenders tended to remember deadbeats. She was counting on the fact that this bartender had seen his share of loser drunks and would not even take note that he left with her. How many drunks had he seen with call girls? It was probably far too many to count. She felt assured because the bartender barely even glanced at her, as he was deeply engaged in conversation with a far younger and prettier customer who had prominently displayed breasts.

Once the bill was paid, Leah took Danny's arm and escorted him outside. The man seemed to revive a bit with the brisk fresh air, and when he realized she was taking him to her place, his gait and demeanor improved exponentially.

As the two entered her apartment, Leah sat her new friend down on the couch and offered him a drink. She informed him that she was going to slip into something more comfortable. This gentleman looked absolutely giddy with his good fortune and was trying hard to figure what the hell he did to be in this situation with such an attractive woman. He finished his drink in one slug and asked for another before she even left the room. Leah poured another and, with a wink, she excused herself. As she returned to the room, she could tell he was really close to being out on his feet, so, to be safe, she poured him another. So far, her game plan was proceeding flawlessly. The happy thought in her head was, "Like sheep being led to the slaughter". Leah then asked him if he'd like her to draw him a bath to which he was eminently agreeable. She poured him another drink and proceeded to run the warm bath.

Once the water was drawn, she assisted him to the bathroom, which turned into quite a ludicrous struggle. Leah, finally able to remove his clothes, assisted him inside the tub which was no easy task. The man's hands were alternating deliberately between grabbing the walls, towel rack, or her tits for balance. During the awkward trip to the tub, she noticed his penis was as wide as it was long which must have been terrible for him, as his penis was about 3" long fully erect. He finally managed to sit down in the tub without hurting himself, promptly asking for another drink. Leah had his glass and the bottle on the kitchen cabinet ready to pour. As Leah poured another heaping serving, she brooded over how this skinny little man was still breathing, never mind continuously groping her breasts. This little dwarf could out-drink a horse any day of the week. She thought of an old fashioned idiomatic and obscure expression for someone that was very drunk, and that person was said to be "Drunk as a lord". Leah briefly tried to recall where she had heard that expression, but soon gave up. It was not as important as what was coming next.

As her gentleman caller lay in her tub in a stupor, eyes rolling around his head and his wits fading fast, she put her plan in motion. Leah pulled her guest's torso forward, yanking his hands behind his back, and worked a rope around his hands. Leah, despite her fear, found herself giggling as she remembered how she learned the particular knot she was about to use. One of her earliest Johns was a man who had washed out of the naval academy only to dress up as a sailor when he was with a woman. She'd tie him up with the knots he had taught her. Leah would now use the best knot, one she was told was called the "Prusik" knot. This was basically a handcuff knot, but much better, and almost impossible to escape. Leah let her mind reflect for just a moment, and she recalled how many times she had tied her "wanna be" sailor up in this very knot. Once her sailor was properly tied up, she would urinate on him to his great delight. This man would pay her big money for these services and he never asked for intercourse. He was as strange as he was polite, which she found oddly endearing.

Returning to the matter at hand, she tied his feet together using the identical knot and observed him closely for a few minutes until she was satisfied that he could not get out. Leah didn't mind if he struggled, as she recalled the Prusik strengthens as you resist. She stuffed his mouth with a rag and then wrapped bandages around his head making sure to cover his mouth, keeping the rag in place. Leah did a sufficient job, and the fact that his resistance was almost non-existent, led her to worry if he was in some kind of earlier than desired distress. She would find out soon enough because she was ready to begin. She suddenly thought of another Double F classic line which summed up how she felt at that moment, saying, "I am as happy as a tick on a fat dog".

Returning her attention to her friend, she saw he had rudely fallen asleep. Leah really wanted this asshole to be awake during her play time, so she drained the hot water and, once it was near empty, she re-filled the tub with cold water. For good measure, she added ice from her freezer box. Within seconds, Danny was wide awake and completely bewildered, terrified, and not surprisingly, he was shivering. Once Leah realized that her victim was processing his situation, she clearly informed him, "If you're thinking of trying anything smart, take a look above you first. You will see a toaster that is plugged in and hanging precariously from a small shelf just above your head. If you try anything cute like give me the slip, I will pull the string and your life will end fairly fast, but very fucking painfully". He looked at the set up, and, in a few moments realized that compliance was his only option. Leah informed him that he was going to pay for the pain that men had inflicted on her. His eyes got bigger when he finally noticed the tray of knives on her lap. Leah picked up the first knife and held it for a minute, staring at it, admiring it. She seemed deep in thought and finally announced, "This is for the countless beatings I've endured throughout my life, and the loss of Daphne who had been a dear friend". His terrified expression was clearly one of "Why me?" and "Who the fuck is Daphne?". Leah took the knife and put the tip of the blade on the side of his lower right calf. After a few seconds of relishing the moment, she pushed the knife into his leg and kept pushing until the tip of the blade popped through to the other side. Her victim agonized; he cried; and well, he bled...

Leah wept. She'd never been so truly content.

Leah had learned in her studies that her friend would bleed out faster from wounds if she removed a blade, and for that reason, she kept the knife implanted. She enjoyed the fact that his eyes were streaming tears, and he was in obvious agony. Leah slowly picked up the next knife and put the tip on his shoulder. She paused for a theatrical moment and then pushed extremely hard. It was tougher in this location, but she finally pushed it through until she reached the handle. The tip of the knife was protruding through his back by maybe an inch or less. The water was rapidly getting quite red. She thought it best to drain the cold water and refill it with slightly warmer water. Leah didn't want this man dying too soon. As she replaced the water, her playmate regained some of his color and then, almost just as suddenly, appeared to fatigue significantly as the rush of adrenaline, alcohol, and mental torture were **taking their** toll. Leah was feeling a bit hurried, so she took the next knife and drove it through the inside portion of his thigh, and the bleeding greatly intensified. To her dismay, she realized she had hit an artery. The tub water was dark red in just a few moments. She could see his life slipping and cursed herself for being so clumsy. Leah didn't want to let him go so blissfully, so she stepped away from the tub and pulled the string to release the toaster from it's precarious perch. Her prey's life ended with a stunning jolt of electricity. It looked like a brutal death, but still much shorter than she would have liked. She vowed to better learn the best places on the body to drive her knives to maximize pain and, in turn, to minimize the blood flow. Leah was determined that the next person would not slip away so abruptly.

Now that play time was over, it was time to work, and this would be the laborious portion of her evening. Part of her plan involved cutting her prey up into manageable pieces for carrying and disposal. Leah was glad about her foresight of having him in the tub, as it made the killing and, more importantly, the cleanup far easier. She used her Christmas tree saw and laid waste to this man's body— a feat which turned out to be far more physically taxing than she had presumed. After a few hours of packaging the body into small but portable portions and lugging them down the street for disposal, tossing the last of the body bags into the dumpster, Leah stood near the dumpster for a few seconds and told her victim to "Rest in pieces". The statement caused her to quietly cackle (just knowing this woman for any length of time, you learn doing anything quietly is a tremendous challenge for her). Leah returned to her apartment and cleaned the tub, floor and the walls. This portion of her evening also turned out to be far more time consuming than she had anticipated. Once her chores were complete, she took a well-deserved bath followed by a very nice night of blissful slumber lasting until noon the next day. She had pleasant dreams of her parents, which she had not had for a very long time.

Leah did her homework and methodically began to develop a new plan. The most important aspect of her strategy involved waiting for the right opportunity, but when motivation is very high, waiting can prove difficult.

During this time of waiting for Mr. Right, Leah wanted to figure out what she had done wrong last time to cause the premature massive blood loss. She put her time to good use by continuing her study of anatomy. In her studies, she learned that she had indeed nicked or severed the femoral artery. This artery is the main artery which provides oxygenated blood to the tissues of the leg. She would not make that mistake again. After extensive reading, she discovered that she must have just missed the Brachial artery, which is the major blood vessel in the upper arm. She knew not to go near the neck, that was common sense, but she read up on the carotid arteries and learned that they supply blood to the brain, neck, and face.

In the following weeks, she would reflect on her time with Danny and, although it was cut short (no pun intended), it was on her terms no matter how you slice it (ok, that pun was intended). This had been her first intentional kill, and would not be her last. While biding her time, she took out a few books on torture. She noticed the somewhat surprised looks on the faces of librarians, but chalked it up to her paranoia. Soon realizing that these librarians see a lot of strange items being researched, so, in time, she just acted like it was normal and the odd looks that she had perceived ceased.

LEAH KEEPS THE BALL ROLLING...

Leah had her "modus operandi" and she was looking to make improvements. She broke down the issues into categories. There was one category that was not a concern, and the other category that made her nervous. The easy category contained aspects of luring a man into her trap, inflicting the pain and terror, which was her favorite part by far, and this fed her motivation. The cleaning up and disposal of the body was laborious work, but far from impossible. She had done that before and could do it again with minimal, if any, concern. Leah was sure that, in time, it would get easier; after all, practice makes perfect. The large tub made a very convenient location to do her work, and any mess she would make could simply be washed away down the drain.

The category that concerned her was partially related to her ability to lure a man to her apartment. Leah had to do this inconspicuously because she was concerned someone might notice her, her prey, or both. Finally, after considerable thought, she put it out of her head, because in her shady neighborhood, everyone kept to themselves. Most everyone in her neighborhood was up to trouble in one manner or another. Leah's biggest concern, by far, was that she might underestimate a target and that he may not be as incapacitated as she would hope. Leah learned that even small men can develop large tolerances for alcohol, as her last victim so clearly demonstrated. She did have a backup plan for Danny, but that was when he was in the tub. What if he had fought back before he got there, or refused to get in? She briefly considered using a gun, but that would be too loud, and gunshots got reported no matter what neighborhood you resided. A knife would not work either; if she's overpowered, how would that help? Leah, feeling that her options were minimal, made a calculated decision. She would make sure the man was out for the count and inside the tub before beginning her party.

Another concern was a fast bleed out, like she had just gone through. Leah didn't want to take these risks only to have her living pincushions continue to die in a minute or two. She wanted the biggest bang for her buck and she would continue to work with her considerable knowledge involving arteries. She'd be far more careful with her knife placement during her next special date. Leah also learned in her reading that it would be a good idea to have a tourniquet handy the next time. This would be helpful on the off chance she made another mistake with her knife. If necessary, she would tie it extremely tight around the bleeding appendage, above the wound. It was her understanding that it would greatly slow down the bleeding and increase her time for fun.

Another concern was the noise that her guest might make before he was tied and muzzled. If she didn't know before, she knew now, drunks with high tolerances can become loud and belligerent, drawing the unwanted eyes of neighbors. Leah would be sure that her guest was gagged securely with gauze, cotton, and tape as soon as she felt the time was right.

A few months had passed since her first party, and Leah was growing anxious for another "special date", as she referred to it in her head. Although she was getting antsy, she vowed to remain patient in her search. Again, Leah didn't fear being captured; however, she realized it was a distinct possibility. She was going to take every precaution possible. If things became dicey, she was not going to go down without a fight. She prepared for the possibility of being pursued and went so far as to pack a suitcase on the off chance she had to leave in a moment's notice. The last thing she would do before resuming her hunt was to draft some rules that she'd follow to the letter, calling them her "Ten Commandments". Leah felt, if she followed every rule for any potential prospect, she'd enjoy a lengthy hunting career and avoid detection by the authorities. She was well aware that the police and Detective Uliasz suspected her in the prior incidents.

Leah Rose's Ten Commandments (in order of importance):

1. Trust instincts;
2. Shit faced (extremely intoxicated);
3. No drug addicts (very unpredictable);
4. Small and weak in stature;
5. No wife/no children/parents deceased;
6. Vulgar/rude speech;
7. Not a regular;
8. Out of work;
9. Over 55; and
10. Not military/police (active or retired).

It would take time and some lengthy conversations to weed out the multitude of candidates, but she remained patient. She knew that drunk men talked a lot. So, it was not difficult to weed out the candidates using her 10 Commandments for guidance.

The flashing returns: the bottles deflect: scenes of violence come and go. Leah is up to trouble again. The picture soon becomes clear.

Leah finally met her perfect man. His name was Josh. Leah found out he had never been married and was proud of the fact that "I never let any bitch get her claws into me," and also added, "If I knocked up some whore, I didn't care and I was not aware of any children". This statement certainly met the vulgar category in spades, and from the way he slurred his words, she could tell he was really on his way to a killer hangover, that is if he made it alive to morning. Upon further discussion and simple observations, Leah could tell he was well north of 50; he was at best 5'5" tall, maybe 130 pounds, give or take, with a severely receding hairline, deep lines by his eyes, and teeth that were in dire need of a brushing (although, not near the level as Ken's).

To my surprise and annoyance, I'm pulled from the vision for just a moment and I hear Ken say, "Man, you gotta real hangup with teeth don't you". *If I responded, I do not recall my reply.*

Slipping back into this vision, I hear Leah's current target say that his parents had been dead for 20 years. Leah, growing more hopeful by the minute, asked about his employer and why she'd never seen him at this bar before. He claimed to be a salesman for the Gordons fisheries and traveled across the country 50 weeks a year. He had just inherited the new sales route from a former employee that had recently killed himself with a shotgun. Claiming, "Everyone leaves that damn place in one manner or another, and I hope to as well, just not in a body bag." The job was lonely and tiresome with the traveling, but he'd only been there a few weeks. At this point in time, he charmingly winked at her with big bushy gray eyebrows and inquired, "How much for a fuck, sugar lips?"

Oh, this man was Mr. Dreamboat. Leah smiled at him, coyly thinking, "I have found Mr. Right at last".

Leah, acting demurely, informed Mr. Dreamboat that her place was right down the street, and they could take the party to her place where they could get comfortable in private. Josh placed some money on the bar to cover the drinks without so much as a glance from the bartender. Leah appreciated how the stars were lining up perfectly tonight.

Once the two love birds arrived at her place, she offered her guest a drink, and he promptly refused, saying, "I think I'd prefer to wait till we're done with our bedroom business." This was more than concerning; it was a direct strike regarding number 2 on her list (the shitfaced criteria).

Leah took a deep breath and decided to give it some time and try another approach. She was very hopeful about this person and didn't want to give up easily.

Leah, hoping to buy some time, offered her guest a hot tub that would relax him and hopefully change his mind about the drink, as well. She could offer him wine and see where that would lead. After just a few minutes of being in the tub, he accepted the glass of wine and soon became relaxed and very sleepy. To coax him along, Leah promised him that, if he changed his mind about a drink or two tonight, she'd be happy to provide her service in the morning. He answered her by asking if she knew how to make a rusty nail. She flashed her sexiest grin (sadly, she was now minus a couple of teeth that she was very conscious of) and replied, "Of course" and she was in business. As she went to look for her whiskey and Drambuie for her special guest, she noticed that Josh was already out like a light. She placed the toaster on its precarious perch above him and began to tie him up with only his dead weight as resistance. But before she got the gag in place, he woke up and began to resist with surprising vigor. It soon got to the point where she had to point out the item on the shelf above his head. Understanding his situation, he begrudgingly complied. Leah's guest was bewildered, to say the least, and she found it odd that he was sporting an impressive erection, but she carried on.

Now, Leah was ready to have some much deserved fun. She really liked how big someone's eyes got when she revealed her tray of knives. Upon her presentation of said knives, Josh's eyes grew large... and then to her great disappointment, the asshole passed out...

This was not acceptable. Leah wanted him awake or, to be more accurate, she needed him to be awake. She went to the end of the tub and pulled him by the feet, and he slid forward below the waterline. This did the trick, as he had to squirm desperately to get his head above water. Leah now had his undivided attention. She took the first knife and slowly pushed it into his calf until the knife reached the handle. The water grew red, and Josh was visibly petrified. Leah thought to herself, along with a cackle, "Wow, the best things in life really are free". Leah's date was beginning to look a bit woozy again, which meant it was time for another water treatment. She pulled him under again. Again it worked. Leah was ready to continue and she held the second knife and slowly pushed it into his other calf. She continued to place knives into his body without causing a heavy bleed. Her anatomy study had paid off, because he was still alive after she placed 7 knives in her guest's assorted extremities. Sensing he was reaching his limits, she informed him that he was a good boy and would be justly rewarded. She then took a long carving knife from her kitchen and proceeded to slowly push it with great effort directly into his chest, hoping to drive it into his heart. She was surprised at how difficult it was to push the blade into his chest. Once she got through the chest wall, she could actually feel his last few heartbeats. As the knife remained fully embedded in her guest, Leah felt as if he experienced the matching bliss that she felt. *However, I'm willing to bet it was not bliss he felt.*

The clean-up was again exhausting; however, it went without a hitch. *It struck me funny because she could have been the eighth dwarf named "Stabby", as she was whistling a happy tune as she worked.*

Time passed with some disjointed visions that didn't make a lick of sense, and I now saw Leah as a woman looking much older than her mid-to-late-30's. The mirror provided an ESP moment telling me her age; otherwise, I would not have guessed. She looked to be in her 40's, if it were up to me to guess. It was deceiving, because she was still attractive, but showing some real signs of age around the eyes and mouth. Leah had been working for The Jackal for several years, and the years were slipping by "muy rapido", as they said in her predominantly Spanish neighborhood. Before she was nicknamed "Wheels" by the patrons of this odd establishment, she was widely known in her predominantly Spanish neighborhood as "La puta vieja", which loosely translates as "The old hooker".

Due to her experience at recognizing trouble makers, combined with her protection from The Jackal, she didn't suffer from beatings as she had in her younger years. Leah's method for obtaining Johns was as simple as it got: she would go to local bars to do her trolling and she'd hope her instincts and The Jackal's protection would keep her alive.

During the previous several months, Leah continued studying different types of torture and concentrated on some that she read about during her quiet times in the public library. She really liked the idea of different forms of water torture, which, as we know, she'd been dabbling in already. She also liked the idea of removing limbs while the person was alive, but she didn't have the resources to pull that off. After much consideration, Leah decided to keep her system, but maybe tweak it a bit when the mood struck. Maybe she could make some changes in her cleanup routine. Leah had really enjoyed her last session with Josh. It was the best time she'd had in years. Leah greatly enjoyed seeing the terror in his eyes. She felt his heart beating through the handle of the knife, and the sweetest part of all, she felt the precise moment his heart stopped. It was a very special moment. She loved thinking that he actually gave her his heart. *If that is not romance, I don't know what is.*

Now that Leah had completed a murder that went like clockwork, she began looking forward to her next adventure. The subtle changes she was pondering would hopefully spice up her fun a bit. Realizing it could take some time to find a man that met her checklist criteria as well as her good friend Josh, she continued her life with a routine and drudgery that would gnaw at her. But the anticipation of her next special date kept her motivated and, most important of all, patient. Leah's employment with The Jackal was proceeding as well as could be expected. Leah cut back on her drug habit, which helped her finances dramatically. Occasionally she fell off the wagon, however, the falls were occurring far less frequently.

With her drug habit greatly reduced, she had become a full blown three pack-a-day smoker, which greatly contributed to her looking far older than her actual age. In addition to her years of hard living, drug use, and smoking, she was also showing obvious signs of malnutrition that she may or may not have realized at the time. It was easy to tell from my observations during the visions that she was declining physically. She appeared gaunt, as if a small gust of wind could blow her over. After her occasional rough treatment, she noticed that bruises, welts, and black eyes took far longer to heal. The one symptom that she most likely didn't anticipate was her decreased concentration. This would be the symptom that would forever alter her future plans and hobbies involving men. The lifelong theme in Leah's life would soon be rearing its ugly head: "All good things must come to an end".

Just like clockwork, the mirror begins flashing brighter than before. The bottles are deflecting differently. What this means, I don't know...

The next fine gentleman that caught Leah's eye was named "Owen" and this piece of shit met her criteria with ease. Interestingly, she didn't meet this creep in a bar, but rather in a grocery store. The low-life was hitting on the young girl who was bagging his groceries. She couldn't have been more than 16 from what I could see. She looked extremely uncomfortable with this person's bombardment of sexual innuendos. The cashier was a young man unsure of how to defend the young lady's honor. He looked as upset as she did, possibly more so. Leah was bagging her own groceries in the next aisle over as she listened to this one-sided verbal assault. The man had asked the young lady to handle his meat with both hands and then proceeded to compliment her firm young melons. He asked several times if he could squeeze her breasts to determine if they were ripe. The lude comments continued to grow more crass as the minutes went by painfully. When he finally finished his transaction, he asked the young lady her name, and she meekly responded, "Kathy". He responded in kind by informing her of his name, which was Owen, further clarifying the pronunciation, "You know, like you be Owen me some round firm melons". This is where Leah intervened to the great relief of the two young employees, as well as a few of the nearby customers who had the misfortune of over hearing the rude interlude. Leah simply made herself heard, and as you know by now, that's not difficult for her to do. She said loudly to this man named Owen, "Jesus, why don't you harass someone that may not be your child, you fucking loser", to which he immediately replied, "Shut up grandma. Go find a Boy Scout to escort you across the street". Rather than allowing that comment to exacerbate the discussion further, Leah just smiled because she realized, at that moment, that she may have a new pin cushion for her knives. Leah pulled a pencil and notepad from her handbag and immediately wrote a note calling him a child molester, and if he'd like a real woman, he should call her up, as she had not screwed a retard in some time. Leah included her telephone number with a postscript on the bottom asking, "Do retards have small dicks?" Leah hoped that he'd take the bait, although, she realized calling this man a retard twice would not help matters and may scare him off. She just found it too difficult to resist. At the very least, she did spare the children some further ugliness and felt as if she'd done her good deed for the day.

Leah thought about the loser as she carried her groceries home, wishing that she got his number. She feared she scared him off, as it is common for a blowhard to run when they are confronted. As she was about half done putting her scant groceries away (smokes, eggs, milk and bread), the telephone rang, and to her great delight, it was the less than charming man from the grocery store. After talking for a bit, they arranged to meet at the corner newsstand later that day to have a coffee and possibly arrange a business transaction. She was surprised that the hostility was absent from him at this time. He even told her that he'd had a real crappy day and just took it out on the young lady. No matter, Leah had already chosen him, because assholes are assholes.

Owen's looks were what I would consider smarmy, and if he were wearing a cheap polyester suit, he'd look like the stereotypical used car salesman. He was well short of 6', rail thin, with a slight and almost feminine build. He possessed far more body hair than any human should have. His hands were small and fragile looking despite the hair on his knuckles. He had obviously not done a hard-day's work in his life. He had black hair that was slicked straight back and thick black eyebrows. He had a constant, sneaky, devious kind of smile. I don't know how to explain the off-putting smile, but it was both prominent and disturbing. He constantly looked as if he'd secretly seen you jerking off in the bathroom or something. Leah took an immediate dislike to him, and to be honest, I did as well. The clincher for this person was, after a short conversation, he stated that he was a disbarred attorney, had ripped off the law firm he had worked for, and left his wife and three children several weeks later. I was looking forward to seeing how Leah would dispose of this schmuck and hoping it would take many knives to get the job done.

During the time between meeting Owen at the store and getting together afterward, he had become mildly intoxicated. At first, his intoxication confused her as they were in a coffee shop, but she soon figured out he was discreetly sneaking alcohol from his flask into his drink when he thought she was not looking. The two of them talked at length, and Leah pretended to like him, which she pulled off by thinking of using her toys on him. Owen learned that Leah didn't play for free, but he had a few dollars to spend to "Get my wood varnished" (his words). As they arrived at her home, she was amazed at how agile he still was. He seemed to have a hand on her ass every second. She wanted to move this along as this disgusting man made her skin crawl. Leah whispered something in his ear, and he stood up snappily, removed his clothes, folded his clothes, and hopped with surprising speed into the tub while sporting a comically thin, hairy, rigid, medium-length penis. Leah thought to herself with a giggle, "My God, his penis is a mini version of himself". She poured him a very stiff drink. Leah was thinking, "I hope this drink is as stiff as his penis. because this guy is bursting with gusto".

I broke from the vision for just a moment and contemplated the crazy visions and ESP moments. Also, I've now taken note on how I have the ability to hear thoughts as well. I've just noticed that, in these visions or ESP moments, I can comprehend thoughts clearly as if they were spoken or narrated to me; however, I cannot hear two people whispering to each other. "What the fuck is that about?" I'm sure if Double F were around he'd claim it was "Nuttier than a port-a-potty at a peanut festival".

Ok, back to Leah. She was taken aback, as well as concerned, by his speed, balance and agility despite his recent inebriated state. Her instincts were telling her to cancel the plans for the evening by feigning illness and sending him home. But she went against her instincts because this guy was otherwise the perfect candidate.

Leah thought of her list again. This guy broke maybe a few of her commandments. She was not afraid of this guy physically. Despite his younger age, she honestly felt she could kick his ass if he got rough. However, he had been surprising her all day and night, so, for extra precaution, she kept a knife close-by.

The warm tub and the flow of alcohol didn't even dent this guy's motor skills, and she soon realized she needed a Plan B. By this stage, stopping was not an option she would entertain. She whispered something inaudible to him while he was in the tub, leaving him with a smile and a renewed energy to his erection.

Again, what the fuck?, I can comprehend a thought, but not a whisper? This is pissing me off.

Anyway, Leah returned with some towels and the remainder of the bottle of wine they had started. She kneeled down next to the tub and in her sexiest voice possible, asked him to close his eyes and relax. He insisted she get in the tub with him, which she did with great reluctance. As Leah was standing over him and preparing to lower herself onto him, she asked again that he close his eyes and relax. To her relief, he complied. As he did as instructed, Leah reached for the towels that concealed a ball peen hammer wrapped inside. Quickly removing the hammer, she reared backwards and struck her guest with all the strength she could muster. My God, did the blood fly. The powerful spray led to her being distracted for just a second, and in that very brief moment, her guest lunged up and, inadvertently or not, pulled the cord attached to the toaster down toward the water. As Leah saw the toaster falling, she instinctively lunged backwards and away from the tub to escape the forthcoming jolt. As the toaster made contact with the bathwater, her left foot was still partially submerged, and the accompanying shock assisted her momentum in knocking her from the tub.

After a brief moment of gathering her senses, she considered if she had been knocked out and, if so, for how long. As she slowly came to grips with what had transpired, she promptly unplugged the toaster. She now heard her downstairs neighbor hollering that he was going to check the fuse box. Leah glanced at her victim, who was obviously dead, and realized she had to get him the fuck out immediately. While she didn't yet comprehend the extent of her injury, in her heart she knew she had sustained something serious. It was purely survival instincts compelling her to act fast. Even in Leah's confused state of mind, the idea of explaining a dead man in her tub holding a toaster didn't seem to be in her best interest.

Leah used her fear and adrenaline, as well as her anger, to cut up and dispose of the body in her usual manner. In her current physical condition, it took a herculean effort. Leah was enraged with herself for proceeding with this endeavor when her instincts were screaming for her to stop. After all, the first commandment on her list was "trust her instincts", and she had botched it badly. She was still very angry with herself when she finally went to bed that evening. She was really worried that she had done significant damage to herself.

Leah woke up the next morning with numbness in her left leg and noticed it didn't look normal. Her leg had a pale look to it and it was dry to the touch. Despite the strange look to her leg, she was thankful there was no pain. She hoped things would be ok if she just took some time to rest.

As the day progressed, Leah noticed her leg was getting darker. It seemed to her that, as time went by, her wound was changing to a gray and black. She was now very nervous and decided to contact The Jackal. Jess always knew what to do or who to contact in times of crisis. It would be a few hours later when Jess finally came to look in on Leah.

Once The Jackal arrived, she was "shocked" at the condition of Leah's leg (sorry, bad place for a pun). It had deteriorated significantly while waiting for The Jackal to arrive. After looking at the injury, the two ladies discussed the situation thoroughly. Though understandably hesitant to call the ambulance, they both knew Leah was in trouble. First, The Jackal convinced Leah that her wound looked serious. Then she explained that she had no idea how to tend to her wound, or even if it could be treated. She told Leah that she was going to summon an ambulance and did so despite Leah's objections.

The ambulance took almost two hours to arrive at Leah's apartment, and her condition continued to deteriorate during that time. The primary reason she had to wait so long was that she resided in a high-crime part of town, and medical, as well as police responses were historically slow to say the least.

Once Leah made it to the area clinic, the on-call physician realized the extent of her injury and promptly diagnosed a severe electrical burn. It was at this point in time treatment began to move at a faster pace. She was soon transferred via ambulance to a major city hospital.

Once Leah arrived at the hospital, her toes, foot and calf were black. The on-call physician told her they'd have to amputate immediately and was hopeful that they could save the knee because a prosthetic would work better if they were able to attach such a device to the knee joint. However, they'd have to wait and see how the first amputation responded. Leah was obviously in shock. She heard what the doctor said, but she didn't fully comprehend it. She was on auto-pilot and would have said yes to just about anything he said.

To Leah's surprise, The Jackal remained by her side and helped make decisions when Leah was unable to. In her deeply medicated state, she realized that The Jackal had progressed from being an employer to becoming a true friend. This was not a common occurrence in their line of work.

The amputation proceeded as planned, and the wound was left open to closely monitor the gangrene. Unfortunately, the doctors soon determined they would have to amputate further up the leg, as the gangrene continued to manifest itself in her wound. If the second amputation surgery didn't happen immediately, she would likely not survive to greet the next sunrise.

The second amputation was a femoral amputation (upper leg). Leah was kept on a heavy dose of pain medication while the wound remained open for observation. As she awoke after the second procedure, Leah was relieved that the face smiling down on her was none other than Jess. Even in her fuzzy state of mind, Leah considered it polite to now refer to her as Jess, rather than the other less pleasant title. After careful monitoring by the hospital staff, Jess informed her that the leg was responding, and the wound would be closed. This news was soon verified by her nurse.

With the second amputation procedure now behind her, Leah would now be on the very long, grueling road to recovery. She doubted she'd ever recover mentally, and physically didn't appear to be in the cards either. The first day that Leah was feeling somewhat coherent, Jess came to visit, slowly closing the door behind her. She said they had to talk. Jess informed her that she'd long thought of Leah as a friend. She was not sure when or why that happened, but she felt a bond with Leah soon after meeting her at the hospital years earlier. Jess tried to lighten the mood by telling Leah that they had to stop meeting in hospitals. Leah, too tired to laugh, managed a smile. She drifted off for just a moment and just as rapidly came to, stating, "Hell, I didn't even want to meet you. I thought you were going to be a Jesus freak", and they shared a chuckle and a cackle. Leah thanked Jess for her friendship. She had always felt protected by Jess and she promised to return the favor should she ever need help. Leah told Jess that she was apprehensive about calling her a friend for quite some time due to the working arrangement. Jess completely understood. Once she sensed that Leah's mind was somewhat clear from the pain meds, she told her they had to talk about the night of the injury and get their stories straight, because somehow the police suspected foul play, and Detective Uliasz was actively snooping around.

Leah continued to listen as well as her partially muddled mind would let her and hoped her shaking hands were not evident to her friend. Jess told Leah that the police had been investigating because of several hinky facts. First was that Detective Uliasz always suspected Leah of earlier felonies. Second, the seriousness of her injury, and third, the ambulance crew had noted suspicious blood splatter at the scene in their reports as well as a pile of men's clothing. When the ambulance medic at the scene had asked if a man was injured as well, Leah appeared surprised at the question and claimed that men were not allowed in her apartment. This statement unsettled Jess and made her realize the depth of Leah's condition, because a pile of men's clothes were less than 10 feet away. As she recalled looking at the neatly folded pants, shirt, undergarments, socks, and shoes sitting on the armrest of the couch, she could not fathom how she had not disposed of them. Leah had reason to be confused. What was her excuse?

The detective and the police were circling her hospital room like hungry sharks. They all knew there was more to this story. Would they find out? That was the question.

Once the door to Leah's room was closed and the two women were alone, Jess pleaded with Leah to tell her everything and assured her she'd continue to help, but she feared telling the police or the detectives something that didn't mesh with what Leah might say. Jess began by asking questions, such as to the identity of the person in her bathroom. Was it a John? Was it a personal friend? Was it Leah's blood they found? What was Leah's story going to be? Did something happen in the tub? That is where the blood was observed. Jess continued to plead with Leah to be truthful, vigorously adding, did someone get violent with you which is why you struck them? If so, where are they now and, most importantly, is this person still alive? Jess asked again for the person's name. She informed Leah that her boys could make the man vanish for good; just tell her a name.

As Jess, with good intent, continued to badger Leah for a name, only one thought popped into Leah's cloudy brain: "I guess I didn't clean up as well as I thought."

Leah continued to feel bombarded by the questions, but understood the reasons. The two women were savvy and understood the importance of getting their stories straight. However, Leah was not sure how to respond at that very moment. Barring some terrible flashbacks or dreams, she had forgotten many details of that night. Leah had been too busy to think of a story because her time awake was spent reflecting on losing parts of her body and taking killer naps that sometimes would cause her to lose entire days. Jess would not let up and persisted on knowing who this person was. Growing agitated, Leah impulsively blurted out in a panic that it was from a man who was a personal date, and he was not a John. Leah knew his first name was Roger but claimed to have forgotten his last name. Also, to add to Leah's stress, she was stunned and ashamed by the fact she chose this particular name from her past as the name belonged to her long deceased father. "Wow, why, from all the names on God's green earth, did I pick my father's name?" Leah still remembered her father as a man that worked very hard. When he died, it changed the course of her life, as well as her mother's. If he had not died as early as he had, would her mother also be alive? Would the fire that her mother started have killed both her parents, and she'd be alone now anyway? Would she have had a better life? Did she somehow hate her father for dying? The question she asked herself last was the most painful. If he had not died, would she be a one legged hooker? What on earth would a shrink think of that chain of thoughts?

After Jess heard the name Leah provided, she stormed out claiming she'd find the bastard and make him disappear. Although Leah greatly appreciated the gesture and that she was trying to protect her, this was really about Jess pursuing some retribution as well as maintaining "The Jackal's" reputation as someone not to be fucked with. This meant she'd have her goons locate and squeeze some money out of the poor, unfortunate, fictional Roger.

Leah felt a little better because she knew The Jackal would not find her dead father, and maybe the lie might actually buy her some additional time to heal from this latest surgical procedure. She figured, after some time, this would blow over. After all, no bodies had been found, nor had any witnesses come forward. Even with Leah's lack of education, she knew this case didn't have a leg to stand on (too soon?). Leah knew a case like this would soon be put on the back burner. She was exhausted from The Jackal's onslaught of questions and was happy that she had left for parts unknown. It was only a few minutes later when she dropped into a sound medication- induced sleep.

A few hours later, Leah woke with a start and a scary thought in her head, "What if the police found one of the body parts?" As Leah's mind raced around on this possible scenario, she looked at where her foot had been and screamed in agitated disgust, "Why does my left foot hurt so goddamn much?, I don't even have a fucking left foot!" Leah had not been told about phantom pain yet, nor had she been told about phantom itches. *The phantom itches would soon drive her to the point of madness, but the drive would be a short one.* This was her state of mind when Jess finally returned the next morning.

The two women continued their earlier conversation and collaborated well into the afternoon. Leah asked Jess a plethora of questions involving what the police might be investigating and knew damn well that her situation looked highly suspicious. She understood very well that she couldn't be arrested for murder on suspicion of a crime. At some point, she thought the police would have to pony up some evidence. Also, it gave her some comfort when she realized that, if the police did have some evidence, she'd have been arrested already. Leah reflected proudly that she had even had the wherewithal to dump her knives in the storm sewer after she had disposed of the last body bag. It had been part of her plan that, if anything ever went awry, she'd toss the knives in the storm sewer. After all, she could always buy a new set. It would not be prudent to have a $2.00 knife set be the cost of losing her freedom. After hearing what Jess knew, which was not much, Leah gleaned from this last conversation that a few small smears of blood had been spotted in her apartment and not the bloody mess that Jess had hinted at earlier. The extent of her injuries, the small amounts of blood, and last but not least, her past history were the reasons she was being investigated.

Finally giving in, Leah spilled everything to Jess about that terrible night. Not a single, sordid detail was left out. The only detail she left out was that this was not the first time she'd killed someone in her tub. Leaving Jess to believe this was a one-time, spur-of-the-moment event.

Somehow, when the long story of that evening was over, Jess was not as shocked as Leah anticipated. She simply took a deep breath and said, "Holy shit. I've wanted to do the same thing my whole life. Men are pigs". Leah impetuously agreed, and they both shared a quiet, cautious laugh. Jess assured Leah that, to her knowledge, she was not aware of any body or body parts turning up anywhere. With that, Jess took her leave and promised to return soon.

Leah remained awake for a short spell and tried valiantly to process the lengthy conversation without much success. Just prior to drifting off, she realized that, to her regret, the evenings she had enjoyed with her special dates were now over. How would a one-legged woman woo a victim to her house and then have the physical ability to tie up her guests and dispose of their remains? She shivered at the thought of the type of man that would try to hire a one-legged hooker...

As Leah dozed off in a roller-coaster mindset, she began to think that she could still meet Mr. Right in the future, albeit, more likely an amputee version of Mr. Right. This positive frame of mind was short-lived, and she soon realized the optimism must be the drugs talking. Nobody had wanted her for a wife when she had two gorgeous legs, who the fuck would want her now? Despite that negative turn, she had a good night's sleep.

LEAH'S LIFE ROLLS ON...

Several months went by during rehabilitation and adapting to a new life in a wheelchair. When, on the day of her release, Jess picked her up and presented her with a special present: a nice, new, shiny wheelchair. It was much nicer than the piece of shit the hospital had provided to her. *What struck me in this vision was the fact that the chair she was given by Jess was not the piece of crap she was then occupying.*

It was during the time of her lengthy rehabilitation that the police investigation fizzled out as Leah had correctly anticipated. A body was never reported, and nobody came forward with any complaints of an attack or suspicious missing persons allegations. The police and Detective Uliasz didn't have any doubt that Leah did something terrible to someone; they just couldn't prove it. The paper investigation only lasted a few months, but, in reality, it had ended well before then.

Once Leah had been home for a month or so, Jess came for a visit and offered yet another surprise, offering Leah a job with her agency. The Jackal referred to her business as an agency because it sounded reputable. Leah would soon learn it was anything but. As we know, Jess was basically a madam, but she also dabbled as a loan shark and arranged accidents for those that could not maintain the agreed upon payment arrangement. The main business for Jess, however, was managing escorts (i.e. hookers). Leah's role in the agency was that of a secretary. She answered calls, arranged meetings, and performed simple tasks for Jess. This usually involved handling some very sordid affairs for The Jackal. For instance, if one of her escorts got out of line, on the first occasion, The Jackal would arrange for a gentleman (aka goon) to rough her up, but not damage the merchandise. The second time would involve a broken arm, leg, or several fingers and a very serious FINAL warning. If the young lady was extremely popular, she'd get dunked in water to the point of near death in lieu of the variety of fractures mentioned previously. The code Jess would use for the water treatment was to "take the young lady to the beach". No matter how popular the young lady was, a third transgression would involve The Jackal requesting Leah to arrange a meeting between a special gentleman (aka special goon) and the young lady in question. The young lady would simply disappear and never be heard from again. Leah was very happy that The Jackal liked her. That woman would be scarier than the boogeyman to have as an enemy. As close as Leah and Jess had become, she never even pondered asking Jess what became of those young ladies that met the special gentleman.

Now, the treatment of her employees was generous compared to the treatment received by the Johns that mistreated her ladies. In a case such as that, there were no first or second warning. It would simply be a send-off to the great beyond.

It was several months after working for Jess that Leah experienced a rougher than usual week because Leah had to arrange two final meetings for employees that she'd known. This upset her greatly, although she had no problems arranging meetings for the Johns that misbehaved. After this particular week, Leah really wanted to enjoy a drink and just sit alone in a quiet bar while she drowned her sorrows. A gentleman (one of the Jackal's special goons) had mentioned a bar called The Last Call. He described it as a very quiet place where the unusual customers kept to themselves for the most part. Leah thought this place would be the perfect location to unwind. If the customers were unusual, who better to visit this fine establishment than a one-legged, retired hooker moonlighting as a secretary for a madam?

Leah visits the establishment and soon becomes a regular. She is so well liked that she is swiftly given a nickname by its patrons. Leah is now and forever will be known as Wheels.

CHAPTER 4

The wall of fame

"Men have called me mad; but the question is not yet settled,
whether madness is or is not the loftiest intelligence–
whether much that is glorious– whether all that is profound–
does not spring from disease of thought– from moods of
mind exalted at the expense of the general intellect."

— Edgar Allan Poe, Complete Tales and Poems

As I watched Leah roll away, I noticed a wall that had many pictures of what I assumed to be favored regulars of this fine bar over the course of many years. Some of the photographs had as few as three people, and some had up to a dozen. The bartender, who I'd barely even noticed aside from his constant badgering about the two drink minimum, mentioned that the photographs were of special customers. I was informed that the bar owner takes these photographs once every four or five years. He also felt it important, for some reason, to advise me with an odd chuckle that "The next group picture day is coming soon. You should dress for the occasion." I felt it in my best interest not to laugh at that statement. He went on to say that only the very special regulars are invited, not just ordinary customers. These statements had me a bit confused because this was my first time in this place, and I had zero intention of ever returning. I contemplated if this guy was off his rocker or just trying to create some business, albeit, in a very creepy manner. I didn't put too much time into thinking about his motive and soon realized that

I didn't give a rat's ass what he was up to. If not for these hypnotic visions providing voluminous detail in seconds, I'd be long gone. As a matter of fact, if not for the shitty weather, I never would have set foot in this damn place anyway.

I took my barely touched beer and ambled over to the wall of photographs for a better look. I stood there gazing at what had to be fifty photographs for several minutes, when I suddenly felt a presence. I looked to the right and then down, Wheels had quietly rolled up to me, which was quite an amazing feat, considering her wheelchair was louder than Stevie Wonder running through a field of whoopie cushions. It must have been my preoccupation with my perusal of the photographs. What made these individuals special? Were the people in the pictures killers like the two individuals that had shared their pasts with me? Is this some kind of Killers' Wall of Fame? I contemplated, "Why are these off-kilter individuals feeling compelled to share their deep and very dark secrets with an outsider? Were these people going to make sure I wasn't going to talk? Was I the mouse that these cats chose to play with because the television was broken and they were bored?" I was growing tired of numerous questions that lacked answers.

As all these questions were banging around my head, I suddenly heard Wheels saying, "Look at the picture on the far left, third one down!" As my head turned to look at it, I heard her say, "The guy in the middle used to like golden showers, and the two on the left were fudge packers."

My response, "You are truly a wealth of information".

I noticed that Ken was walking toward me via the scenic route. He began his journey looking in my direction, but walked around a few of the booths in the restaurant portion of this building while on his trip toward me. As he finished his circuitous route, he sat down on a stool that was a few yards from me and just said, "Christ, come on, Wheels. He don't give a shit who you fucked or pissed on. Let's just tell him about some of these guys in the pictures, because with this weather, there ain't a goddamn other thing to do." He abruptly added, "Since Gerald is too fucking cheap to have the TV repaired." Everyone turned to look at the bartender, Gerald.

It was apparent that Gerald wanted to stop the talk of him being cheap as he recklessly chimed in with, "Hey, Wheels, why don't you tell our guest how many men on that wall you gave handjobs to?"

Ken, retaliating, nipped that question in the bud (thank God) by stating that the photographs began in 1910 with the first owner and continued up to the present owner, whom he referenced as the cheap bastard behind the bar. Gerald responded with a vigorous polishing of the mug he'd been working on since I'd arrived. He mumbled something that I didn't hear.

Ken continued with the history of The Last Call and mentioned that a photograph was taken in the similar location in front of the mirror since the 1920's or so. Ken went on to say, "Much of the bar's interior originated in Chicago. Once the original owner of The Last Call passed away, after about 20 years in business, the estate sold the actual bar, mirror, and some other odds and ends to a new owner on the east coast. The only original items remaining to date are the bar, mirror, and that fucking mug that Gerald has been rubbing forever."

Gerald adds to the conversation by stating, "It ain't the place that's special; it's the mirror".

I consider asking what is so special about the mirror; however, I realize that, like all my other questions, it would likely go unanswered.

I glance back at the wall of pictures and notice that Wheels was in many photographs dating back 20 years, give or take. I also noticed Ken in many pictures, as well some of the other characters sitting in this bar that I've not yet had the pleasure of meeting.

I tried like hell to avoid it, but a question was burning in my noggin, so I finally asked the question that I'd been dreading. "What makes these people worthy of the wall? What makes them so special?".

Gerald, the bartender with the obsessive need to keep one particular mug polished, simply muttered "Not sure you are ready, young man. Ask me again later."

Feeling frustrated again with the lack of a response to my questions, I turned toward the bar and took a sip of beer to which Gerald loudly proclaimed, "Fucking finally".

Ok, I barged ahead, "Let me ask one more question; hopefully this one will warrant an answer."

"Don't get your hopes up", answered someone sitting behind me, startling me because I'd barely recalled that there were others in the bar.

"The visions I've had of Wheels, and the photographs displayed, show her in a very nice, well-kept wheelchair. Can I ask why she's now using a wobbling piece of shit?" Taking a quick breath, I drove on, "Jess gave her a nice one, which I see in many photographs, and the last picture she's using the indistinguishable piece of shit she's in now."

"Goddamnit", Gerald explodes, and I could tell he wanted to throw the mug he'd been working on all night, but he soon regained his composure and resumed the vigorous polishing.

Leah cackled and, after regaining her composure from the accompanying coughing fit, announced, "Oh, Gerald, why don't you give our friend an answer to that question?"

Gerald hollers out, "Jesus Christ, how many times do I have to say I'm sorry, Wheels?"

"Not looking for another apology, Gerald. I've told you countless times that I've accepted your apology. I would just like our friend to know the answer to this question".

"Ok, ok, I ran over the fucking thing after one too many drinks".

"I'm just glad I was not in the chair when you ran it over", announced Leah.

"Oh, yeah, thank God for that", Gerald responded with biting sarcasm. It was said in such a tone that you had no doubt that he wished she was in the wheelchair when he hit it.

In almost a whisper, and very un-Leah-like tone, she said, "Just to set the record straight, it was far more than one too many".

Wanting this awkward exchange to pass, I stated sarcastically for all to hear, "Let the record reflect said clarification", and I lightly banged my beer down, doing my best to impersonate a judge using his gavel. I soon realized that it could have been a bad decision when you consider the company I was in.

"Ok, I got an answer, and we're on a roll", I exclaimed. I again look at all the people in the photographs and a new question pops into my head, "Is there anyone in these photographs that disturbs you guys more than the others?"

As if they were a chorus with perfect timing but lacking anything even remotely close to harmony, the entire bar hollered out, "Charlie Chop-off".

"Who the hell is Charlie Chop-off?" I asked to nobody in particular, because the answer came from everywhere.

The bar got very quiet after that thunderous answer I had received, Gerald, while still polishing his mug, slowly walked away. Ken just muttered, "That crazy son of a bitch made us look like Boy Scouts". Leah rolled away claiming, "My old friend Freddy would have said he was crazier than a dog in a hubcap factory."

Wheels continued, "This guy was hunting in the early-to mid-1970's. He was attacking young Spanish and black boys in New York. I believe he killed five or six of them. He would stab and slash them and when he was done, he'd remove their private parts..." At that moment, Wheels, looking visibly shaken, took a moment to gather herself and then continued...

"As you may have gathered, we're not a crowd that really gives a damn about minorities one way or the other; however, no child should suffer the way these boys did. The police never caught this degenerate, but they had a couple of suspects, and if memory serves, one was named Soto and the other Gonzales. Both of these men were solid suspects and were far from contributing members of society, but they were not the murdering pervert chopping off privates".

"Why did the mutilations and killings stop?"

Wheels rolled over and proudly exclaimed, "We stopped him".

I asked, "Care to elaborate?"

Gerald chimed in with his input, "No".

Wheels, after another moment to compose herself, continued by stating, "The actual killer was, indeed, Hispanic and entered the bar in late 1974, just in time for our special picture to be taken. It didn't take long to realize that he'd be in our picture and, most of all, we collectively determined that it would be his last picture. You can see him in the picture, third from the right in the fourth row. He's smiling because he's in the clear with the police as they were actively pursuing Mr. Soto, who had a rich history of frequenting the Manhattan State Hospital dating back to the late 1960's. Also, Mr. Soto had a history of abusing children, uncontrollable violence, burglary, narcotics possession, and if that was not enough, heroin addiction. He would eventually be diagnosed with schizophrenia and found not guilty by reason of insanity. He was soon remanded to a high-security mental institution. After his arrest and institutionalization, the murders stopped."

"So," I asked, "Maybe they did have the right guy and the mirror was wrong?"

Without warning, Wheels stated the following response slowly with strong emphasis, "The mirror is never wrong". She put additional emphasis on the word "never" by dragging out the pronunciation uncomfortably long.

After a short hiatus dominated by a long awkward silence, the conversation was taken over by Ken where Wheel's had stopped. As he continued the narrative, he stated that the group quickly determined it was the perfect time to eliminate the true Charlie Chop-off. "We collectively thought that, since Mr. Soto was in custody and the murders stop, the police would naturally assume they apprehended the true killer. The police would cease to investigate and would soon consider the case closed, which is exactly what occurred."

Thinking it would be stupid to continue my questioning on this topic, I did so anyway, "What did you do to him?"

Again, Ken chimed in, "He had an accident and slipped into the concrete mix and was mistakenly poured into the steps leading to the back deck."

How unfortunate...

Leah stated with dripping sarcasm, "Yes, it broke our hearts".

CHAPTER 5

Scott

"It takes a very long time to become young."

— Pablo Picasso

After our little discussion about the wall of fame pictures and Charlie Chop-off in particular, the gang kinda spread out again, and Leah slowly wobbled away in her wheelchair. Loudly announcing for all the world to hear about how hot she was back in the day...

Without warning, the large double doors to the back kitchen crashed open, causing everyone in the bar to suffer a near heart attack. Gerald yelled at the young man, in a pissed off voice, "You'd better stop banging the goddamn doors, or you're gonna find yourself without a job."

The hurried young man just smirked and replied, "Promises, promises".

Gerald then told me under his breath, "Fucking kid's right. I hate interviewing people for this minimum wage job".

The young man was cleaning the booths in the restaurant section, which I found odd because it didn't look like anyone had dined there for a decade... or two, or three. I recognized the solid and sturdy commercial tableware as Syracuse China. The only reason on God's green earth I would recognize these otherwise nondescript dishes is because the Masonic Lodge that I belong to features the same design. Each plate is decorated with a grouping of diamond shapes on the corner. Since I've been a member of my Lodge for several years and washed many plates, I'd know these dishes from a mile away.

The young man worked his way around the booths and circled his way back toward me and as he drew close, the flashes from the bottles began anew. What was I going to see this time? Is this another sick bastard like the first two people? What is that annoying goddamn flashing that precedes these horrible visions of the people in this run-down tavern? Why don't I go to the police and report these sick murdering fuckers?

It didn't take long to come up with an answer for that, realizing that I'd sound nuttier than these people. "Officer, you need to arrest these people".

The officer would ask, "For what reason?"

And I'd claim, "I saw these fine, tax paying citizens murder people in a vision." At that point, I'd be thrown into the loony bin, jabbering incoherently about killers and magic mirrors until my wife convinced the authorities I was normal. (Hmm, I wonder if she would?).

I never really interacted with this young man as I did with the others, but we made small talk about something innocuous like the weather, or some damn thing, as he was now haphazardly cleaning the bar area around me. I saw his story in depth within a matter of minutes, or maybe it was seconds?. I glanced at the clock because it was chiming the hour, and I was in complete shock how it could only be 7 p.m.. This meant I had only been there 30 minutes. Could that possibly be right? My mind was racing, I found myself thinking of lyrics to the Foreigner song "Double Vision"; the line in particular was "I live all of my life in a single minute". I briefly entertained in my mind if this band ever stopped in this bar, and if they moonlighted between gigs murdering people? I again looked at the Wall of Fame pictures, but I don't see any rock band members. That would have been a great addition to the wall and to my story.

As I sat pondering the song and its relevance to the visions I'd been experiencing, the young man, who I learned is named Scott, accidentally bumped into me in his haste to finish his shift. I made a comment about being sorry for being in his way while sitting motionless at the bar. He either didn't get my snide remark or didn't care to respond. He nonetheless continued hurriedly in his tasks...

The mirror is lightly flashing, and the deflecting of the bottles is barely noticeable. It is not nearly as ominous as the others I've seen...

I am now seeing the young lady he's going to meet after work, and he's hoping to get lucky. I'm not told in the vision that this is the young lady he plans on nailing tonight, but I know it is thanks to the mirror induced ESP moment. The quick vision I had of his last attempt with this pretty young lady leads me to believe that tonight could very well be his night, as he just missed the night before (you guys know what I mean). The young man is hopeful, I can tell, but every young man is hopeful in youthful endeavors, especially when breasts are involved. The young man is of average height, brown hair, and I have no idea what color his eyes are, but he was a fairly good looking young man. I'm sure, if he does not get lucky tonight, he will have plenty of luck in the future. After all, every dog has his day. My mind wandered to my youth, in particular, the victories and the failures with young ladies. Suddenly, I discover that I am far more affected by the vision of this lovely young teenage girl than a man my age should be. Once realized, I look away from the young man in embarrassment, only to meet the unnerving gaze of Gerald. He added a creepy wink and walked away actively polishing his mug. I ruminate, "Did everyone in the bar know what I was thinking of and the reaction?" If someone there didn't know, Leah sure clarified the matter, announcing loudly, "If that girl's boobies got you excited, mine would have killed you". The bar erupted in laughter.

A FUN ASIDE...

As an aside, I do realize that "polishing his mug" sounds like slang for "jerking off", and maybe I will add it to my ongoing list begun when I was a teenager. Off the top of my head, my list has the following gems: polishing my bayonet, waxing the dolphin, arguing with your Henry Longfellow, badgering the witness, killing Kojak, clubbing a baby seal, evicting the testicular squatters, getting your pole varnished, going blind, jerkin' the gherkin, keeping the optometrists in business, milkin' the bull, punchin' the midget, releasing the olympic doves, slapping high fives with Yul Brynner, stroking the salami, yanking your Yoda, and, last but not least, my favorite of all time, taking little Elvis to Graceland, just to name a few.

I realize I am about to witness this young man's life, and the fact that he is so young compared to the collection of old farts, has beens, and never was's (wow, is that a word?) in this place gave me an extra sense of dread. This young man can change his course in life, but I have a feeling his terrible future is somehow cast in stone. The others in here are older, and the damage has been done. This young man has a future, although, it'll be a wild ride judging by the collection of mentors from hell. It is becoming more apparent to me that there are a few other people in this bar. I ponder if I am going to discover their terrible secrets as well. With dread, I realize that time is moving slowly. Hearing every story in the world would take only minutes in this place. I contemplate, "Is this some kind of crazy 'Twilight Zone' episode?" Here I go again — more damn questions without answers.

The first vision accompanied by an ESP moment indicated that Scott played little league in his hometown. He played third base and left field for the White Sox, wearing number 8. For some reason, the powers of the mirror felt it necessary for me to know this information.

A very special moment in Scott's life was brought to my attention right off the bat. A little league game that he thought of frequently. It happened shortly after his parents separated. Scott was standing in left field waiting impatiently for someone to hit something to him, when suddenly he heard a familiar sound that he immediately recognized. It was his father's piercing yell. Scott looked closer and saw that his grandfather was the recipient of the tongue lashing. Later, he found out to his amusement, that what had set his father off was his grandfather receiving a speeding ticket while on the way to the game. What drew my father's ire was that, when the officer pulled Scott's grandfather over, in his true fashion, he made a light joke. The officer apparently didn't have a sense of humor as the joke didn't go over very well. When the officer had approached his window, Scott's grandfather asked, "Officer, was I driving too fast or flying too low?" The officer, without so much as a grin, issued him the maximum ticket. Scott's grandfather was allowed to proceed to the game, but was warned strongly to slow down.

A FEW SHORT STORIES FROM THE FRONT

Scott's grandfather was the classic "glass is half full guy", and luck surrounded him despite his traffic ticket. Scott's grandfather was an amazing man, and Scott looked up to him. Although, I didn't see visions of Scott interacting with his grandfather, whom he called "Pop", courtesy of the mirror and its ESP powers, I do know some of the stories he told Scott about his participation in WW1 with the 102nd Yankee Division. Pop was a patriot through and through and had actually volunteered for military service during the Mexican border conflict which preceded WW1. This Mexican conflict involved Pancho Villa and was basically an American dress rehearsal for World War 1. It was not long after his time with Pancho Villa that he was called to serve in "The war to end all wars", more widely known as WW1. I promise not to digress too long here, but the stories are amusing and, for some reason known only to the mirror, I was made aware of them.

The first story involved his grandfather (Pop), and at this time, he was in a cave in France. This location had been in German hands before the Americans joined the fight with the Allies. In a short time, the Allies pushed the Germans back toward the beginning point of their mission. It was during a particularly rough day that Pop was finally able to get some rest in a bunk that was dug into the side of a very deep, dark cavern. As he lay down and began to drift off, he noticed what looked like some letters or newspapers tucked into a crevice within the wall. As interested and tempted as he was to read whatever the paper contained, he realized that his eyes were just too heavy from fatigue and that the light was not near adequate for reading.

Furthermore, on what little writing he saw and not recognizing any French words with which he had some familiarity, he presumed the material to be German. Just prior to drifting off to sleep, he planned on grabbing the papers when he woke because there were two things you dealt with in this war: Death and boredom. He figured, if he was not dead, he'd have something to look at in the next trench, hoping, maybe some Frauleins.

The next morning came fast, and he was up, dressed, and out on patrol before he knew it, and in his haste to join his squad, he forgot to grab the paper lodged in the wall. Realizing it later, he was greatly dismayed because he really wanted to read or look at something, even if he didn't understand what it was saying. It may seem to the reader a trivial matter; however, the boredom of trench warfare was never ending. Later that day, while marching to the next section of the "front", he and his squad heard a distant explosion. The direction was difficult to discern because they were in a valley, and the sound echoed around them, seeming to come from everywhere. Later, he would learn that a soldier had tripped a booby trap set with newspapers. He would later find out this was a trick the Germans used when retreating from a formerly held position. Pop was sure that the paper jammed in the wall was the one that killed several American soldiers. It was in that moment that he considered himself to be a lucky man, even as he stood in the middle of a world war.

This battle where Pop discovered just how lucky he was occurred during the Meuse-Argonne Offensive. This was the final Allied offensive in which 1.2 million American men participated across the entire Western Front. The lives of his friends seemed to be rapidly dwindling before his eyes. This battle cost 28,000 German lives and 26,000 American lives. It was the largest and bloodiest operation of World War I for the Americans and second only to the Battle of Normandy in American history.

Just to give you a quick idea of how many people died in the war to end all wars, approximately 6 million Allied soldiers perished (the majority from England, France and the United States) and approximately 4 million Axis power soldiers (the majority from Germany and the Ottoman Empire) These numbers do not include civilians killed or the millions of returning soldiers that died in the 1918 pandemic which began toward the end of the Great War. The scourge that would kill millions worldwide and was more commonly known as the "Spanish flu". It would be revealed that this flu killed more people in the first 24 weeks than the Black Death killed in a century.

It was during the Meuse-Argonne Offensive when Pop's patrol was taking a breather in yet another formerly German held trench, and he was on watch looking out over no man's land. Basically, this is the land between your army and that of the enemy. His watch had been very quiet for several hours, and the slightest noise would put him on high alert. It was well into his watch duty when he thought he heard something several yards away; it was subtle. He hollered out, "Halt! Who goes there?" He heard the noise again and again he announced loudly "Halt! Who goes there?". This second challenge drew the attention of an officer who ordered him to give the proper warning one more time and challenge for a password. He was ordered that, if the correct reply was not provided, he was to take a shot toward the direction of the sound. It was just seconds after receiving the officer's instruction that both of them heard the familiar noise. The proper challenge was offered as the officer instructed, and no password was returned. At that point, Scott's grandfather took a single shot in the direction of the sound. The two of them clearly heard a guttural sound, followed by a body landing. There were no words called out after the shot from either friend or foe. The next morning the scouts that had returned intact from no man's land reported no enemy in the area. Pop and the officer who had ordered him to fire went to investigate the area. The two of them crawled over the trench, being extremely careful of snipers, and soon located the dangerous enemy. It was a cow with a bullet hole in his head. The two of them carefully and deliberately returned to the trench and had a very good laugh.

One more short story of Pop's time in the war, and I promise, we'll get back to the main storyline very soon. This story involves a Scouting patrol that would venture out into no man's land. The soldiers were chosen on a rotating basis due to the very dangerous mission. Every soldier would get his turn to investigate this very dangerous area. It was not something you looked forward to because, if a shelling began while you were out on patrol, you would most likely not return. The main objective of these evening patrols was to get as close to the enemy line as possible to determine and report if they were retreating to a stronger location or digging trenches. Digging could mean a couple different possibilities, both not good. The Germans could be digging a new trench to best attack from during the next offensive. Another dismal aspect of digging meant they could be tunneling under your line and filling it with explosives. As you can tell, it was important to know what the enemy was up to. While on patrol, it was common practice that, if you did spot an enemy patrol inside no man's land, you would try to remain undetected or leave the area as slowly and quietly as possible, taking careful note of their location. The last thing in the world you would do is fire your rifle or make any kind of noise, because that would cause a shelling or at the very least a machine gun burst. No man's land was a plethora of craters and not a place to be with bombs flying around you. Every Allied soldier hoped that the enemy would take the identical precaution when patrolling this very dangerous piece of real estate.

On this specific evening, with very little light from the moon, Pop crawled out of the trench leading a patrol into this area with four soldiers crawling closely in a line behind him. As he was roughly halfway out into no man's land and just feeling his way through the mud, bushes, shrapnel, and body parts, he bumped his head into something solid. He had no idea what it was, but it was so loud to him, he kept his head down, said a quick prayer, and listened. For the first few moments, all he heard was his own breathing, and as he lifted his head to look straight ahead, his eyes having adjusted to the darkness, he made out a face about approximately two inches from his own. The face he was looking directly into was wearing a German helmet. Pop noticed instinctively that the enemy was motioning a "quiet" or "shh" gesture to him. Pop understood that he could not shoot or make a noise; however, he sure as hell would not surrender! What was going to happen? His heart was in his throat. The two of them looked at each other for what seemed like an eternity, but in reality was just a few seconds. The German, with a slowly developing smile, slowly reached out with his hand to indicate he'd offer friendship in lieu of a bullet. To their mutual relief, Pop complied with the gesture. The German pointed to Pop and then pointed to Pop's side of the front and then pointed to himself and his side of the front. It was understood: they would both return to their own side alive if everyone kept their wits about them. Pop gave a discrete signal with his foot to the men behind him, and as one, they turned around and crawled back to their trench. Once they reached safety, he told his comrades what had happened out on patrol. It was obvious that the German patrols were taking similar survival precautions while out in "no man's land".

So, once again lady luck strikes for Pop.

Now, finally getting back to the game in question, the really great thing about this specific day was the fact that, shortly after his grandfather arrived, Scott got his first hit of the season—a ripping double over the head of the short stop and between the left fielder and center fielder. Judging by the pace Scott was running, if he had any speed, he'd have had an easy triple; however, it was a really nice hit. The next batter cleanly singled to right field, scoring Scott easily. Scott's teammates enthusiastically greeted him at home plate and congratulated him. His grandfather came down to the dugout, as well, and gave Scott a big hug while his father was still in the bleachers talking to an attractive mom, completely oblivious to his son's accomplishment. It didn't bother Scott in the least. He had both feet firmly planted on cloud 9. Pop truly was a lucky charm. Not only was this Scott's first hit, it was the first win for his team in the first five games of the season.

Immediately after the game, the team voted Pop the team good luck charm and gave him the game ball.

After each little league game, despite the outcome, there would be a trip to Marie's Diner, which Scott, as well as all the other players, thoroughly enjoyed. Marie, the owner, seemed to be about 100 years older than Moses and looked like Mother Teresa (minus the habit, of course). Everyone in town loved her and supported her diner as much as possible. Many mothers would sneak into the back kitchen and clean some dishes for her as Marie worked every facet of her business by herself. Her prices for hot dogs, hamburgers, and especially candy seemed to reflect the 1940's, not the 1970's. Most people realized this and tipped well. Even Scott's cheap-ass father gave Marie generous tips.

Another fond childhood memory for Scott was the Christmases when his father was still home and the parties with friends and family. The tree that his father put up was an artificial tree with tiny blue lights. Scott never understood why his father chose that color, but he had to admit it looked quite pretty and peaceful. It was a classic suburban Christmas tree. He does not remember the gifts too much, but he did recall the normalcy of his family before things turned to shit. Maybe that is because the normal life that he had enjoyed was now gone, never to return.

Scott's life in these mixtures of mirror induced ESP moments and visions began to manifest itself negatively for the young man when his parents officially divorced. Scott was about 12 or 13 at this time. The divorce was ugly and caused primarily by his father's wandering hands, and his mother becoming unhinged. The divorce was expedited when his mother began to find comfort in a bottle on the nights his father went "bowling" with his friends on Thursdays. The friends were kindly referred to as "Your father's whores" by his mother when she was knee deep in a bottle. Scott's mother strongly suspected that he was not bowling as he had claimed, and that if he was bowling, it was not pins he was knocking over. She took out her frustration with the bottle to such an extent that Scott would often find her deeply inebriated. On many occasions, she'd be passed out on the kitchen floor when he got home from school. If he did decide to hang with his buddies after school, he would more often than not find his mother almost comatose upon his return. He soon learned not to bring his friends home.

Beginning a month or two after the divorce became official, Scott would visit his father on the weekends. This generally consisted of visiting his father's girlfriend and her family on Saturday. The girlfriend, whose name was Liz, was a widow who had three daughters. The youngest was a few years older than Scott; however, she was not interested in becoming friends or just being cordial due to the understandably awkward dynamics. Scott did like her, nonetheless. The middle daughter he found to be a total bitch, and the oldest was a non-issue, as she was married and out of the house. On Sundays, Scott and his father would watch old black- and-white Abbott and Costello re-runs in the morning and then watch the NY football Giants lose (that's what the team did very well in the 1970's up to the early 1980's). Scott's visits to his father would taper off as his teenage years progressed because he felt terrible leaving his mother alone, not to mention his anger and resentment at his father for destroying their family. Scott knew very well that visiting his father made his mother feel bad. God forbid Scott had fun; his mother would lay a guilt trip on him like only a mother can. To make matters worse, it was also becoming obvious that his mother could not maintain the large house on the small amount of money she had received from his father in the divorce agreement. She tried hard to find a job, but things didn't go well for her as she slipped further into depression and heavy drinking. Scott remembers, and still has nightmares about the evening his mother wanted to take him to the local Drive-In while she was deeply intoxicated. He begged her to just stay home and sleep it off, but she insisted, and they took a terror trip to the movies that involved so much swerving, he's amazed to this day that a cop had not spotted them. To his relief, she slept through the feature movie, intermission, as well as the second movie. Once the traffic cleared out, she was able to safely drive them home. To this day, he does not recall what feature movie was playing that night.

It was about a year after his parents' divorce when his mother began to date a very cocky, abrasive, short, and stocky man named Spike. I know that sounds like a cliche name for a story like this, but honest to God, that was his name. There was no indication in these visions or memories as to his real name. This man looked to be Italian, but I'm not an expert on ethnicity. This little man had claimed to be a prizefighter in his day, and I will say his nose looked like he had been on the receiving end of some extensive punishment.

After only a few months of dating, Spike moved into the home and he was always around. Scott didn't know whether this interloper had a job or not, but he surely noticed that, financially, this man Spike was a man of one extreme or another. He would have wads of money, or no money at all. Once Spike moved in, he soon brought his dreadful, evil-tempered cat who I will elaborate on later. Also moving in a couple months after Spike was his daughter, Brenda. Unlike Spike and his damn cat, Brenda was a pleasure, and her smile just lit up a room. He didn't have some kind of twisted puppy love for her; he just liked her from the get go. The actual reason for Brenda moving in was not known to Scott, but he figured it was possibly a rental situation that would help his mother hold onto the house. Scott noticed the fact that, every Friday, there was an envelope of cash on his mother's desk. Brenda never had to be asked; the money was paid on time and without fail. Also moving in, as I said before, was Spike's cat, and this vile creature paid rent as well. The currency used was torture, misery, and a shit load of bloody bites and scratches.

FRED "THE FUCKING FISH"

Scott's father had had a 55-gallon fish tank in the living room, which Scott fondly recalled was a family Christmas gift a couple years before the divorce. However, when the day came and his father was officially out of the house, the tank actually went to shit. Scott's mother saw the tank as something that her ex- had loved; it brought her joy to see it fall into such a sad state. Spike convinced Scott's mother that it would be best to sell the tank when all the fish finally died, thinking it would not take long given the state of its current condition. Scott had to admit a few years later that, due to the financial crisis he and his mother faced, it was prudent to sell the tank. At the time, however, Scott did his best to keep the tank going and to keep it as clean as possible. This would prove difficult, as either Spike or his mother would turn off the filter when he was at school or outside playing whiffle-ball or touch football with his friends. This hastened the deterioration of the tank, and the fish population plummeted to a total of one. Somehow, Scott's favorite fish, a very large white goldfish named Fred, continued to live, and this frustrated Scott's mother and her boyfriend Spike to no end.

One day, when Scott had returned home from a weekend visit with his father, he was greeted at the door by Spike. As Scott ran inside the house looking for his mother, who was not home, he was told by Spike that the tank had been sold and the last fish had to be removed from the tank. Adding insult to injury, he went on to say that the fish was flopping around the backyard and he handed Scott a hammer with instructions to take care of the fucking fish. Spike assured him that a quick hammer blow to the head would immediately kill him, thereby putting it out of its misery. Scott didn't want Fred to suffer any longer than it already had. Grabbing the hammer like a shot, he bolted out the back screen door and ran to the fish, slugging it very hard on the head as Spike had instructed. It was soon apparent that the fish didn't die immediately upon being struck, nor did it seem to die at all. To his horror, the fish continued its struggle to live. Scott swiftly grew frustrated as the blows to the head accomplished nothing. He tearfully covered the fish with leaves and dirt so he'd not continue to witness the fish struggling to survive. Later that day, Scott held a private funeral for Fred. The only attendees were Scott and Brenda. The eulogy provided by Scott was short and to the point, "Here lies the toughest fucking fish that ever lived".

Brenda quietly added, "Amen," immediately followed by, "Don't swear".

This was just an ordinary goldfish, and I'm sure a shrink could find plenty of dark suppressed, memories to pull out of Scott's undeveloped adolescent brain. Professionals could theorize at length as to why this simple fish's death really unhinged him. From my untrained mind, this incident truly devastated him and he actually pulsed and vibrated with hatred for this asshole in his life named Spike. The idea of ramming that fish-gut covered hammer deep into Spike's brain was something he would love to carry out. Maybe someday, just maybe.....

That very evening, Scott heard his mother and Spike arguing about the fucking fish as Spike now referred to Fred. Although his mother seemed to be mad as hell about how Spike had handled the matter, it was too late for his mother. This event was the straw that broke the camel's back. Scott had now officially lost respect for her because she was the one responsible for letting this monster into their house. The surprising event that really lifted Scott's spirits was the fact that Brenda blasted her father, really laying into him with verbal shots that hurt and stunned Spike tremendously. It was a truly beautiful tirade she lambasted her father with. Brenda compared his actions to those of a demented, fucked-up monster and she added language that would make a sailor blush. Brenda's verbal attack continued, and she went on to call him a sadistic bastard and said that she prayed that Scott would not end up a fucking psycho like him. Just as she turned to storm off, she screamed, "Every life you touch turns to shit". Scott was perplexed by that comment because he suddenly realized he didn't know as much about Spike or his past as he had thought. That evening, as Scott tried to sleep, he wrestled with what lives and how many lives Spike had "turned to shit", as Brenda so aptly put it. In the end, that act of kindness and support led to a very restful sleep.

Scott realized everyone in his life was weak or unavailable. His mother was spineless and using the bottle to fight her own demons. Scott's father had moved on to a new whore (as his mother often claimed), and in a short time, he had adopted her children as his own. Scott's grandparents lived far enough away that frequent visits were not common, although plenty close enough to see on holidays. Scott's middle school teachers barely acknowledged him as his grades and attendance rapidly declined. Brenda quickly became Scott's rock, and he soon loved her like a sister. It was comforting, but unfortunately for him, it would be short lived. Fate was about to crap on Scott again.

It was an ordinary Friday night when Scott knocked on Brenda's door to tell her that dinner was ready. She didn't respond to the light knocking which caused him to knock a little louder. Scott knew Brenda was in her room because he saw her enter about a half hour earlier. He slowly opened the door and called out to her again just to make sure she was not getting undressed or something. He glanced over toward her bed and saw that she was taking a nap. Scott figured she was very tired which was why she didn't hear his mother calling or Scott's knocking. He went over to her resting form in order to shake her awake. As he approached her, he saw a needle with its poison plunged deeply into her arm. Scott stood by her, transfixed. She was ghost white, and what struck him was how peaceful she looked. He continued to look at her for what could have been 10 seconds or 10 minutes. Just as suddenly, Scott ran out of the room to tell his mother that something was wrong with Brenda, and she needed help, while knowing full well that she was beyond help. His new sister, best friend, and his only steady influence was gone.

In no time, the police and the ambulance arrived, soon to be followed by the wake and the funeral which was sparsely attended. Scott would learn later that Brenda had been a recovering drug addict, and her death was a horrible relapse. What he'd learn later is that drug addicts frequently burn bridges, which was why her funeral was so lightly attended.

Scott didn't think worse of Brenda for her difficult past; he had really cared for her and was devastated from the loss of his self-appointed big sister. This information was provided by a mirror induced ESP moment, as I didn't witness any visions on this matter. Unlike the other ESP moments, this one had a very strong emotion attached. I could swear that Scott was trying to block this memory from me, but since I don't understand anything that's happened tonight, who knows? If a psychologist ever tries to unlock this memory or time period in his life, it could become extremely dangerous for the doctor.

Brenda's appearance gave death a different image than what Scott had always imagined. Death was supposed to be gruesome and macabre, like the movies always portrayed. She was supposed to have protruding eyes, bugs crawling out of her, tongue hanging out, blood oozing out of her nose and ears; however, he saw only peace. Other than her pale face, he didn't see anything that was Hollywood material. Scott asked himself why Brenda would do this, but each time he'd try, it would end without an answer.

Several months after Brenda had passed, Scott's lack of friends became more evident, but he had one good companion — David O'Connor. I would go out on a limb and bet money that he was Irish, as he had nine siblings, red hair, and a killer devious sense of humor. The two friends were opposites in almost every aspect, but they got along swimmingly. Scott was the instigator, and David was the follower in all their endeavors, which would usually get them both in frequent trouble. No matter how stupid the prank was, Scott could count on David following his lead into any plan with both feet running.

BROWN UNIVERSITY FOOTBALL FAN TAKES LOSING HARD...

Another moment that had a big impact on Scott was when he and David were both roughly 14 years old, and their parents allowed them to take a community center bus trip to the Yale Bowl in New Haven, Connecticut.

They were going to watch an Ivy League football game between Yale and Brown University. David's mother transported the boys to the departure location. From that point, the boys were on their own. It was a feeling of independence for the boys, and the game was quite exciting, won by Yale in the final seconds of the game, which is what usually happens in this annual event. The boys relished participating with the Yale students, chanting, "What's the color of horse shit, brown-brown-brown".

It was just after the game ended when Scott and David were entering the men's room at the stadium before heading to the bus for the return trip home. As they entered, they witnessed a commotion by one of the stalls. Scott worked his way closer through The Last Call of adults to get a better look with David closely following. Someone had opened the stall door because blood had been spotted on the floor — a lot of it. What they saw was the corpse of a young man dressed in full Brown regalia (jacket, hat scarf and even a pennant lay on the floor). Scott recognized the familiar, peaceful, and pale look on his face that Brenda had. It was the peaceful expression on this young man and Brenda that resonated with him. He didn't seem to notice the ugly needle that had been fully expunged of its lethal heroin into Brenda's arm or the shiny razor blade still stuck in this young man's arm. This was uncanny to him. Why was death so beautiful? Lastly, he remembered turning toward David, who had been annoyingly tapping on his shoulder, and then finally getting the chance to say, "These Brown fans take losing hard". They shared a boisterous laugh which understandably drew the ire of the surrounding adults. The two boys were vigorously escorted away from the stall. They left the restroom after using the urinal and never again mentioned the incident.

Of the two young decedents discovered by Scott, he'd not witnessed their actual moment of death, but he frequently found himself daydreaming what it might look like. He was desirous to stare into the eyes of a dying creature. His first thought was Spike, but he instinctively realized that would not be a good idea. What drove his curiosity was contemplating how many expressions a dying creature might have. Would it be fear, anger, horror or sadness during the throes of death? Would there be several emotions, just one, or something entirely different?

It didn't take long for Scott to think of one way to answer his questions regarding the moment of death. If you recall, I mentioned a cat that Spike brought with him when he had moved in. This, fucking cat was a burdensome pain in the ass. Seeing a living creature die and getting rid of that cat would be fucking awesome. However, the icing on the big beautiful cake would be his revenge for Fred, his beloved, big, white fish. It would be three birds with one stone.

The cat's name was Tazzy, which I can only assume was short for Tasmanian Devil. When Spike was not around, the big white cat was referred to as "Kitler" by the family because it was a mean fucking cat. Also, adding to its namesake was that it had a distinguishing small black spot under his nose. Knowing he was an outdoor cat, and outdoor cats get killed, struck by vehicles or eaten by all manner of wild critters, the opportunity to remove this goddamned cat had many avenues. He just needed the right plan...

After much thought, Scott decided to act on his carefully devised plan and put out a bowl that had two baby mice inside. Scott knew damn well that this crazy cat would be by and would not pass up two warm, tasty morsels. Once the evil beast made his appearance, Scott would then don the two large welding gloves that he found in the garage. The gloves had belonged to his father and, for what reason, he didn't know. His father couldn't hammer a nail straight, never mind weld something. Scott required the gloves because the second stage of his plan called for him to pick-up Kitler as it devoured its meal. That mean fucking cat could scratch like goddamned crazy, even when not fighting for its life. With the bait set, Scott waited and waited for that cat from hell to show up. No sooner had he briefly dozed off, he awoke with a start to see Kitler licking his chops. The damn cat seemed to be saying, "Thanks for the meal asshole", and very much looked like the cat that ate the canary.

As the cat was busy cleaning the mice innards from his chin, Scott very slowly removed the welding gloves. He then reached slowly for a golf ball sized rock that was less than an arm's length away from him. Once the stone was grasped, he whipped a hard side-arm throw at the cat. It surprised even Scott that the projectile struck that fucker extremely hard in the ribs.

The evil beast was writhing in pain. Scott re-donned the gloves in a hurry, wrapped his hands around the neck of Kitler, and squeezed as hard as he could. The experience was exhilarating. He could feel and see the fear in this awful creature, and, most exciting of all, he could feel and see the precise moment the animal died. Scott noticed the cat had a combined look of terror and rage while it was in the throes of death. At the very last moment of Kitler's life, Scott saw a sad form of surrender in its eyes, just a fleeting moment, and then the cat was gone. "Oh well", Scott announced matter of factly, "Animals don't have souls anyway". Scott put Kitler in a bag and took a long happy stroll deep into the woods, dumping the cat in a stream far from his house.

It was several days later when Spike noticed that his crappy cat was missing for longer than its usual two or three day furlough and sent Scott out to look for him. Once Scott was out of earshot, he loudly exclaimed, "Why can't this guy search for his own demented pet?" (If you could call that evil beast a pet). Scott was very tempted to retrieve the carcass so Spike could see the dead animal in all its gory glory. It would be extremely satisfying to Scott to see Spike's heart break, but he thought better of it. He didn't want to rock the boat with this asshole and would pick his moments leading to his eventual victory with caution. Killing that damn cat was a small victory and hopefully, in time, there would be more victories.

About a week after the cat's dissolution, Scott went out again and took cat food under the guise of looking for the beast. Spike was starting to think his pet was gone and was quite depressed about it, which thrilled Scott to no end. He was damn near chipper and decided to hike to the exact location of Kitler's remains in order to bask in his victory again, as well as out of morbid curiosity. However, the unholy beast was missing due to the high water flow from the recent heavy rain, or maybe a hungry scavenger took care of the remains. Seeing the beast gone was a bittersweet moment.

As Scott stood at the spot where the damn cat had been, he reflected on the fact that Kitler had cost more to care for than Fred the fish ever did. Scott stood by a moment and remembered that Brenda would be pleased, because she hated the damn cat as well. Just before taking his leave, he thought, "If there really is a devil, he now has a cat."

Although, by now, I should know that the flashing comes without much warning, this one really surprises me with its amped up intensity. Along with the surprise factor, this mirror show along with the bottles now has an entirely different vibe. The flashes are similar to that of

a camera causing you to see spots afterward. I will put that thought aside: the picture is coming into focus...

SPIKE GETS THE POINT...

It was now a couple months after he cashed in Kitler's nine lives. Spike's terrible treatment of him continued and even intensified. The abuse Scott received was primarily psychological, but physical threats were often made.

It was on a particular Friday night at the dinner table that Spike had informed Scott he needed help with a foundation of a house that needed cleaning after a construction job. The job would be very dirty, as they'd be hauling up heavy tools and and all manner of garbage, such as coffee cups, sandwich wrappers, and soda bottles that the construction crew left behind. The clean-up had to be finished by the weekend, as construction would resume on the following Monday. The worst part was that the house was in the middle of nowhere, and Scott was not looking forward to being alone with this asshole for an entire weekend.

It turned out, the house was indeed in the middle of nowhere. There were no other houses in sight and the driveway was longer than the street Scott lived on. His instincts were telling him something big was about to happen, not necessarily bad, just something monumental.

As Scott and Spike stepped out of the pick-up truck and approached the foundation of the house, they could see the floor joists had been unexpectedly started. This would make the clean-up a bit more challenging, and they would have to carefully walk on some beams to get to the portion where they could safely drop down into the foundation to commence their work. As Spike instructed, Scott circled around the back and was happy to find a ladder leading into the basement. He thought briefly that he should call out to Spike and tell him about the ladder, but then thought, "Fuck him. Let him find his own way down". Meanwhile, Spike was walking hastily across the floor joists and trying to locate a safe way down. As Scott was climbing safely down the ladder and reaching the bottom without incident, he heard the sound of cracking wood followed immediately thereafter by an anguished cry for help. Scott ran over, having no idea what to expect, and saw Spike impaled in the shoulder with what looked like a two foot section of rebar protruding from the foundation. The wound was through and through, and Spike was bleeding slowly but steadily. He was yelling for Scott to get help as he could not get off the re-bar without causing more damage. However, Scott approached and sat down comfortably on an old rusted red tool box. He could not contain his ear to ear grin, telling Spike he had some confessions to make since Spike was going to bleed to death in this disgusting basement. Scott suggested that Spike quit his complaining and to shut the hell up and listen for his last few minutes. As Scott began speaking, he was looking at the blood flow and figured the rebar might be preventing a faster bleed out. He was going to goad Spike into wrenching his shoulder and exacerbating the blood flow with confessions to the asshole forthcoming. It should not be very difficult and would prove to be pleasurable. If not, this man would bleed out slowly, no skin off Scott's back.

Scott began by telling him quickly but succinctly how he killed Kitler and relished describing the blow-by-blow details and even added some extra editorial changes just to torture him further. Spike replied with harsh language, but sadly without moving his body much. He claimed he had known Scott killed his cat because Scott was a sick fucking loser like his father. (Scott had to admit later, that shot hurt). He collected himself and responded with a chuckle before adding a real ball-busting gem, "Did you know I could have saved Brenda? She was alive when I entered the room. Did you know that, asshole?" Also adding, "I pushed the rest of the poison into her arm." The look on Spike's face was one for the ages, mixed equally with shock, horror, and utter despair. This was the moment Scott was looking for. The blood flow had slowed down, but with that latest piece of information, Spike lunged to such an extent that he almost dislodged himself from the re-bar, but this caused the blood flow to practically spurt like a fountain out of him just as Scott had hoped. Scott, now happy with his efforts, saw that time was short for Spike and clearly stated as if he were making a public announcement, "Fred the fish had more fight in him than you do. Just fucking die. I got shit to do today". He briefly considered using a hammer to finish him off like he was told to do with his fish, but that would be very hard to explain.

Later, Scott would regret using Brenda to torture Spike because she was, in fact, very dead when he entered her room. He just said those terrible things to further torment the asshole and to wrench his injury. If his objective was to crush this asshole in his time of death, he was wildly successful. How could you regret a perfect victory? As he would say later, "Sometimes ya gotta break a few eggs."

Scott waited patiently for Spike to die and he even whistled a song from a famous 1946 Disney movie, "Song of the South" called "Zip-A-Dee-Doo-Dah" sung by James Baskett. It was indeed a wonderful day, my oh my.

Once Scott was sure Spike was dead, he kicked him for good measure and then proceeded slowly to the distant neighbor's house for help. It took great effort to act upset about this event when, in his heart, he'd not been this happy in a very long time. He doubted that the happiness generated during the liberation of France could match the elation he was feeling. Scott could have driven Spike's vehicle to the neighbor's house, but, "Hey, I'm not old enough to drive. I would not want to break any laws", (grinning at that thought). While on his long (and very slow) stroll to the neighbor's house, he considers that Brenda would not have approved of his actions today, but what the hell, she left him for drugs. Everyone left him for one reason or another, not always in death, but they left him nonetheless.

Scott was able to eventually contact the ambulance, and Spike was pronounced dead at the scene. The police investigated, but everything seemed to be as Scott had tearfully reported, and foul play was soon ruled out. The police noted that Scott did the appropriate thing by contacting the ambulance as fast as he was able.

A few days later, Scott continued his performance, claiming to be too upset to go to Spike's funeral, and politely bowed out. Everyone understood Scott's choice, considering the horrific scene he had witnessed and his valiant attempt to contact medical assistance. When his mother had finally left for the service, Scott turned up the music on his stereo and danced with the joy he had not possessed in quite some time. After several dances, he laid down on his bed to reflect on his good turn of luck. He finished his day by reaching under his mattress for his dad's old playboy magazine which he had pilfered long ago. He masturbated three times to Miss March 1977 (Isn't youth amazing?) before his mother returned from the funeral. Upon her return home, she found him deep asleep with the Playboy on his chest. Scott's mother took the magazine away, but hey, that would not dampen this spectacular day of celebration.

LIFE "POST" SPIKE

It was shortly after Spikes glorious curtain-call that things really got difficult financially for Scott and his mother. The house was becoming impossible to maintain financially and it was in a deep state of disrepair. The lawn needed cutting more often than not, which was primarily due to Scott's laziness about chores. He was entering his prime teenage years which meant he knew everything (or thought so). He continued to do the minimum at school and faced staying back a few times during his middle and high school years. It was a pattern where he would work very hard at the end of the school year and manage to pass to the next grade by the skin of his teeth. Scott remembered fondly a history test in the 7th grade. He needed to score 115 points out of a possible 121 to pass. He got 117 points, tops in his class. The information about the test is another example of the ESP moments that I somehow know due to the will of the mirror.

To understand this troubled young man a bit further, you should know his mother a bit. She was an Irish Catholic and was extremely timid, especially without her asshole enforcer boyfriend sticking by her side (get the point? Spike did). Scott had never in his life heard his mother swear, unless, of course, she was drunk. More often than not, she was far more likely to withdraw into a bottle than fight back with words. However, there was one occasion that he would always remember fondly. Scott had been talking back to her one day and really letting her have it with his unending flow of teenage pearls of wisdom. The lecture had something to do with some mundane aspect of her life that Scott thought she needed to improve. Scott's mother, having heard enough, exploded like a loaded keg of dynamite (the booze probably helped), "You think you're so smucking fart!!!"

Well, what followed was a very long, awkward silence, then Scott said, "Did you just say smucking fart?". They both began to laugh uncontrollably and soon forgot what led to the argument. That hilarious reply actually helped alleviate some (not all) of the damage to their relationship. For all the reasons mentioned, as well as Scott growing stronger and more determined, he would become the man running the asylum.

Mother and son eventually lost the house and found themselves in the coming years moving from one crappy apartment to a steady stream of worse apartments. They did have an improved relationship from that earlier referenced "Smucking moment", all thanks to a long piece of rusted rebar.

Scott's story continues on a bit, but consists of trouble with the law, primarily constituting typical teenage behaviors. I had not seen visions of him killing cats and dogs, but I know somehow that he has been doing this with increasing frequency. This, I understand, is a sign of things to come, and I anticipate he may be headed toward serial killer status at some point in his near future, just like the lovable old cronies in this bar.

Scott's story ended on this evening with him running up to his mother after school and telling her that he'd gotten a job as a pot washer in a restaurant called The Last Call.

Startling everyone, as Leah tends to do, she burst out with a long cackling laugh mixed equally with an accompanying coughing fit and, after a moment to recover from the episode, she loudly proclaimed, "Holy Christ Scott, you have to share the initiation story from when you joined our group. Oh my stars, that's a funny fucking story". This statement was followed by another long bout of laughter from the entire room.

Scott energetically interjected, "Did you really say 'Oh my stars'?" How fucking old are you, Wheels?"

Avoiding the crack about her age, Ken chimed in and added "Oh hell yes, ya gotta tell that story".

Ken continued, "The initiation prank played on you was an absolute classic", adding his toothless smile for added emphasis.

Gerald gave Scott a directive, "Share the story or you're fucking fired", which drew a round of laughter by all.

Scott looked exasperated and he knew the gallery of patrons would bust his balls until he complied. As he began telling this amusing story, I noticed that Scott appeared to be annoyed, but seeing his grin, it was obvious he was willing to share the story. This indicated to me that he found the ruse played on him as funny as it was embarrassing. The giggling in the room also set my mind at ease. It was refreshing that this story was not told by the mirror nor the ESP moments that had been so prevalent. Scott's story held the same hold as the mirror did. It truly was a great story, and I'd have to agree, it was the prank of all time. Just as with the mirror, I soon noticed that the background sound faded; the giggling from the monsters in my mist faded.

SCOTT'S INITIATION

It had been a short time since Scott had been employed at The Last Call, and it was soon apparent that his "darker" interests were very similar to the clientele's as well as the owner's. On this specific day at his new job, he came into the bar with great excitement and wanted to share his successful request for a date with the big-breasted girl he'd been wanting to ask out for several weeks. Scott informed his new friends in the bar that the young lady accepted his request to see the latest "Star Wars" movie that was showing at the drive-in; however, this particular drive-in was in a town and stretch of road he was not familiar with. One of the regulars, a man with an extremely dry demeanor and an even drier sense of humor, stepped up to the bar and told Scott that he drove that area of the state several times a week and knew exactly where this theater was. He offered to give the young man directions.

Scott, thinking he was going to have to purchase a map, was grateful for the directions. Gerald nonchalantly slid Scott a piece of paper and a pencil to write the directions down. The man provided easy steps to follow along with landmarks to keep an eye out for. Scott was extremely appreciative and thanked the man wholeheartedly for his time. The instructions would prove to be deadly accurate; however, they were just not quite what Scott was looking for. As Scott went on to say, on this stretch of road, there is indeed a drive-in, and it was showing an extra run of "Star Wars"; however, about a mile prior to this family drive-in, there is also an adult movie drive-in. This kind gentleman didn't feel the need to share this little fact, so, Scott drove his date down this road and saw the drive-in sign, pulled in, paid, and was thrilled to find a good spot in the middle of the third row. Scott immediately thought the place seemed sketchy and more than a little creepy; however, he figured that extended run theaters were not as polished and clean looking as first run movies. Putting aside his doubts, they settled into their seats and looked forward to seeing "Star Wars" together. While Scott and his lady friend had been driving to the drive-in, he had been telling her that their date was a good omen, because they were probably the only two people in the world who had not seen the hit movie yet.

Now, let me set the scene for this movie. It involves a birthday party for a young child about to commence (don't worry, the children were just implied). The young, pretty mother made her entrance in the movie, and she had breasts that would rival Dolly Parton's, and she was wearing a dress no self-respecting mother should ever wear. The scene has her discussing arrangements with a clown who was hired to entertain the children. It is discovered, to her shock, that she does not have the money to pay the clown for his services. The clown threatens to leave, but the mother insists her child wants a clown for his birthday; could other arrangements be made? (Insert bad porn music here). The clown tells this young mother that, if she turns his frown upside down, the kiddies will get their show (resume porn music here). The clown bends the mother over the table and enjoys some home cooking - if you get the picture.

Scott, at this age, was streetwise beyond his years, but at the same time, he was floored at what he was seeing. His young, pretty date sat still, not knowing if this was an inappropriate prank, or a misguided attempt to get into her skirt. The two of them were equally speechless.

Once they got over their shock, and before the clown's frown turned upside down, Scott simply muttered "This ain't 'Star Wars'". He mumbled an apology to his date, started the car, and the young couple departed the theater.

The room thundered with laughter, and I must admit, it was a masterful prank.

Scott acknowledged the laughter with a good natured bow and left to finish his work in the kitchen. As he did so, he humorously exclaimed, "You old fuckers suck", causing even more laughter. I'd say it was fair to say that, if he needed directions in the future, he would buy a map.

Shortly after Scott entered the kitchen, we were all startled by the sound of breaking glass. Scott had dropped a beer bottle and, with a loud exclamation of "Goddamn mother fucker" and his rushing to the supply room, which was just beside the kitchen. He returned to the spill, hell-for-leather, with mop and bucket in hand while still swearing up a blue streak. He worked fast to clean this mess and, just as impetuously, he left on his mission to deflower his girlfriend with the lovely young breasts. Gerald slyly grinned at me as he somehow knew I was getting an erection from thinking about the young lady's breasts again. However, he just mumbled loud enough for all to hear that he's gonna fire that kid if he doesn't watch his fucking language. The remaining people in the bar let out a tired and forced laugh, except for Leah, who simply announced that "The day he fires someone is the day I'm gonna gang bang the Harlem Globetrotters". After a moment of silence, Gerald said dryly with a faint grin, "Didn't you do that last weekend?"

Wheels response to Gerald's jibe was non-verbal; she just leered at Gerald, slightly leaning to her left side, and let out a very weak fart. The non-verbal response was very un-Wheels like, as everything this woman did in life was loud. Her flatulence didn't measure up.

Scott's story will no doubt continue, but what unfortunate souls will be in the path of his story? As much as Scott seemed like a troubled young man, I really hoped that he'd get his shit together before life makes the decision for him.

I truly believe that this is wishful thinking and that his path involves killing, and he will continue until jailed, captured, or killed. I hope I'm wrong... and I really hope he gets to those pretty breasts tonight.

CHAPTER 6

Baxter Forberg

**Never hit a man with glasses. Hit
him with a baseball bat.**

— Author unknown

There was a gentleman at the bar next to me who'd not said much of anything to this point. If he were not such a physically imposing man, I wouldn't have even noticed he was there. He made the stool he was sitting on look comically small. It reminded me of when, as parents, you would go to your child's kindergarten teacher conference and sit in the little chairs. Anyway, he had long, straight, blonde hair with more than a smattering of silver. His eyes were blue, and if he'd been wearing a helmet with horns, I would guess him to be a modern day Viking. He looked well over 6'5" and probably in the neighborhood of 260 pounds. His shoulders and arms were massive, his legs like tree trunks. This looming giant seemed to be in his mid-40's, but he may have been older. I contemplated if he might have been an athlete in his younger years. Had I guessed linebacker in football, I would have been wrong. We had barely said a word to each other during the entire time I'd been there. As he rose from his tiny seat to use the men's room, we exchanged one of those "**man-he**ad-nod acknowledgments". It was the type of silent communication that women take as indifference; however, we men know the simple head movement speaks volumes and covers every topic from "how's the family" all the way to "sorry they put your dog down".

NOT QUITE THE WALTONS...

I had witnessed, through my ESP moments and visions with Ken, Leah and Scott, that they all had less than idyllic childhoods for one reason or another. However, that was not the case with Baxter. He had had a pretty average start in life compared to the others, unless you consider an overbearing father a deal breaker. Baxter's mother was the stereotypical mother who kept a nice house and could bake a mean apple pie, but other than that, she was nothing exceptional and barely registered a blip on the character of the man he is today. Baxter would frequently chew-over why his father didn't bust her balls for being marginal, as he did with his two sons. Baxter's significantly older brother lovingly referred to him as "Whoops" for reasons I'm sure you can guess. He was not the best brother in the world, but nothing that would be considered horrible by any stretch. The two of them had their moments of fun, but the older brother was what Baxter's father would refer to as a "Jack-of-all-trades, and a master of none". Honestly, from what I knew of Baxter's brother through the occasional ESP moments, it was a valid assessment. However valid it may have been, it just was not very nice, and it cut right to the core of his brother like one of Leah's knives. I'm not sure why I don't know the brother's name; maybe the mirror is less than impressed, as well.

Baxter's hard pushing father was determined to make him a success, and deep down, Baxter wanted to make his father proud. It was discovered early that Baxter had an incredibly strong arm and could throw a rock through a brick wall. After watching his son throwing stones in a pond one day, Baxter's father decided that baseball would be the avenue to direct Baxter's success. It would either be success at baseball or bust for young Baxter. Mediocrity would not be accepted for this man's younger son, and the emphasis was going to be pitching. Baxter's father would be on his ass every step of the way, pushing him harder and harder as the years progressed. On many occasions, Baxter resented his father's presence, but eventually came to the conclusion that his dad just wanted the best for him. Also, he noticed many of his friend's fathers were never around very much. In Baxter's mind, his father's constant, looming presence showed that he cared for him. His father coached every little league team he was on right up to the town major league level.

Once Baxter reached high school baseball, he initially got a little relief from his overbearing father, but not much. His father still attended every game but not every practice, and Baxter's high school coach soon noticed that his pitching and hitting improved dramatically when the father was absent. For Baxter's sake, as well as the team's, the coach tried to talk to his father about the pressure of performing with a parent that constantly looks over the child's shoulder, however well intentioned. The coach made every effort to do it as diplomatically as possible, stating that many boys performed better when parents missed the occasional games. Baxter's father claimed he understood that parents can be overbearing and promised to take the coach's comments to heart. Thinking he made his point, the coach was soon disappointed when he saw Baxter's father at the very next game, as well as every single practice thereafter. Also, the coach found it strange that the father was so insistent that his son pitch and would not allow him to try other positions. The kid was an absolute natural power hitter. If Baxter had become even mildly proficient at another position, he may have played every day, rather than just scheduled pitching days, pitch drills, or the occasional pinch hit situation. The coach would try to work Baxter onto the field, claiming to be short-handed (hoping Baxter's father would buy that), but whenever he tried, the father would come down from the bleachers to give the coach an earful.

WHO'S ON FIRST?

Baxter's loftiest baseball moment in High School was technically a failure with his bat; however, that would not do the story justice. Even in failure, it was the drama and excitement that made this moment a town-wide point of pride, and Baxter the town hero. This was not an observation that I saw in a vision; it was entirely an ESP Moment. The memory is so vivid, even years later. Immediately, I knew that he was not scheduled to pitch in this game as a starter due to pitching rest regulations that are strictly enforced to help save young arms. He would, however, be available for relief (3 innings maximum) "if necessary". Anyway, the "if necessary" scenario was not looking promising as the team found itself getting its usual early drubbing. This was not too surprising, as Baxter's team rarely made the state tournament, and they were matched against the top seed in the final matchup of the season. The last game of their season was always against this particular team, and it was that town that was the top seed. Baxter's team needed to win this annual game to qualify for the district tournament. This year, the game would be held on Baxter's team's home field, as the annual event alternated locations each year. The team they were playing had triple their population and usually beat Baxter's team soundly, whether home or away. It was said that town historians could not remember their town defeating the larger rival.

It appeared as though it was going to be the same as usual when Baxter's team found themselves down 18 - 3 in the sixth inning. Their turn at bat had arrived and they had to score a minimum of 5 runs to avoid a mercy loss, which simply means that, if after 6 innings a team is behind by 10 or more runs, the game would be over. Most of the crowd understood another drubbing was coming to a conclusion, and many were getting ready to leave.

The comeback by Baxter's team started slowly. The first batter hit a grounder to the pitcher, which resulted in an easy out. The next batter hit a chopper toward the 3rd baseman, who in his attempt to short hop the ball, missed it entirely. The left fielder surprisingly failed to back his teammate up, allowing the ball to slowly roll to the inattentive left fielder, thus allowing extra bases to be taken. The next two batters were walked, and the crowd was beginning to sit down again, as the bases were loaded with one out and Baxter up to bat. The crowd anticipated a clutch hit and did not need to wait long. The first pitch was low and inside, and Baxter drove it down the first baseline, easily scoring three runs. He was very excited and caught up in the moment and did not hear his father berating the third base coach for not sending Baxter home. The coach was right not to; the solid part of the batting order was due to bat, and the team and crowd had perked up considerably.

The next batter hit a single, and Baxter scored easily. The team now trailed 18 - 7. The other team took this opportunity to switch to their all-state pitcher who, to everyone's surprise, struggled to find the strike zone. He began by walking the first two batters. The next batter hit a deep ball in the gap of left center field. It would turn out to be an inside the park home-run. The score was now 18 – 10, but just as abruptly, the opposing team's pitcher found the strike zone and the next two batters struck out. Baxter took the mound and struck out the side (meaning, he struck out each of the three batters he faced). The score remained 18 - 10 with two at bats remaining for the home team. Baxter's team scratched out two runs in the second to last inning and, although they were creeping back into the game, it looked to be too little too late. The score stood at 18 - 12 with one full inning remaining.

Baxter struck out the first batter of the inning and then he ran headlong into some trouble. In a mixture of wildness and improper pitch locations, he gave up three runs. A timeout was called by the coach and, after a short chat with his young pitcher, Baxter bore down and struck out the next batter on three pitches for the second out. The third out was registered in exciting fashion. Baxter threw a pitch right down main street, and the hitter slammed it over the center fielder's head. The ball caromed off the wall, spinning directly to the right fielder whose hustle allowed him to play the ball perfectly off the wall. He threw a dart to third base, nailing the runner for the third out. The score stood at 21 - 12. It was now the bottom of the 9th inning. Baxter's team decided to go out swinging. The first batter promptly rapped a double into right center field, advancing on a wild pitch. Baxter was up next and he again hit the first pitch for a round tripper, easily clearing the right center field fence The score now stood at 21 - 14 with no outs recorded.

It was soon obvious the opposing pitcher had again lost the strike zone. Baxter's coach made yet another adjustment to the game plan and told the players to make the guy pitch until he found the strike zone. The next two batters walked, followed by the first out of the inning. The next batter was struck by a pitch, and the bases were now loaded with just one out in the books. The opposing team again changed pitchers which resulted in a quick stand-up triple being struck. The score was now 21 – 17, and you could hear the excitement in the air. The next batter hit a deep fly to center field which sacrificed the runner on third to score, inching the match ever closer. At this point in the game, there were two outs with the bases empty. The current batter was one of their stronger hitters and masterfully tricked the opposing team with a perfect bunt single. Baxter was on deck and he could hear his father screaming for him to swing for the fences if he got up to hit. The batter drew a hard earned walk after fouling off several possible strike three calls, and now the table was set to do some real damage — runners on first and second, two outs, and Baxter was up again. The coach yelled time out and spoke with him privately about 10 feet from the plate. He implored Baxter to look at the outfield and take notice that the outfielders were as far out as possible and to ignore his father's pleas of swinging for the fences. Baxter returned to the batter's box; however, all he could hear was his father's booming voice begging him to swing away. He took a deep breath, collected his thoughts, dug in his cleats, and took a mighty swing at the first pitch with determination to win the game and gain his father's respect.

The ball was hit hard, and, as the ball travelled toward the gap in right field, the opposing team's center fielder and right fielder raced to the ball with everything they had. Baxter was running hard; his base runners in front of him were running hard; the coach and crowd were cheering loudly. As Baxter approached second base, he could see the head and shoulders of the third base coach slump down in despair. Baxter's heart broke. The center fielder had made an amazing snow cone catch against the wall. The catch was in the local papers the next day, but not with the intention of glorifying the catch, as incredible as it was, but to show how close Baxter came to winning the game. The team had lost; however, they were cheered as heroes. Had Baxter hit the ball just an inch or two further, he may have been the town's new mayor.

To Baxter's surprise, as he headed toward the dugout, head down to shield his tears, he soon noticed that everyone was standing and cheering him. Even the opponents were cheering him because he had put on a show with a sterling effort. Everyone was shaking his hand and patting him on the back. The opposing team's coach gave him a fatherly hug and told him that he could not be more proud of an effort, even if it were from his own son. Baxter would never know that it was this opposing team's coach that notified the minor league scouts about his potential. It was a truly nice gesture.

Baxter, looking for his father, noticed he had left the bleachers, and he knew getting a pat on the back from him was not going to be in the cards. Baxter got a ride home from a friend's family. His father didn't speak to him for several days and began using a new hurtful nickname for him: "Mr. Marginal".

Continuing on, Baxter had maintained the high velocity fastball estimated to be in the mid 90's from high school all the way to his AA days; however, the lack of a second pitch began to be more pronounced, as the talent level he faced improved faster than he did. He could get away with one damn blazing-fast fastball when he was younger, but the opponents improved and learned about timing. He tried to develop the elusive second pitch and tried them all, such as a curveball, slider, or even a changeup. The only time he enjoyed success as a pitcher was when he managed to paint the corners (i.e. consistently hitting the corners of the strike zone, not just down the middle all the time). To summarize his problem, his pitches were just too damn straight, and all a batter would have to do is be patient and wait for their timing.

The two AA (semi pro) teams Baxter played for remained patient with him because of his consistent velocity and the fact he was a tremendous pinch hitter. The two teams Baxter spent time with worked with him to develop additional pitches that would make his go-to fastball pitch even more devastating, but to no avail. If the elusive second pitch had been developed, he may have made it as a starter, but the fastball was all he would ever have.

Baxter's years in the minors were as exciting as they were frustrating. He worked hard to make the bigs, and his father put a lot of added heat on him to reach the next level. As time passed, the pressure became overwhelming, and the stress was going to kill him unless he found an outlet. Baxter was not handling it well, and, in his second year, began to use his fists to unwind. It felt good when he did the hitting for a change, because he was getting clobbered enough in the games, and the retaliation was "just what the doctor ordered". Unfortunately, he drew the ire of his first AA coach who once had high hopes for him and didn't want Baxter to injure his throwing hand doing something stupid. Subconsciously, Baxter was working on an outlet to relieve stress that didn't involve fist fights or knocking drunks or hookers around. The answer was closer than he thought.

One evening, a couple hours after another bad outing, he had been walking in a rainy and humid night trying to forget the deluge of hits he surrendered. It was a typical game. He'd made it through the first nine batters easily (striking out the side in the second and third innings). The next time those hitters came through the order, they belted him unmercifully. They now had him timed, and he got the hook in the 5th inning.

Baxter's first two years in the minors with the AA Smokies were not eventful. He would show just enough promise to remain on the roster, but not much more. He needed to go above and beyond if he wanted to get an invite to AAA, not to mention the bigs. He was in search of an answer. Year three would be the beginning of that search, but he'd do it with a new team. He was traded for basically a bag of balls during the offseason without so much as a postcard from his former coach. Baxter was sure it was the last drunken bar brawl that hastened his departure. He was happy to hear from his new coach just two days after the trade. The new coach welcomed him to the team and promised to help him find a second pitch.

The mirror is flashing. It's intense., As usual, the bottles deflect, but soon, it tapers off. Scenes of violence, featuring what appears to be a club or stick, come and go, then, as usual, the mirror reveals the truth...

RX YOU DON'T GET OVER THE COUNTER...

Baxter is walking toward his hotel through an alley behind a nondescript bar he had just left. As he was in no particular hurry, he noticed an old wooden bat lying on the side of the alley. He picked it up and took a few lazy swings and promptly noticed that it felt kinda right to him. It was very comfortable in his hands, and soon his swings picked up in intensity. He placed the bat on his right shoulder, and after walking just a few yards with his new wooden friend, he noticed a small, frail looking hobo that was pissing on the back of a building like a racehorse at the Kentucky Derby. The hobo was completely incoherent, as he could barely stand, but had a seemingly endless stream of piss. He was oblivious to the massive, looming presence behind him. Baxter was truly amazed that this wavering person was still upright. Without even putting much thought into his forthcoming action, Baxter stood behind and to the right of this unfortunate person with the 10 gallon bladder. He proceeded to get into a hitters position and took a mighty swing, striking the hobo directly on the side of his head with devastating force. Baxter stood there a moment, observing this person slowly rolling around on the ground in an impossible attempt to regain his senses. Baxter exclaimed excitedly, "Now that's how you hit high cheese" (a high fastball that is difficult to hit). Baxter looked down on his victim and was surprised to see he was still urinating. He turned and resumed his walk to the team hotel with the bat on his shoulder like a soldier marching with his rifle. He was singing as he left. The song is a favorite of mine, "I Can See Clearly Now", a popular song from 1972 by Johnny Nash.

The next day, Baxter climbed aboard the team bus as they were headed toward another shit-hole minor league city. The coaches were quite surprised that Baxter was clowning with the other players far more than usual. It was well known that Baxter usually kept to himself after a bad outing, and recently, his outings were, for the most part, dreadful. On this day, he was happy, bordering on jovial, and anxious for his next game just a few days away. Baxter didn't know, but two days after he left this city, an article reported in the back pages, "Homeless man assaulted in back alley - No motive and no suspects". This homeless man would not live longer than a week.

On the day that Baxter finally did get on the mound, the weather was spectacular, and he had a hopping fastball. His other pitches were only slightly better than normal, which is not saying much. Baxter would end up pitching one of the best games of his minor league career (again, not saying much). He made it to the seventh inning, allowing 6 hits, 3 walks and 4 runs scored. As he left the field that night, his superstitious coach approached him and said, "Whatever you did differently this week, keep it up!".

Baxter gave his coach a brimming smile and responded with, "Don't worry coach, I'll keep knocking 'em dead," and he strolled away with an ear-to-ear smile on his face.

The third season for Baxter continued with some improvement, but no significant gains on the second pitch he needed to compliment his fastball. Basically, his improvement with the team came with his bat and pitch locations on his good nights. He was now beginning to have a few more good games than bad games. The AAA team was taking notice, but they were well aware of his history of "inconsistent" performances. Baxter was going to have to find that damn second pitch, or at least develop consistency to hit his spots better in order to keep his ugly innings to a minimum.

As Baxter's third season came to an end, all things considered, it was looking up for him and the team.

It seemed Baxter had found an outlet that lifted pressure off him and he had a nice new toy to play with so he could focus without his father's shadow always ominously hovering over him. Baxter was taking care of that dark cloud with the help of the good luck charm he found in the alley. The bat he had found and broken in on that fateful night with the hobo was a good luck charm, as well as the highly unorthodox but effective stress reliever that he had been searching for. Baxter, being as superstitious as his coach, wanted badly to give his bat a proper name. He thought with a chuckle, "It would have to be smashing". The bat didn't have a brand stamped on it or even a size indicator, but Baxter measured and weighed the bat as 40.5 ounces and 35.75" long. He suspected it was homemade and felt in his heart that the bat was destined to be in his hands.

If what he remembered about his hero, Babe Ruth, was true, he had used a bat of very similar size, and the idea thrilled him. Baxter had heard so many stories about Babe Ruth from his father and grandfather that he felt like he'd personally seen the baseball icon play. The Babe was an American icon and went by many nicknames, such as Babe, The Big Bam, The Bambino, The Sultan of Swat, The Rajah of Rap, The Caliph of Clout, The Wizard of Wham, The Colossus of Clout, Maharajah of Mash, The Behemoth of Bust, The King of Clout, The Colossus of Crash and the King of Swing. Thanks to his new bat, he now felt a kindred spirit with the Babe because they both began their baseball careers as pitchers but flourished as tremendous hitters. The difference he didn't care to admit to himself was the fact that Babe Ruth was a great pitcher, and the Babe could play the outfield extremely well, unlike Baxter.

As a pitcher in a league where there was a designated hitter, he still had ample opportunities to use the batter's' box. Baxter was a far better batter than the average pitcher, as they tend to be poor hitters. However, if a batter was needed on one of his "off" days, he'd gladly step in. The coach was thrilled with his attitude. Not only that, Baxter assured the coach, "I'll take extra swings at night to practice". He claimed practicing at night was just good luck, but, it was the only time he could find appropriate practice partners.

In his first pinch hit opportunity with his new bat, he hit a solid "two bagger" (double) and if he was not in love with his bat before, he was now. He looked forward to the extra practice he'd get that night and maybe soon he'd be inspired to give his bat an appropriate name.

That night following the game, at around 11:00 p.m., he went out for a walk and told his roommate he was going to take a few swings with his new lucky bat at the local park. He'd be back in a couple hours at the most.

As Baxter left the hotel, he strolled towards the shadier section of town. To his chagrin, he failed to locate a suitable pitch to hit (i.e. victim). He did stop at a bar for a beer and sulked a bit on the misfortune of not finding some practice time. After the beer, he returned to the hotel, and, on the following day, he got promptly pummeled. Baxter got the hook before the first out was registered in the second inning. It was easily the worst performance he had experienced on any level.

He really wanted to find a scenario to relieve some stress on a consistent basis; however, he was very aware that he had to be careful. He knew with the cities and towns that he traveled to, the right practice partners would present themselves. He just needed to remain patient.

More flashing bottles deflecting scenes of violence wielded by a larger than life man. The face is not visible, but I know damn well, it's the big man sitting next to me named Baxter.

The next shit-hole city Baxter's team traveled to was a former mill town down on its luck. Baxter was very hopeful, and his patience paid off in spectacular fashion. He had been strolling a red light district when he saw an older woman by herself. Judging by her well worn outfit, she was working her trade without much success. Baxter briefly contemplated, "If this woman had a 50% off sale, would it help her gain customers?" He abruptly deduced that it would not. Anyway, Baxter approached her and asked how much a blow job would go for. The dreadful looking streetwalker replied, with a very raspy smoker's voice and a smile, that it would cost $25.00 with her teeth or $35.00 without her teeth, popping them out to show him. It took great effort to not laugh in her face, taking a moment, pretending to consider the offer. Baxter thought to himself, with a barely contained chuckle, that he'd not give her that much money to blow the Pope. However, the insane price didn't matter; he was going to get his money back anyway. After the moment or two of mock contemplation, he agreed to the lower price and handed her the money — 24 singles and 4 quarters. Baxter asked her to walk to the darkened corner, which actually was only about 20 feet away, and to take her top off. He went on to say, "For $25.00, I should at least get to see some titties". He informed her that he had to take a leak behind the dumpster and would join her soon. Baxter didn't have to relieve himself; he wanted a couple extra moments to pull the bat from his coat without her becoming suspicious. He then approached her from behind with his bat while continuing to tell her to keep looking away from him because he was bashful about his very small penis (which he actually was, and why I had to find this out, only God and the mirror know).

The streetwalker stood waiting for him while trying not to giggle about the "small penis" comment. She was about to ask where he was when she was struck in the back of the head with prodigious power. The trajectory of the bat was slightly upward, and with the power of his swing, the impact actually lifted her off the ground. Her skull was crushed and made a strange sound that thrilled Baxter. He had never heard a sound quite like this one, and I must say, to my embarrassment, that it was both exhilarating due to the impact and sickening because of the mess it made. The victim, or shall I say "practice partner", likely didn't hear him loudly exclaim, "Wow, that's a dinger" (more home-run lingo). The woman landed on her feet like a demented cat. She then stumbled forward a few feet and dropped to her knees for just a moment, most likely climbing the stairs to the pearly gates. Before she could fall forward on her face, she was struck again from the front with brutal force. This woman now lay dead in a backwards, collapsed, kneeling position. She certainly didn't hear him exclaim, "Hell yeah, baby! That's a four bagger!" (Yep, another home-run term). Baxter stood there feeling extremely satisfied. He then bent over his latest victim to reclaim his $25.00 and took an additional $17.36 from the woman's purse. He proceeded back to his hotel with a very pronounced spring in his gait.

Baxter returned to the team hotel after washing the bat carefully in a local fountain. He popped into the bar, as it was not quite curfew. He was in a jovial mood and decided to buy a round of drinks for the few teammates still at the bar discussing the next day's game. He hung out with them until curfew. Baxter was still in an excited state and had a hard time getting to sleep. He kept thinking about how hard he hit that woman in the alley, and how she had actually lifted off the ground. Just before he finally drifted off, his last thought was how his new friend (the bat) had knocked Alice Kramden "Bang zoom to the fuckin' moon". It was at that moment that his lucky bat would be known to him as Ralph Kramden, or Ralphie for short. Many of you will remember this character from "The Honeymooners", brilliantly portrayed by Jackie Gleason. It was the perfect name...he drifted off dreaming of pitching "no hitters" for his favorite team in the World Series.

The following day, Baxter pinch-hit for a struggling teammate in the 7th inning and ripped a missile for an easy triple. The hit rifled between the left fielder and center fielder. As Baxter stood on third base, he lamented that, if he had any talent with a glove, he'd already be in the bigs as an everyday player. He also questioned why his father was so damn hung up on him pitching. If he'd have worked him at catcher or third base, his strong arm would have helped just as much as a pitcher. At this stage in his baseball career, he was realizing that he'd most likely never develop the second or third pitch that would complement his ace pitch (the high heat).

The next day, it was his turn to pitch, and he had a decent, yet underwhelming, effort. He pitched five innings — 9 strikeouts, allowed 4 walks, and gave up 5 runs. His team won, and he was congratulated by his coach and given the game ball. Later that evening, Baxter received a positive call from his father which was as surprising as it was rare. It seemed as though everyone was happy with his performance, but he had expected more. Afterall, he and his friend, Ralph, had just knocked Alice "Bang zoom to the moon", and his expectations were significantly higher.

As Baxter's story goes this season, it would have its ups and downs, but in the end, his third season revealed the anticipated promise he and his father had been waiting for. Also, it was the first time he'd been on a team that finished over .500 for the season. Maybe year four would be his moment? The minor success he'd experienced this season was boosted by his new best friend, Ralphie.

YEAR 4 - TIME TO PUT UP OR SHUT UP!

The team and the local fans looked forward to continuing their success from the prior season. Baxter's first two years in the minors were with the Knoxville Smokies. They had given him two years to work on a second pitch, and when he failed to do so, they traded him to the Birmingham A's. The Smokies had rarely let him hit, as it was their mission to develop the ongoing elusive second pitch. He was not bitter about his time with the "Smokies", but he did do well when his new team played them. The A's, on the other hand, let him hit in exhibition games, and he fondly remembered from his high school days that he could knock the shit out of the ball. He had always assumed that his prolific hitting in high school and little league was based on the level of pitching, but he still saw the ball very well and was always comfortable in the batter's box. The negative aspect in the first two weeks of his time with the A's is that they learned, just as soon as the Smokies did, that Baxter could not catch a cold in a hospital ward. He was truly a dreadful fielder and was very fortunate that teams didn't bunt on him.

The coach had called him several weeks before the upcoming fourth season to advise him that his chances of making the bigs had been dwindling and reasoned if the pressure was getting to him. The coach suggested that Bax (typically what he was called by coaches and teammates) would get more opportunities to hit off the bench as his bat had really picked up last season. The coach continued telling him that it might relieve some of that pressure and assured him he'd pitch just as often. The coach further claimed the reason for his call was to inform Baxter of his greater responsibilities this upcoming season and to be in shape for their reporting date.

Baxter was thrilled with the news, not paying much heed to the negative portion of the coach's message. He assured his coach that he'd be in great shape for the upcoming season and he would work with the new players as well. The coach would soon learn that Baxter was a man of his word; he arrived at camp in amazing shape. He'd been working in a lumber yard since the end of the prior season, and his arms and hands were stronger than ever. He had even been swinging his new favorite bat when the opportunity arose, using an old tire hanging in the backyard. The tire was not nearly as satisfying or effective as the extra "on the road" training he had enjoyed late last season.

Baxter's fourth camp began with great promise and would even garner some second looks from AAA. He was instructed to keep working on that second pitch, and they'd give him strong consideration for the AAA team because they were in dire need of a long reliever. (A long reliever is a pitcher that comes into a game when the starter gets hit hard early or sustains an early injury.) This long reliever would bridge the gap from the early portion of the game until it was time to bring in the relief pitcher.

If not for his blistering ability to hit, his one pitch repertoire would not have been enough to keep him on the roster past year two. However, his clutch and powerful swings and powerful fastball had always made him a fan favorite from little league right up to the minor leagues.

As camp wound down and he'd made the roster, Baxter realized his progress, motivation, and momentum were beginning to wane. He felt it was now time to relieve some stress and work his lucky charm, Ralphie.

He needed to resume his special nighttime regimen that had paid such handsome dividends the prior season.

The team's first road trip was to Asheville for three nights, and he was looking forward to some significant batting practice. It is worth mentioning that he did find it odd that his unorthodox batting practice actually helped his pitching, as well, if not more so. The adrenaline gained from his training partners gave him that little extra juice in his arm that he needed to be competitive.

The team arrived early in the day of their first night game, and he was not scheduled to pitch until the third game. Baxter had ample time to find some batting practice and to relieve the stress that life and his father were unmercifully dumping on his shoulders. It also gave him the opportunity to think things over about his training program. This time to reflect usually resulted in him making a pledge to himself to not push his luck and be patient when looking for training partners.

Their first game was a bad loss and a harbinger of things to come for that season. Immediately following that game, Baxter took his bat and went out for a stroll. He was hoping to get some extra swings at the park with his new best friend, Ralphie.

Oddly, the mirror is dormant...

Baxter walked the streets for over an hour and didn't run into a single pitch to hit. (I think by now you know what I'm referring to). With great reluctance, he called it quits. He was in a foul mood the following day and when he found out that he was going to have to pitch on short rest, his demeanor worsened. He was on the ropes in the first inning and struggled to make it through the second inning. Baxter learned the next day that a scout from the A's had been there just for him. The scout left unimpressed, as even Baxter's patented fast ball was lacking its usual pop. Much to his relief, he didn't get a call from his father.

A couple days after his disappointing game, he was having dinner with his teammates. When the players began to head back to their rooms, Baxter announced that he was going out to do some lucky evening batting practice at the park. Much to his chagrin, his teammates wanted to join him, since he had been hitting a blue streak. He knew damn well how superstitious baseball players were which soon resulted in Baxter relenting to their perseverance. He was left frustrated once again.

If there was a bright spot for Baxter, it was that, after his teammates joined him for evening batting practice, the entire team's batting collectively slumped the next day. The team produced a total of 2 hits for their final game in this dreadful series. Baxter realized that there was a silver lining after all, because now his superstitious teammates would avoid Baxter's training regimen like the plague forever more.

The team left Asheville very frustrated and, aside from some sporadic powerful hitting and pitching displays by Baxter, the season would not get much better for the team.

About one-third of the way into the season, the team experienced a few wins and headed to Memphis for an important road trip, feeling pretty good about themselves. This road trip would be four games in three days, with a Saturday double-header.

Baxter's team won their first game on this trip; however, Baxter was on edge. That night, he told his coaches that he was going out for some extra swings and would return in an hour or so. Not wanting to take the chance that his teammates would accompany him, he slipped out the back without being noticed.

Baxter headed for a local strip joint that was not known for their high end ladies. He observed a pimp escorting a young lady into a very nice car and also noticed the not-so-subtle hand-off of money. Baxter took note of the woman as being very attractive, although a bit plump for his taste. However, she carried her weight well, with large breasts, dark hair, and big, pretty eyes. She had full lips which he found very alluring. As the young lady departed, the pimp stood alone smoking a cigarette on the dark corner waiting for his employee to return. Baxter approached him and asked if he could discuss a price for the chubby brunette, informing the pimp that he had time and didn't mind waiting for her return. The pimp, with the his golden toothed smile, assured him it would not take long. The John that just took the young lady was famous for working fast. The pimp inquired cautiously as to why he was holding a bat. Baxter assured the gentleman that he did not want to get mugged, and the bat was just for protection, saying to the cornerside businessman, "If you don't give me shit, I won't give you the bat," to which they shared an awkward chuckle. This explanation seemed to relax the businessman, and he agreed to step into the darker portion of the street to discuss the transaction in privacy.

The Flashing returns, but it's slower somehow: the bottles deflect in a corresponding manner. The scene in the vision begins as if half speed, but things then return to normal...

Baxter was thankful that he had the bat because the pimp was a fucking massive guy of Middle Eastern heritage. If this guy's size didn't scare someone half to death, his looks sure would. The golden-toothed pimp was wearing a sleeveless shirt revealing freakishly strong looking arms, but not the type of arms you'd get at a gym. Also, he was wearing cut-off shorts of an obscenely short length revealing more male leg than Baxter or any straight male would ever care to see. He wore sandals with white socks and on his head was a Hartford Whalers hat. His face was scarier than his ensemble, which was no easy feat. He had a long, thick scar on his right cheek and a short thick scar on his chin which criss-crossed the cleft on his chin resulting in a jagged cross. The pimp claimed, while pointing to the strange scar, chuckling, that he was the real Mr. T. Baxter asked what the "T" stood for, but the man just stood there as if he'd never contemplated the answer. As he stood there dumbfounded by the simple question, Baxter took pity and just asked, "Can we head over to where it's more private to discuss this transaction further?"

The pimp continued to walk toward the darkened alley with Baxter following closely. Once they were well hidden from prying eyes, Baxter struck him in the back of the legs with Ralphie, and the man dropped to his knees like a ton of bricks. The man with the self-appointed nickname of Mr. T began screaming uncomfortably loud for Baxter's taste. Realizing he had to act immediately, Baxter took his batting position and waited just a few seconds for Mr. T to turn his head. When his head turned, he was immediately struck solidly and squarely in the nose with the bat. Baxter exclaimed, "That, ladies and gentlemen was a frozen rope" (a solidly hit line drive). He considered striking him again, but there was no need for that. The man was already dead as a fucking door nail. The swing that killed Mr. T was a quality one and left Baxter feeling on top of the world. Baxter rifled through the man's wallet, mainly to make this assault look like a robbery or a turf invasion matter. Baxter was very happy to find over $300.00 in the dead man's pocket. He had been reluctant to reach into the pockets because the shorts were disturbingly short, but he was rewarded for his bravery. As Baxter departed, he contemplated what his father always preached about practice paying off. He felt a good game coming in his future. His batting practice was brief but very rewarding.

As he left the alley and his big, ugly batting practice partner, he turned to see the vehicle returning the young lady from her date. She had been whisked away just minutes earlier, and Baxter thought to himself, "Wow, that guy is really fast". Upon his last glance at her, he noticed that she appeared to be looking for Mr. T.

The next day, Baxter was scheduled to pitch, and his anticipation was driving him close to insanity. When the game finally started, his fastball was popping, and he hit the corners beautifully for 6 innings. The opposing team began to time his pitches in the 7th, and he was finally pulled from the game after allowing the first two batters to spray solid singles. He left the game allowing 6 hits, 3 walks and just 2 runs. Baxter's teammates saved him with timely hitting and solid relief pitching which netted him his third pitching win of the year. It was by far his most commanding win in AA ball with a final score of 3-2. Everyone was happy for Baxter — his coach, his teammates, and especially his father. This performance really typified his luck, though there were no scouts at this game, and his performance would be relegated to a report that barely garnered a glance.

A few weeks slipped by since Baxter's last "extra practice", and he had been doing quite well. The scouts were returning to see him more frequently than ever. While he didn't have a second pitch, he had improved on hitting his spots around the plate with his usual heat with increasing consistency. This resulted in fewer base runners, and when hitters began to time him, the damage was not nearly as extensive.

The team was now in El Paso, and the season was moving toward its halfway point. Baxter was beginning to grow restless for some extra practice. On this particular evening, he wanted to try something different to spice things up a bit. He had really been hitting very well; however, he noticed that teams were moving the infield back and shifting the outfield heavily to the right, as he was a well-known, natural, "pull" hitter (meaning a hitter hits with power primarily to his dominant side of the field).

Baxter's coach had taught him some techniques that would help him counteract the extensive defensive shifts he found himself facing with greater frequency. He needed to push the ball to the opposite field and, to do that, he'd have to practice timing a pitch better and adjusting his feet a bit. Baxter would also learn to adjust his arm position, which would hopefully delay his swing a split second, thus pushing the ball to the other side of the field. It is far easier said than done, but Baxter figured it was worth a shot.

Baxter had a plan but needed the luck and timing to obtain a "training" partner. This was the night he'd get to put his plan into action.

The Flashing returns and it's explosive The bottles deflect most of the early images. The scenes appear upside down or sideways. The vision soon aligns itself. and we see what Baxter is up to...

Baxter brought his team bag with him on his evening walk, when he was fortunate enough to find a well-dressed and polished looking young man who Baxter deduced to be a rich college kid up to mischief. The young man expressed that he needed cab money to get home because he had blown his money on beer and coke. Baxter asked the young man for his help, saying he was willing to pay him a few dollars to just pitch some soft tosses for him to practice bunting. He explained to the young man that, like most baseball players, he was very superstitious, and it was his preference to practice in dimly lit areas because the dim light made him concentrate harder on ball location. The young man readily accepted the offer. Baxter led him to a small field that was a few blocks off the beaten path and was illuminated by just a single street light about 20 yards away. Announcing to his new partner that the location was perfect, he removed his bat from the bag and asked his new partner to grab a glove and a few balls from the bag. Just as his new found partner reached into the bag, he received a crushing strike to his ribs. The young man dropped and crumpled into a fetal position while crying out in a strange, muffled, wailing sound. Baxter could feel through the bat barrel that several ribs had been broken. Before this young man realized what was happening, his mouth was duct taped, and his wrists and ankles were tied with short pieces of rope. It took great effort for this young man to breathe, never mind fight back. As he came to slightly, he was already hanging upside down from a tree branch. What this poor bastard comprehended is unimaginable, but Baxter was currently doing "play by play" in a low but audible voice for his own entertainment.

"Bax Forberg pinch hitting for second baseman Joe Simms with the bases loaded in the bottom of the 9th inning. The game is tied with one out, and the infield is in". (Due to bases being loaded, the only options were to go for a double play or a force at home). Baxter continues in his announcer voice, "Forberg will have to be careful of this junk ball pitcher as the ball has a lot of movement" (as did his practice "partner", who was currently squirming a lot). Baxter lined up behind his partner, remembered his coaching tips, dug his cleats in, and struck his partner in the ribs again. Realizing his form was awkward, he made corrections to his swings several more times, both high, low, inside, and outside. After each and every swing, he would continue his play by play using the appropriate baseball lingo. His form progressed, and when he finally stopped due to fatigue, he appraised his slowly spinning partner, noticing the large puddle of blood and the fact that the young man was very dead. He lamented, "I guess you do get what you pay for".

Baxter cut down his partner, removed the rope and tape, and looked through the young man's wallet. He was amazed to find well over $400.00. "What the fuck was that about?" he thought, "This guy didn't need money." He briefly considered if the kid was a fag, but didn't put much more thought into the situation because the money was a great bonus. "Looks like I'll be buying the boys another round or two of drinks tonight", he thought. Baxter gathered other items from the victim's wallet and other pockets and placed them in a plastic bag, which he threw out in a garbage bin located a few blocks in the opposite direction of his team hotel. It was his practice to begin his return to the team hotel after an "evening practice session" in the opposite direction on the off-chance that someone had noticed him.

The next day was not a pitching day. He did get to hit in the game, but it was a meaningless at bat since they were losing 9-1. He struck a "Texas leaguer" (a flair hit that lands before the outfield and just over the infield) to left field and he turned it into an easy triple, catching the other team in a drastic shift. He stood on third base, and his smile ranged from ear to ear. Baxter's coach was equally proud, but privately lamented the young man's inability to field anywhere near as well as he could hit. However, he was happy for the young man that had the weight of the world on his shoulders applied by his overbearing father.

Baxter's turn in the rotation came the next day and he performed well by using the high heat and hitting his spots with unusual frequency. He made it to the 7th inning — 6 hits, 2 walks — and gave up 3 earned runs. However, due to his teammates' poor hitting, he lost the game 4 - 3. That evening, his coach called him into his office and assured him that the "bigs" were paying attention again and to keep up the good work.

The next day, on the front page of the paper, was an article about the death of a young man that was assaulted with a blunt object, according to the local police. The article further stated that the county coroner would confirm COD in a few days. The young man was attending the local college and had been out celebrating his engagement to his high school sweetheart. The police were combing the area for any possible witnesses, and a contact telephone number was provided. The article described the attack, which featured too many fractures to specify, and also stated that the victim had been restrained while the attack occurred. The police asked the public for its help in this apparent over-the-top robbery and manslaughter case as well as additional charges of assault. The article suggested that a more sinister motive was possible and that police would continue to investigate.

Baxter didn't worry; he knew the area was void of prying eyes, and, on the off chance someone had witnessed the attack, the wandering drunken locals were likely to have been too inebriated to see straight. Baxter did have a very brief regret (actually a few seconds) which was that the kid appeared to be doing well in life. But then thought, "Hey, sometimes life sucks." He had no intention of stopping his extra-curricular practice sessions. As Dad always said, "Patience is a virtue". On that note, he made a mental note to call his father that night.

The results with his latest "practice companion" were long lasting compared to his other practice sessions. The college boy's assistance began a wicked hitting streak for Baxter, resulting in his call up to AAA just a few weeks afterward. I will not go into this short lived promotion in detail, because whatever I write, sadly, would be longer than his stint in AAA.

To summarize, the issues that led to his rapid rise and fall were a combination of factors. First, the talent level rose another notch, which meant that only a top effort from Baxter would yield moderate success, and to constantly be at the top of your game is a difficult pace to keep in any profession. Second, the practice session with his college-aged friend was wearing off. Third, he didn't have the freedom to pursue his extra sessions, as the AAA team had strict bed checks and frequent meetings that were mandatory and could be called at any time. Finally, facing different players, different cities, and different expectations led to a terrible, albeit short, slump at the worst possible time. Baxter's less than stellar total statistics in AAA were as follows: The only pitching appearance ended with him not surviving the first inning. He got four at bats (pinch hit situations) and struck out each time, looking like he'd never swung a bat. Baxter's father had driven several hundred miles to witness his son's rise to the AAA, and, before the four game series was over, his father gave him a lift back to his AA team, where he finished out the remainder of the season. It was the longest ride of Baxter's life despite the fact his father didn't say a word. After a few hours of silence, he began to hope for the inevitable lecture because a lecture would inevitably end; the silence seemed eternal.

The team welcomed Baxter back, and his coach was consoling. Baxter politely listened to the coach speak but all he could think of was how much one of his extra practice sessions would have helped. His team was now in Montgomery, which was not a town that Baxter performed well in historically. He was determined to change that bad mojo as soon as possible! Furthermore, with the season close to ending, it was imperative to end on a positive note.

The flashing returns energetically. The bottles deflect and, as usual, they are matching the intensity. Just as the eyes adjust, the picture becomes terribly clear...

Baxter was in a hurry; he didn't bother bringing his bag of supplies. He just grabbed his bat, and if anyone asked where he was going, he'd just say, "Going to get some evening swings". However, nobody asked.

Baxter proceeded to a favorite drinking pub and had just one beer. He didn't get drunk on nights that he was prowling, but one beer wouldn't kill him. After nursing his one beer for about a half hour to wait until it was dark out, he departed, acting like he had had a few too many. He sure noticed the gorgeous woman leaving ahead of him and was glad to be following her. She was very pleasing on the eyes.

As he exited the bar, he sensed he was being followed (after all, he was not as drunk as he appeared). This unnerved him and excited him equally, and although he was still behind the attractive young lady, she was a non-factor to him. He was now a target of the gentleman following him closely, and it was intoxicating. Baxter allowed himself a small, secret smile and proceeded to an alley that even hardened muggers would shy away from. Baxter knew where he was going, but would his new practice partner follow? Was his pursuer a mugger? Was he a homo? He didn't know the answer, nor did he care. Baxter would have his fun tonight, and it would have a twist. For a brief moment, he thought of his childhood hero, Sherlock Holmes, saying, "Dr. Watson, the game is afoot". As he turned into the dark alley he'd been looking for, he proceeded to kick some boxes trying to give the impression that he had stumbled and fallen. In the few moments he had, he hid just around the corner and waited with his bat in position. He was desperately hoping his victim would keep advancing. How far behind him was this mysterious tail? How tall was he? To his brief annoyance, he contemplated if the woman was still nearby. Baxter, recouped his concentration despite the questions running through his head, swung his bat when the time came, and struck his new friend right in the Adam's apple. He actually saw his bat travel well into the man's neck, and, although not a killing blow, it sure as hell fucked this guy up. Baxter's pursuer dropped to his knees and grabbed his neck as if signaling he could not breathe.

Baxter exclaimed, "Ok, now that practice is over, it's time to hit a tater" (home run lingo). The man's eyes were closed from the pain or the fear (or both) as Baxter set up into a proper stance and took the most vicious swing he could ever take. He struck his prey flush in the forehead. It was, without a doubt, "a bomb" (i.e. very long home run), and the Sultan of Swat would have been proud.

After Baxter admired his handiwork for just a moment, he vigorously rifled through the man's pockets to see just who this mugger was and to hopefully find some cash. As he reached into the man's pocket, his heart went ice fucking cold. Without even seeing it, he knew, he knew, he goddamn well knew. "Fuck, fuck, fuck". It was a police badge. He pulled out the shield with his trembling hand to discover it belonged to a detective. Suddenly, finding himself panicking and contemplating, "Did this guy have a partner?" But then, if there was back-up, they'd have been there by now, and he'd be wearing cuffs and getting a hurried ride to the station. After cleaning the shield of prints, he grabbed Ralph Kramden and walked as fast as possible directly toward his hotel. He was too damn nervous to bother with the doubling back crap that he had always done in the past. He didn't dare run or to even turn around. Baxter had never been so frightened.

Although the remainder of the season was only a few weeks, Baxter slept like shit, and his pitching and hitting failed him more so than usual. The killing of the detective just added to the stress, rather than releasing it. Baxter's entire world was teetering. He could only think of how he let his father down again. As the season wound down, he noticed his coach distancing himself and he sensed his baseball career was going to end very soon. He didn't know if the police suspected him, and not knowing was very unsettling to him. He found himself looking over his shoulder a lot.

Baxter was an avid reader of the local papers, albeit, usually just the sports section, comics, and the stock portfolios. However, he was now looking for updates on the undercover detective that had been reported murdered while trying to catch a serial rapist. The detective had instead run headlong into an ambush, resulting in his demise. The papers went on *ad nauseum* about how great this detective was. Baxter thought it was overkill (sorry for the pun). As far as the papers were concerned, there were no suspects, but the police are famous for withholding information from the press. The only lead they had was that the officer left the bar shortly after a very tall patron had left the establishment. Baxter knew this was weak, but was there more? The uncertainty was really wreaking havoc with his nerves and, for the next several months, it would keep him awake countless evenings.

As for his baseball career, it was over. He was not invited back to his former double A club, nor did he try to pursue other teams. On occasion, he would observe his former team from far up in the bleachers and would depart as quietly as he had arrived.

Baxter soon got a job with the city sanitation department and, to date, he has not taken out his old friend, "Ralph Kramden", for a trip down memory lane. Baxter didn't need to worry about baseball any longer, and his father was dead. Aside from the bad dreams and bumps in the night, Baxter was living a quiet life without the constant pressure bearing down on him. He was doing well at the time I met him. However, if this man has a trigger somewhere in his brain, he is still plenty big and powerful enough to cause some real fucking damage.

Baxter keeps his friend, Ralph, in the hallway by the front door, which surprised me given how much he fears being apprehended. Even years after his playing days, if he hears a noise in the night, he'd think the police were outside his door waiting to smash him with the justice that their fellow officer justly deserves.

CHAPTER 7

Mr. Trivia

"Excessive intake of alcohol, as we know, kills brain
cells. But naturally, it attacks the slowest and weakest
brain cells first. In this way, regular consumption
of beer eliminates the weaker brain cells, making
the brain a faster and more efficient machine. That's
why you always feel smarter after a few beers."

— Cliff Clavin (Cheers)

As my latest tale of gruesomeness came to an end, Baxter stood up and asked
forgiveness. I replied, "What the hell for?"

The response was a belch that would be the envy of any young red
blooded American boy and was deliberately followed up with, "Oh, not for
the belch, but for this", His face reddened and then he let out the most toxic
fart you've ever heard or smelled. I was sure that somewhere in the universe,
an angel was weeping. He grinned before turning toward the men's room
to a chorus of "boos" and the waving of napkins to dissipate the toxic cloud
that had been so crudely blasted into the room. The only person that found
this act amusing was Wheels. She just sat on her wheelchair cackling loudly,
her gesticulating stump waving about wildly.

As I turned my gaze from Baxter making his exit off the "stage of horror",
I realized that Gerald was standing right in front of me inquiring, "You been
here 45 minutes, you gonna drink that fucking beer or what?"

I disregarded his comment as I was fixated on making sense of the stories I'd been subjected to by visions along with the ESP moments. The visions were all horrifying, and I can recall them in detail. The ESP moments were not all gruesome, but they seemed to fill in gaps left by the visions and they were oddly helpful.

I then snapped back to Gerald's comment about the time, "How on God's green earth have I only been in this fucking twilight zone of psychopaths for 45 damn minutes?" Yeah, I know. More goddamn questions...

As I was sitting down and trying to contemplate everything that had transpired on this very perplexing evening, I saw some flashes being lightly scattered by the mirror and the bottles. The flashes reminded me of when you see lightning far off in the distance. Within a few seconds, a man entered the bar looking well-dressed; however, the clothes looked like they had some miles on them.

I felt a tapping on my arm and I looked to see who it is. At first I didn't see anyone, but now knowing better, I glanced downward to see Wheels looking up at me. She leaned over toward me and whispered, "Whatever you do, don't ask that guy a question and, just to be safe, don't even look at him, because that is an open invitation to this crazy bastard". Sadly, I looked and, the room groaned.

I announced to nobody in particular, "Come on, when someone says to not look at something, you always look. What the fuck".

The well-dressed gentleman took my glance in his direction as an invitation, as Wheels had forecasted, and immediately approached our section of the bar. As he drew near, he had a big smile and introduced himself as Bob Cullen, who I would soon learn was simply known by this bar as Mr. Trivia. Personally, I would have named him Cliff, after Cliff Clavin from Cheers. You'll figure out why very soon.

Just to give you an idea of what he looked like, I'd say he was in his mid-30's, but looked older due to his prematurely receding hairline made even more pronounced due to his jet black hair and clean shaven, pale skin. He was a slight looking man; I'd say he was close to 6 feet, but wispy thin. His weight could not have been more than a buck fifty. He had a long narrow nose that bent to the right side. His mouth looked like Mick Jagger's, and his teeth looked capped. This was an odd looking fellow, to say the least.

Mr. Trivia pulled an empty stool up close to mine and, before sitting down, he shook my hand with a vice-like grip. It was unexpected for such a slight man. He asked if I'd wet my whistle yet, and I assumed he meant if I was drinking my beer.

I replied, "I am working on it". He then asked if I knew the origin of that phrase to which I responded that I didn't. (A loud groan filled the room).

He felt the need to immediately provide me with the answer, "Many years ago, in England, pub frequenters had a whistle baked into the handle of their ceramic cups. When they needed a refill, they used the whistle to get some service. I'd say this pub should practice that method; the service here is brutally slow".

Gerald, only a few feet away, put in his two cents, "Bob, I got some trivia for you: how many facts can you tell before my foot goes so far up your ass that, every time you brush your teeth, you'll also shine my shoes?"

This drew a hearty laugh from the peanut gallery, but Mr. Trivia just continued on, nonetheless, "Gerald, mind your P's and Q's, I'm talking to our guest". Again, without pausing, Mr. Trivia plowed ahead. "The origin of minding your p's and q's also originated from English pubs (insert louder groans and some swears here). You see, in England, beer is served in pints and quarts, and if someone got unruly or impolite, like our friend Gerald here, the bar manager would yell at them, 'Mind your pints and quarts, and settle down.' This saying eventually changed to 'Mind your p's and q's'".

Several napkin balls were tossed into our area, and Ken, who had not said a word in quite some time, said, "Jesus Christ, Bob, would you just shut the hell up?"

Although, personally, I found this man amusing in a quirky way, I could definitely tell that he'd get on my nerves in short order. Judging by the looks of the other patrons, Mr. Trivia was on their last nerve right now. I also noticed that this guy was different than everyone in this bar. He was loud, brash, and, since I first glanced in his direction, he had not shut his trap for one minute. Although I found the man intriguing, I could clearly see that he didn't fit in with this group. The other patrons of this bar seemed to feed off each other's vibes, talking when the mood struck or the occasional joke when the time seemed right. This man was a verbal bulldozer; he'd just plow ahead with his trivia. Like I said before, the perfect nickname for this man would be Cliff Clavin. However, unlike the TV Cliff, this man was not intimidated by women; he hated them. I guess a deeper thinking person could say that maybe he was intimidated by women, which created his hatred, but I'm not that deep.

Mr. Trivia plowed ahead, "Aren't you glad you called me over?"

"Nobody called you over," declared Wheels.

"Didn't you? Well, I guess before this crowd gets violent, maybe you want to take a look at the mirror. It's my turn to share".

The Flashing returns; however, it's not as intense as with the others. The bottles deflect as they had in the other visions. I'm getting snippets from differing viewpoints of a victim, and it's only one female victim unlike the other visions. The scenes are just as quick, and in just a few moments, the picture becomes clear...

Soon, I'm made aware by the mirror induced ESP moment that Mr. Trivia had a sister that was a couple years younger and clearly the favorite of their parents. She was the baby of the family and, whatever she wanted, she got. Bob didn't really resent her too much because even he had to admit that she was cute as a button. He was equally guilty in doting on her, as well. He did figure out fairly soon that if he wanted to be noticed, he had to verbally shove his way into his parents' life to make his presence known. He began mildly with tall tales of his school days at the dinner table and, as he grew older and his vocabulary increased to what one might consider highly advanced, he began to spout off facts into every conversation possible.

During his years in high school, his habit of blurting out facts didn't help him develop friends, but he was seen by the teachers as a kid just trying to find himself. In college, his habit grew far more annoying. Teachers tolerated him due to his solid grades, but his fellow students did whatever they could to avoid him. He had, by this time, become a social pariah.

A very small glimpse in the mirror showed Mr. Trivia in an office where he seemed a bit younger than he does now, but not much. The office looked like the inside of a trailer and, as the vision seemed to pan off, it revealed a run-down camper supported by concrete blocks on a construction site. It was never confirmed by the mirror, but my impression was that he lived in this dump, as well. He was dressed in a blue suit and a faded yellow tie, and I briefly consider if he's color blind. He finished whatever work he had been doing and bounced out of his seat and began singing "Strangers in the Night" made famous by the legendary Frank Sinatra as he proceeded to the bathroom. I see him slapping on some cologne. It seemed as if he has plans for the evening.

The vision became a bit disjointed for a moment, but I now saw him in what looks like a hotel bar which was soon confirmed by the all-knowing mirror.

He was sitting next to a heavy set blonde woman with massive breasts prominently displayed in a tight v-neck sweater. His eyes were glued to her cleavage, but she didn't seem to mind or care. He was not talking to her; he appeared to be discussing matters with the woman's breasts. He was, as his custom, talking non-stop, and she appeared to be enjoying his endless trivia. As soon as she responded to one of his quips with a giggle, he fired off the next one.

I'm viewing this particular vision from where the bartender would be standing, almost as if through his eyes.

Mr. Trivia's date appeared to be very interested in this man's endless stream of facts. At some point in this verbal assault, she managed to say that her ex-husband never spoke and she resented always having to be the person that broke the silence. She then reached for the bowl on the bar that contained M&M's. Mr. Trivia tore his head from her breasts just long enough to notice. He informed his lady friend, "Did you know that M&M's actually stands for "Mars & Murrie's? Those were the last names of the candy's founders".

The bosomy date let out a quick chuckle and she gave Mr. Trivia a not so subtle hint that she'd like the date to progress to dinner as she was quite famished. She found herself coughing to break his gaze from her breasts and repeating the request to move on to a restaurant. He suggested a nice place about 15 miles down the road. When the woman asked if there was anything closer, Mr. Trivia responded, "Did you know that William Faulkner refused a dinner invitation from John F. Kennedy's White House, stating, "Why that's a hundred miles away. That's a long way to go just to eat". With that amusing fact out of the way, they stood up and took their leave.

I now saw this couple as if I was looking from the hood of the car, which I was obviously not doing, but that was the angle of my vision at this moment.

Mr. Trivia was still spouting off his litany of facts in rapid fire speed. I could detect that this woman was showing the first signs of annoyance, speculating if he would ever tire out.

Anyway, they were on a dark portion of road, and Mr. Trivia stated that he needed to stop at his work site to pick up a document. It would only be a moment. As they arrived at the trailer, it's very dark, and the woman's instincts are tingling: should she be concerned? As they enter the trailer, he asked her to sit down while he looked for the document. He gave her a drink to enjoy while he located the papers he needed. She reluctantly took a sip. Soon, she was unconscious.

MISS IVANNA BOOBMORE, COME ON DOWN...

The next scene has this woman sitting on a couch in the trailer with her hands tied behind her back with what looks like thick boot laces. Her ankles are tied in the same manner. She was not tied to an object, but between her build, what she is wearing, and how low the couch was, he figured it highly unlikely that she could spring up and surprise him.

Mr. Trivia was standing in front of her with a lamp aimed at her face. His appearance and mannerisms were that of a wannabe game show host. In his right hand, he was holding an old ladle as if it were a microphone. He began by thanking her for being a contestant on the "You Bet Your Life" show. The woman was completely bewildered and still groggy from the Rohypnol Mr. Trivia slipped into her drink.

He began by announcing the rules to his fantasy game show like it's been on for years. "As our loyal viewers know, the rules are simple. We will ask you up to seven questions. Answer four questions correctly, and you live. If you answer 4 questions incorrectly, you'll have a dream date with a cement mixer". He continued, "Furthermore, the contestant must keep in mind, you have one chance to answer a question, and it must be in the correct form. Whatever you say first is your only answer, so, think before you speak".

The formerly flirtatious and demure woman suddenly turned ugly as she was beginning to understand her situation was perilous. She struggled to gain her feet, but unsurprisingly, he easily pushed her down again. She howled, "I knew you were a freak, damnit. Why do I always find the freaks?"

"Ok", said Mr. Trivia. "Enough about me. Let's find out a little about our lovely, large-breasted contestant".

"Asshole!" she shouted, spittle flying.

"My goodness, that is fascinating. Let's begin. First question, This is a true or false question. Listen carefully. Obsessive nose picking is called Rhinotillexomania?"

"Fuck you"

"Oh, I'm sorry, that is not the correct answer. The answer is true. I'm sure you'll get the next one. "Now, make sure you take your time with your answers. Don't be so hasty. Here comes another true or false question. That thing you use to dot your lowercase "i" is called a tittle. True or false?"

The angry contestant, still not grasping the true depth of her situation, shouted, "You're a fucking weirdo! Take me home immediately!"

"Oh, I'm so sorry. That is not correct, either. That brings you to two incorrect answers. While we break for commercial for our sponsor, Boulder Holders, remember ladies, put your breasts in their capable hands".

As Mr. Trivia broke for his mock commercial, he went to a closet and pulled out a pair of lawn clippers and promptly removed the contestant's right index finger. He apologetically said, with mock concern, "I think you need to realize the seriousness of your situation before we return to the show. Ok, ladies and gentlemen, we are back to 'You Bet Your Life'. I'm your host, Howard Humpalot. Our lovely contestant is struggling to answer some questions, but she seems ready to make a comeback. I have a feeling she's put her finger on the problems she's been facing. Let's go with question number three, In the 1970s, Mattel sold a doll called Growing Up Skipper. Her breasts grew when her arm was turned, true or false?"

Through clenched teeth, the lovely bleeding contestant responded, "True".

"Yes, absolutely correct, I thought you could answer a breast themed question correctly. See what can happen when you put your pretty little mind to something?"

Turning flamboyantly around one hundred eighty degrees, as if to face a fictional camera again, he announced, "If you've just tuned in folks, our contestant has one correct answer and two incorrect answers. Let's remind the viewing audience of what our guest can win with just three more correct answers." He ran a few feet away, portraying the off stage announcer, "Why yes, Dick, Miss Big Boobs can win precious oxygen for the rest of her life. However, if not, she gets a date with the Grim Reaper. Now, back to our host".

He ran back to his former position. "Yes, thank you, Mr. Announcer. Back to the game. We have one more true or false question, then it gets tougher with the multiple choice portion of our game. Are you ready?"

She was glaring at him with pure hatred. She fully understood her predicament at this point in time.

"Ok, ready or not, here we go, True or false, Jane Jetson, of the famous Jetsons cartoon, was a teen mom, true or false?

"No"

"Oh, I'm sorry, that's incorrect. The judges will not accept your answer as it's incorrect and not in the correct form, either true or false. For the audience's clarification, on the Jetson's program, Jane, his wife, is 32 years old. Daughter Judy is 16, so, when you do the math, that makes the mom a 16 year old tramp when Judy was born".

The large breasted contestant again tried to get to her feet, only to be easily pushed down yet again. Her anger was now turning to fear, with good reason.

"Ok, in this portion of the show we announce the fact that there are no consolation prizes on our program, so let's see if our contestant can stave off her date with the Grim Reaper".

Mr. Trivia continues, "As the viewing audience is aware, this portion of the show switches to a multiple choice format, which will change the odds of our contestant's ability to answer the following questions. The true false questions' odds were 50/50, but now we are going to switch to the multiple choice portion of our show, which will give her a 33% chance of success. The odds, like her breasts, are stacked against her. Let's continue. Since she is facing death, this is a great question, and, please, listen to the question in its entirety and wait for all the options to be read…"

Looking down at his hand, as if reading the question from a card, he asks "What causes a death rattle? Would it be…

a. Erratic heart beat
b. Fluid build up in the lungs
c. Kidneys shut down?"

She shouted out with wavering hatred and fear, "B, fluid buildup in the lungs, you asshole."

Mr. Trivia announced that they will take a commercial break while the judges discuss her answer, as asshole might not be accepted. He walked over to the counter where the lawn clippers were and proceeded to remove the contestant's left index finger. The woman was sobbing and apologizing for the asshole portion of her answer.

"Ok", Mr. Trivia continued. "Welcome back from our commercial break. The judges have discussed the last answer by our contestant and have agreed that the answer is correct. Remember, we do want our contestants to succeed. Now, to summarize, our lovely contestant has three incorrect answers and two correct answers. Now, for what might be her last question, how long does the brain survive after the heart stops beating? And remember, wait for all the options to be read.

    a.   30 seconds to a minute
    b.   3 minutes to 7 minutes
    c.   10 minutes?"

As the last answer was announced, she blurted out, "B, 3 to 7 minutes," which caused Mr. Trivia to jump up and down in mock excitement, announcing, "Yes, that is the correct answer, and now we are at three correct and three incorrect. This is what makes our show so exciting. It looks like our contestant has made a comeback with her medical knowledge. We will now proceed to the last question. This is indeed going to be for all the marbles. Now, for the last question, I ask that the audience remain quiet and let our contestant concentrate. Here we go. Which of the following famous individuals was born on August 15, 1769?, was it...

    a.   John Adams
    b.   Queen Victoria
    c.   Napoleon Bonaparte?"

Mr. Trivia was now humming some made up game show music as his contestant sat bewildered. She had no idea of the right answer. It was really beginning to hit her that, even if she guessed the right answer, she was not getting out of the trailer alive.

Mr. Trivia waited a moment or two while pointing to what I believed was a make believe timer, then said, "Tick tock, young lady".

The woman seemed to know her fate and decided to take a shot. Her response was firm and through gritted teeth; she stated, "John Adams".

Mr. Trivia made a loud buzzing sound and said "Oh, I'm so sorry. Let's give our contestant a big round of applause, Ms. Boobmore started slowly and made a gallant comeback." As he said this, he turned toward a shelf and opened a box. To his astonishment, when he turned back with a pistol, she plowed into him, knocking him backwards. As he fell, his head struck the counter, knocking him out cold.

As he slowly came to, he recalled what happened. He remembered she had somehow launched herself at him and even remembered that her hands were free. He had no idea when she had untied her restraints or how long he'd been unconscious. Was it minutes or hours? He tried to think clearly through the pain and realized that, if it had been hours, the police would have been there by now. He made a mental note to himself: if he managed to get past this evening unscathed, he would buy a damn clock for his trailer. His last thought before getting up was, "How the hell did she get out of the restraint with two missing fingers?"

Gaining his feet, he cleared the cobwebs from his head and swiftly cleaned the blood from the back of his head. He now raced out of the still open door of his work trailer. Where the hell was she? The trailer's location was fairly remote. However, the main road leading to town was just a mile or so away. He tried to reason why she had not used the telephone. Maybe she just wanted out as fast as possible, but that was just a guess. Maybe he had removed her dialing finger, allowing himself a brief moment of humor. Returning to the present situation at hand, he knew he had to find her fast and he was wasting time. The only direction she could take that would lead to the road was just to his right, so he figured that was the first place to look. It was pitch black outside, with minimal moonlight, but he began a cautious jog in that direction. When he was about 30 yards from the highway, he saw his game show contestant. Not a split second after seeing her, she was brutally struck by a semi while she was trying to wave it down. Allowing another moment of levity, he chuckled and said "Problem solved".

The truck had locked up its brakes after striking the woman and came to an eventual stop some 30 or 40 yards up the road. The driver abruptly exited the cab of his truck and he was shaking and screaming profanities that, "The crazy broad came from nowhere." Oddly, I'm seeing this portion of the vision from the driver's viewpoint and I actually feel his fear running down my leg. I'm also privy to the fact that he has 5 kids at home and a wife that was fooling around on him. This man was clearly enveloped by pressure. He did not know what to do, but it was obvious that he wanted to make this accident disappear.

Sensing a golden opportunity manifesting out of the ashes of ruin, Mr. Trivia informed the badly shaken driver that he had just happened to be there after a late night of work. Maybe something could be arranged? This caught the driver's attention; he understood immediately, rashly inquiring, "How much for you to forget this?"

"This is a death we're talking about; tell me what you have."

The driver, sensing the seriousness of the moment and too afraid to haggle, said "I've got two grand in my truck. Will that get it forgotten?"

"Get what forgotten?"

"Jesus, the damn lady... oh, I get it". He then ran to his truck and pulled out an envelope loaded with cash and handed it to Mr. Trivia. "We square?" asked the driver.

"Just one more thing".

The driver, sensing he was gonna get hit up for more money, asked, "Come on, buddy, it's all I have".

"No, don't worry; we're good. Just need some help moving the body to a better location".

"Oh". The driver was visibly relieved and seemed to begin breathing normally again.

From this point in the vision, it got a bit convoluted and I saw them dropping her and shoveling dirt onto her. The mirror informed me that a foundation was going to be poured on top of her the next morning. To this day, she's never been found.

As the truck left the scene, the sun was just beginning to pop over the horizon. Mr. Trivia took a deep breath and said, "Damn, almost got cancelled in the season opener."

Realizing the vision was over, I jokingly said, "What, just one?" and managed a half-hearted smile.

Mr. Trivia smiled and just said, "Hey, the longest journeys begin with a single step. Don't you worry; my journey is going to be a long one. My show will run for many seasons."

He continued by saying in a prideful manner, "I'm going to stake out the fatties with poor self- esteem, make sure I alienate them from their families, and when the time is right, it's show-time. I'm even working on a fake microphone, wheel, and scoreboard, to give it some realism. It takes a long time to find a contestant, and I'll bet Ms. Rose would agree", but before she could respond, he added, "but it's best to be safe."

CHAPTER 8

The Anti-Sam Malone

Life doesn't imitate art, it imitates bad television.

— Woody Allen

The bartender had been fairly quiet, with a couple exceptions up to this point in the evening, aside from the numerous times he felt obligated to remind me about the two beer minimum and a couple loud give and takes with Wheels. A couple of times, I saw him strike up a conversation with one of the bar cronies. If the other person engaged with him, he'd soon grow bored and would stare over the person's head, lost in his own thoughts. It was obvious that he was not listening to a word the person was saying. He broke away from his last one-sided conversation and headed in my direction. As he stood in front of me, he leaned over, again reminding me in a low, almost inaudible tone, "Buddy, that fucking beer ain't gonna drink itself".

He immediately reminded me of an older Sam Malone from the show Cheers, but the physical similarities were where the comparison ended. This man completely lacked the charm and sex appeal of TV's Sam Malone. He had the good looks akin to everyone's favorite bartender and, like "TV" Sam, his hair was very well-kept. Although his hair was thinning, it still retained its brown color with what looked like a reddish tint and a smattering of gray by the temples. I would have to say he was 5'10" or so, but he had a stoop to his shoulders, and I figured he had been taller in his youth. The fact that he wore dark glasses had struck me as odd earlier in the evening because the restaurant/bar was already gloomy; however, I soon figured out why. He was clearly imbibing heavily as he worked. I could only assume that he wore the glasses to keep his customers from realizing how loaded he was. However, his mannerisms, gait, and attitude spoke volumes, and glasses were not going to hide the fact that he was soused. I also noticed a slight drawl, but I could not figure out the origin, not that I put much time into it because I really didn't care. I had known this man's name was Gerald from hearing the patrons speaking to him and learned that he had owned the establishment for several years. He was fully functional, but truly fucked up at the same time.

After the short reminder about the speed at which I was drinking, he wandered toward the window to look at the snow. He mumbled, "Damn it" and immediately returned behind the bar, vigorously rubbing what had to be the cleanest mug in New England. As he approached the bar, the mirror had a cloudy look, almost as if a storm were approaching. There were no flashes in the mirror which meant the bottles were similarly inactive.

It was at this time that Gerald removed his glasses and again leaned uncomfortably close to me, so close that I could smell the mix of alcohol and the sardines he had been eating. He was looking directly into my eyes with an intensity that seemed to bore into my brain like a drill when he smugly asked if I was ready for some big boy visions. He asked this question with a smile that was not in any way warm or friendly but resonated strongly in the form of a challenge. After I tactfully shook off the effect of his breath, which would knock a buzzard off a carcass from 20 yards, I informed him that I was ready...

Announcing to the bar, "Now the boy becomes a man", then his sinister laugh filled the bar. He stepped aside and ordered me, "Concentrate and look directly into the mirror, it works better that way".

I responded with, "What works better?" But I knew what he was talking about. As the odd flashes commenced, I reflected upon, for what had to be the 100th time, why he was still polishing that fucking beer mug with his towel? The few patrons from hell that were here were drinking from bottles, except for Wheels., She was using an old, nasty, plastic cup that I would not even use to give a urine sample.

The mirror's stormy appearance was swirling and almost hypnotizing. The bottles by the mirror seemed to be rising up and down as if on waves. I knew I had another story to view and I guessed it was going to be a doozy. I waited for all the flashes and deflecting to begin.

No sooner had I considered the possibility, the flashing returned and the bottles did their usual routine. Mixed in with the quick scenes of violence were what I'd call horizontal red lines of varying lengths. Also, not only were these new shapes manifesting in the mirror, they seemed to be pulsing, almost like a heartbeat. The new show was starting, and, unlike the others, there would be no preamble to this man's story. It was time to dive into the deep end of the pool. As I was transported into this new hell, I still managed to hear the odd cackling and coughing from Wheels. The interference from the bottles and the new lines had tapered off. The picture was clearing again. The forbidding story had begun...

I find myself in the passenger seat of a vehicle and immediately I can tell that, not only was the flashing and deflecting by the bottles different, but this current vision was different, as well. Most of the previous visions appeared like I was watching the events unfold on television from the comfort of my recliner. However, this time I was there, and the visions were far more intense and somehow crisper, I was not sure why, but that word seems to fit. I could not only see and hear this new tale of horror but I could now touch and smell my surroundings. I could actually feel the material of the seat I was in; I could smell the stale cigarettes in the car's ashtray. Later on, when I was walking, I could feel the gravel beneath my shoes, the chill of the air, and the sun in my eyes. This was far more than just a vision; it was as if I were traveling with this person on a different plane, and I was now somehow more than a witness to the atrocities forthcoming. I could feel this man's rage, excitement, as well as the plethora of other fucked up feelings this monster possessed.

I would further say this new experience was similar to an empath's, but it's more, because I made an additional unwanted observation. Early on in this vision, one of us farted, and I sure as hell know it was not me. How could I hear and smell a fart in a vision? I'm sure this is far too much information for the reader, but it does show how matter-of-fact the vision was. These forthcoming visions are far more disjointed than the others, but for what it lacked in transition, it more than made up for in laser-like intensity and clarity.

HAVE A HOLLY, JOLLY CHRISTMAS...

I see a young teenage couple sitting in a diner, and, judging by the decorations surrounding their table, it's obviously Christmas time. I am suddenly informed, via an ESP moment, that it is December 20th, 1968. The young man has straight, dark hair combed toward his right eye. He is wearing a rumpled suit and tie, and although he is somewhat disheveled, it is obvious that it was not for a lack of effort. He was clean-shaven and looked like an altar boy. His skin was free of the blemishes that usually plague young men of his age, which I'm sure contributed greatly to his youthful and almost angelic appearance. Despite this seemingly less than stellar description, he had a quiet confidence that the smitten young lady across from him found very attractive.

The pretty young lady sitting across from the young man also has dark hair. She has big, brown eyes, delicate features, and a small mouth. Her hair is tumbling out of her updo adorned with purple bows that match the dress she is wearing. The short dress is a dark purple and the collars and cuffs are white. She is quiet, but I do hear her reference the fact that she has been looking forward to their first official date, and she was delighted her parents granted her permission. She has felt guilty sneaking around with him for several weeks and lying to her parents, and for using her friend as a ruse to meet up with him. Their difficult discussion aside, they seemed to greatly enjoy each other's company. They were soon holding hands while they waited for the waitress to bring their hot chocolates. It was a scene that, I'm sure, Norman Rockwell would have painted with his usual bucolic detail.

The lovebirds were talking about their plans for that evening in hushed tones. The young lady had told her parents they were going to a Christmas concert at Hogan High School and she felt guilty about lying again, especially since they had finally let her go on this date. The young man promised her that, after this evening, there would be no more lying. This brought a large smile to the face of the young lady. He went on to say the reason for wanting to be alone is because he has something very private to talk to her about and, if they go to the dance, he wouldn't get the opportunity. It soon became apparent that, after consuming their hot chocolate, they would depart to a private location. The smitten young couple discussed several different locations and soon decided on a place called Lake Herman Road. This location featured a turnout and was known as a lover's lane location. The young lady thought this spot would be appropriate, as she had heard from her friends in driver's ed class that the spot is very isolated. Furthermore, she was assured that the police had not yet caught onto that location.

At this point in the evening, I'm well past feeling as if I'm intruding on their private conversation. I am dismayed to unexpectedly notice that a man in his late-20's or early-30's is sitting next to me in the booth. I had not noticed him when I was listening to the couple discuss their plans. This man, I just noticed, is sitting on the bench to my left; however, he is not interacting with me in any way. It feels awkward. This very familiar man that I recognized, but had not yet identified, is listening to the young love birds with laser-like intensity. He's holding a cup of coffee close to his mouth with both hands, accentuating his glare. The young couple fail to notice the danger in their midst. I now notice him lean away from me, and he releases flatulence for everyone to hear, earning a stern reprimand from the cook behind the counter. The offending party mumbles an apology, but it's obvious by his smile that he is anything but remorseful. I smile, not because he got reprimanded, but because I have solved the mystery. This flatulent person next to me is the younger version of my bartender. I suppose I could have guessed Baxter because of his recent toxic bombing of the bar. However, I knew damn well it was the bartender because of his shady demeanor as well as the clincher: he left no tip for the waitress. Ken had been right in his earlier statement that this man was extremely tight with a dollar, unless he is partaking of alcohol.

The scene changes. I am in the passenger seat of a late-1950's, 4-door, Chevy Impala, and my young buddy Gerald is driving. Oddly, he has not acknowledged my presence to this point. I can see and feel him next to me, but, at the same time, I am somehow not there — a feeling that is quite unsettling. As we travel together on a dark and secluded road, I see a light brown Rambler station wagon directly in front of our car as it slowly pulls into a gravel turnout. The area is pitch-black, and there are absolutely no lights in sight. Gerald recklessly maneuvers our vehicle behind theirs and exits rapidly. He walks in a determined manner toward the young couple's driver's side door. He begins yelling instructions for them to exit the vehicle. And, before I know it, he's blasting a .22 semi-automatic pistol into the window in order to expedite the process. It is shocking to me, because I had no idea, until this moment, that he has a weapon with him. Gerald then circles around the back of their car, and, when he gets within a few feet of the passenger's side of the vehicle, the young lady bails out like a shot. She flees from the attack with surprising quickness, with the young man on her heels in his attempt to escape out of the same door. Gerald matter-of-factly shoots the young man in the head at point blank range, killing him instantly. The young man barely exits the vehicle before being slain.

My attention is now on the girl as she flees, and I'm hoping she makes the treeline and possible safety. As the young lady is about twenty feet or so away from the vehicle, and roughly ten feet from the trees, Gerald takes careful aim at his prey and put 5 bullets swiftly into her back (three high and two low, all on the right side), killing her instantly. Gerald stands for a brief moment and waits, most likely looking for signs of life. Not seeing movement or hearing a cry for help, he promptly steps over the dead paramour without looking down and returns to our vehicle. As young Gerald enters the car, he fumbles in his pocket with shaking hands for his keys. This is the only indication of nervousness that I've witnessed so far. Once locating the keys, we leave the scene immediately. There are no witnesses and, as we take our leave of the grisly scene, I feel his euphoria. It is emanating from him in waves. I realize my assumption of nervousness was incorrect; it was excitement making his hands shake.

As the two of us sit in silence traveling away from the shooting, my mind is racing. Why did he do this? What had the young couple done to deserve being slain in such a crude manner? I contemplate if he is a cop or a soldier that returned from the war mentally unsound. He shot very well, and his stance was very police or military-like. The five shots he fired were quick, all struck her in the back with precision. The police or military would call it a "Nice shot grouping". Furthermore, pistols are not as accurate as a rifle due primarily to the far shorter barrel. However, his form was unwavering, and he hit his moving target with ease. I attempt to contemplate these questions further, but it appears that the mirror is becoming active again, drawing me to another event, and it's clear that this sick fuck is not done sharing his tale.

This latest flashing returns with a fury. The bottles do their usual routine. This time, however, mixed in with the quick scenes of violence were vertical red lines of different lengths. Also, not only were these new shapes forming in the mirror, they were also sizzling, like bacon frying in a pan. As I am transported into this latest adventure, the bar is now ghostly quiet. The interference from the bottles and the new vertical lines have tapered off. Here we go again...

SOME PEOPLE GET A REAL BANG OUT OF THE 4TH OF JULY...

I find myself as a passenger in the green car with young Gerald again behind the wheel. We are following what looks like a light brown Corvair from a distance of roughly 50 yards. It is difficult to tell, but it looks like there are two people in the front seat, and if I had to guess, a woman is driving and a man is in the passenger seat. Unlike the first couple that we were introduced to in the restaurant, this is my first interaction with this twosome. Gerald and I follow this vehicle for several miles from varying distances, and as the roads become more desolate, Gerald begins to look around. Whatever is coming is coming soon.

The date is easy to determine as the distinctive odor of fireworks' smoke hangs in the still air, and the accompanying haze clings to the road like a heavy blanket. It is quite late, and, if I had to surmise, it is around midnight, give or take an hour. We are within a few miles of where the first killing occurred at Lake Herman Road. I see a sign for Blue Rock Springs Park in Vallejo, and the Corvair we are following pulls off the road and parks. Gerald aggressively positions our vehicle alongside the other car with surprising speed. Just prior to exiting the vehicle, he becomes fidgety. He appears to be concerned about something behind us. He is mumbling something about headlights behind him that I fail to see. Gerald, with his typical aggression, pulls away with smoking tires leaving the bewildered couple behind in a cloud of dust and the smell of burned rubber. After we drive ahead for a spell, he eventually finds a spot to turn around and we back-track past the vehicle we had previously pulled alongside of to where he thought the lights were coming from. Gerald looks around the area and, not seeing anyone, he curses his own nerves and calls himself a "Nervous Nelly", which is oddly corny language for this particular young man.

It is shortly thereafter that we return to the vehicle and he parks behind the Corvair, rather than beside it like the first encounter. Without delay, he exits the vehicle and approaches the Corvair's passenger side door. He is carrying a large, heavy flashlight and a 9 mm Luger which I realize is a different weapon from his previous attack. Without saying a word to the young, confused couple, Gerald approaches the driver's side door and aims his flashlight into their eyes in order to disorient them. With his confused prey trying to make sense of the situation, Gerald fires five shots into the car, striking both victims. In the next moment, I am viewing the same action from behind Gerald and slightly toward the front window side. The young couple tries in vain to shield themselves. The look of terror in their eyes is surreal. The young man briefly tries to shield the woman, but soon realizes the bullets are going through him and striking her as well. He almost instantly goes into self-protection mode, making himself as small as possible. I'm sure he is understandably scared shitless. Gerald, thinking his fun is over, walks rapidly from the scene, pausing for a brief moment before opening the car door. I can only assume he hears crying or moaning coming from the vehicle and he returns to the victims' car and shoots both victims twice at point blank range. It is now time to leave.

As we take our leave, I realize that, at certain points during the second attack, my vantage point had changed. The last position I found myself in was leaning on the hood of the car and looking into the windshield to see the last glimmer of life up close and personal. As I had witnessed this latest attack, I felt the still warm steel of the hood, the ground beneath my feet, the chill of the evening air, and the overwhelming smell of fireworks smoke still draped in the air, now mixed with gunshot smoke.

The next thing I notice is Gerald in a telephone booth delivering a message that appears to be rehearsed. The booth is at a gasoline station, and he's speaking to the Vallejo Police Department. He is claiming responsibility for the murders of the night before as well as the murders six and a half months earlier. I hear the entire declaration as I am behind him and the telephone booth is wide open for all the world to hear. He is not concerned.

In an ESP moment, I would learn that Gerald was greatly disappointed to hear that the male in the Corvair survived the brutal attack despite having been shot in the face, neck, and chest. I also learned that, while the shooting and killing was euphoric for Gerald, the call to the police took his excitement to a higher level. He was sexually aroused by the call; however, I thank all the gods, and especially the power of the mirror that I didn't have to witness that. Knowing is nauseating enough.

I was still reeling from my last horror show when I was hurtled into another of the mirror's latest light shows. This time, rather than lines, the flashing forms resembled a sizzling, jagged red circle. The bottles are very active, as they usually are, and they seem to be trying to block the mesmerizing oval shape forming in front of me, however, unsuccessfully. Here we go again...

ROMANCE ON THE LAKE...

I have to believe it's later in the year, following the last attack, but this time the powers to be didn't provide a date. My best estimate for the time of year would be late September or October, as it is significantly cooler outside. Gerald's car was the same, but he now wore dark pleated pants, a dark blue coat that looked like a windbreaker, and dark brown work boots.

As usual with this unsavory character, I'm a passenger, and we're on a lightly traveled road. I see a small sign that reads "Lake Berryessa" which is in Napa County. I observe Gerald as he stops and exits the vehicle on the shoulder of the road. He opens the trunk and removes some odd garments which he carefully dons with his back toward me. His movements make me think he's performing an important ritual of some sort. He has been keeping his back to me, but I can clearly determine that his actions are not related to shyness. He appears to have no idea that I'm standing just a few feet away from him. In this brief moment in time, I reflect on how strange it is to be a voyeur to these disturbing, nonsensical attacks. I would much rather be like John Belushi in the movie Animal House, watching that pretty coed taking her top off from his perch on the ladder, but, nope, not me.

Anyway, we resume driving for just a short time on a deserted road when Gerald abruptly parks behind a white 1956 Kharman Ghia with a black vinyl top. Considering it's 10 years old, it's in pretty nice shape. As we exit the car,

Gerald goes to the trunk of his vehicle and makes adjustments to his already strange appearance. I note that he is placing a dark hood of some sort over his head, and the top is kinda squared off, almost as if he has a paper bag or box on his head. He then adds a pair of clip-on sunglasses, which I see him fastening from behind. Just before we depart the vehicle, he adds something to the front; I can tell there is writing on it, but I'm not in the proper location to see it. The two of us are walking briskly toward the lake with me following about five yards behind.

I feel the sun on my face and I can feel the damp grass below my shoes. It's almost slippery, I briefly contemplate, "Can someone slip during a vision? Also, if I do fall, can I hurt myself? Are there injury lawyers in this altered state?" After these nonsensical questions to myself, without answers of course, I return to my vision.

I glance around and notice how beautiful it is outside, and, as the ground begins to level from the predominantly downward slope we had been walking, we approach a small peninsular portion of land. I'd learn later that this section is an island in the wetter months of the year. It is connected by a sand dune to Twin Oak Ridge. How do I know this specific information? I've got nobody to thank but the mirror.

As we approach a clearing, we can see two trees out on the point by the lake. I see a young couple lying down on a blanket. The young man is on his back, and the young lady is lying on her stomach with her head nuzzling his shoulder. The couple has chosen the larger and shadier tree of the two near the water's edge in which to enjoy a quiet and, most likely, romantic respite together. This couple seemed older than the first two love birds, but not by much. They appear to be college age compared to the previous couples that looked to be attending high school. I'm thinking of yelling a warning, and I really want to, but I know that it would be futile, as these events I'm experiencing have already occurred. I'm only present in some form of cosmic body and taking a bewildering field trip with a very otherworldly and disturbed person. I briefly contemplate that maybe I'm in the world's most fucked up time machine, but soon realize that is even more ridiculous than my other theories.

As Gerald and I draw closer to the couple from behind the tree, it becomes apparent that they were reminiscing about old times and the dreams they had shared before going their separate ways. It is at that point that the woman hears our approach due, primarily, to Gerald's trudging through the leaves with all the stealth of a blind elephant sneaking up on a bag of peanuts in a china shop. The young lady informs her male companion that someone was behind the tree. The young man loudly says something about it being a rude place to take a piss. He then adds nervously, "Hey, man, we're in a forest, and you have to pick that tree to take a leak?" I am a bit further in the young couple's line of sight; however, their focus is solely on what is happening behind the tree. The young lady still has her head resting on the young man's shoulder, but she is clearly concerned and contemplating getting up, but fear keeps her down. The young man asks the woman to check out the situation because he doesn't have his specs. I think he sounds like Sherlock Holmes or something. Also, even more glaring, it seems cowardly to ask a young lady to check out the strange pissing man behind a tree. This man has a rich, kinda snooty voice. The woman only refers to the disturbance by the tree as one person even though she was looking right at me. As I think on this further, she is staring through me, not at me.

As she is about to get up to investigate what the stranger was up to, Gerald makes his appearance from behind the tree. The young lady, still in her prone position, spots the pistol and squeezes the young man's arm, whispering something to him which I can only guess is, "The person behind the tree has a gun." The young man remains aloof and doesn't so much as move, unless you count his mouth. He starts rambling on and on about not having money, but offers his brilliance to Gerald if he needs help, because he is pre-med-this and pre-law-that in college. As the young man converses with Gerald, he keeps addressing him as "Mac", like how a person calls a stranger "buddy" or "pal". The young man goes on and on about his education level and how he could help Mac. It was getting irksome for both of us. For a brief moment, I am hoping Gerald would hand me his gun so that I can off the college boy myself. The young man tells Gerald that he can get him help with no strings attached.

It is obvious that Gerald is getting edgy when the medical advice takes a turn toward legal advice. Bad things happen to strangers when Gerald gets edgy. The gun reappears when the brazen young man tries to call Gerald's bluff by daring him to prove the gun is loaded. Gerald displays the fully loaded clip, and this is when I realize it's not the familiar pistol he had when he blasted the young teenage couple with a Luger. This pistol looks like a .45, but I'm not sure, as my attention is hastily drawn back to the terrified couple. They are beginning to realize they may be in more trouble than they first thought. However, I think the young lady realizes this well before her dumb ass college boyfriend does.

Gerald is growing increasingly agitated with this pompous young man and informs the couple that he is a convict from Montana where he killed a guard and stole a car to escape. He needs their vehicle because he knows the pigs will be looking for the car he has stolen by now. Gerald further claims to need money to get to Mexico, which I knew was bullshit because his car was not stolen, he had not been in prison, and he sure as hell was not going to Mexico. Gerald then pulled out several pre-cut lengths of rope from his pocket and told the young man to roll onto his stomach. The college boy complains that they could freeze to death overnight if they cannot escape the knots. After some brief, ineffective protesting, the young lady ties her date up as instructed. Once the young man is tied up, Gerald ties up the young lady with very tight knots. He then returns to the college boy to check his restraints. He is visually annoyed that the knots are very loose. Gerald refastens the ropes extra snugly, drawing an audible wince as he listens to the young man coaxing his date to stay calm by expressing repeatedly that, "It's just a robbery". It is at this very crucial moment Gerald has a change of plans that didn't involve the pistol. I felt as if I actually see the light bulb over his head light up. The very second that the young man completes his reassuring comment, Gerald begins stabbing the man in the back. I'm guessing that Gerald perceived him as the bigger threat and wanted him dispatched quickly. The stabbing is exceedingly aggressive. It requires great effort to finish the young man off. In fact, one of the stabs actually pierces the young man's lung. There was a faint sound coming from the wound that I think, in all the excitement, I am the only one to notice. After five or six stabs, Gerald finally finishes with the annoying young man. Then he and I look over at the young lady.

She is in a deep state of panic, her eyes filled with terror. It appears that she fainted for just a moment and, although she is not able to fight due to her restraints, she wiggles just enough to piss Gerald off, and his anger flourishes anew. He stabs the young lady approximately five times in the back. In the midst of the assault, she manages to turn herself around. Despite her efforts, he continues his assault with about five additional wounds to the front. He is really worked up with her, more so than the young man. In his frenzy, I find it peculiar that he stabs her in the arm and the groin in addition to the stabs to her chest. The failure to physically resist doesn't mean she is obligatory to her attacker. It is certain that her resistance is what put him into this nonsensical state. She does get some screams out, of which Gerald and I are keenly aware.

To my knowledge, he still has not noticed the very slight high pitched wheezing sound coming from the young man's chest wound. I consider that he just assumes the young wannabe doctor or lawyer will be dead soon. Gerald knows that his time is growing short, and once he felt the young lady is properly dispatched, he takes a well-deserved deep breath, admires his handiwork with an odd smile for just a moment, and we take our leave.

As we are in the process of leaving the scene, we traverse the quarter mile or so at a brisk walking pace back to his vehicle. As usual, I am following close behind and trying to figure out why my viewpoint never changes as I am usually positioned behind him. Meanwhile, the short escape hike leads to a sign indicating it is Knoxville Road. Gerald locates the young man's vehicle and draws a familiar symbol on the passenger side door followed by a location, what looks like dates, and a reference to a knife. It read as follows:

⊕ "Vallejo/12-20-68/7-4-69/Sept 27-69-6:30/by knife.

Holy shit…

My mind began spinning for the briefest of moments. I'm in the bar again. The flashing is painfully intense and pulsing as if it's alive. Is this…

I'm instantly returned to the vision. Gerald turns… It's the first time I see him from the front since we departed his car for our hike down to the lake. I see a symbol on his chest. It was the infamous Zodiac symbol.

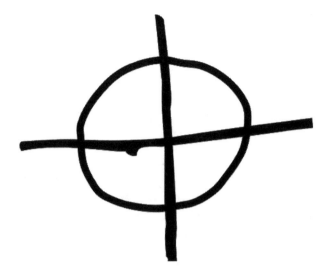

It takes a moment, short enough for a flea to fart, and I thought, "I've been taking a cosmic joy ride with one of the most prolific serial killers of all time. Just like Jack the Ripper, this infamous killer was never apprehended".

After I shake myself from my mind-numbing revelation, I contemplate the fact that this last attack was conducted with a knife and not the customary handgun. I tried to recall from my reading about the Zodiac as to whether or not he used a knife in any of his attacks, but could not recall that detail at the moment. The non-serrated knife he used in this latest attack was about 10" and had a wooden handle.

Why did Gerald deviate from his weapon of choice? I could surmise that maybe it was more hands on with the knife or more, of a challenge, which created greater excitement? But that would merely be a guess. With help from the mirror, I knew what he was processing in his head after these latest murders under the shady tree. He initially thought it would be exciting; however, it was just too physically taxing and burdensome. It was a far riskier manner of killing which was proven by the screams that came from his victims. It was not the screams that bothered him as such, but the amount of energy necessary to finish the job. Between the anticipation, adrenaline, and the amount of energy expended, he was left thoroughly spent. These factors weighed on him, and he vowed not to use a knife again. He found out later that a man and his son were fishing nearby and had heard screams and were cautiously looking for the source of the distress and shouts for help.

Gerald also learned later that the man was hesitant to run to the rescue for fear of running into an ambush, and he was worried about his son possibly getting caught in the crossfire. The father and son had gotten to the scene shortly after the attack and contacted park rangers. As Gerald and I carefully escaped the scene in his vehicle, we drove by many police cruisers. To be honest, I'm not sure why they didn't stop us.

During our departure from the latest attack, the tension radiating from Gerald was palpable. It was roughly 8 p.m., and after about 25 or 30 miles of driving, Gerald decided to stop at a Napa Car Wash on Main Street. It was here that he made a telephone call to the Sheriff's office from a pay phone.

As I witnessed this call from a distance, I noticed the call was brief and to the point. Gerald's head looked to be making up and down movements, as if he were checking off points in his head as he spoke. I would have to ascertain that this was a rehearsed declaration similar to the call he made after he attacked the first young couple. The difference with this call was that he purposely dropped the phone without placing it on the cradle before returning to the vehicle.

Gerald soon learns from a radio broadcast that the young lady was conscious when the police arrived but was listed in critical condition. Her prognosis was grim, but should she survive, it was more than likely that she could provide a close description which troubled him greatly. A few days later, he was relieved to hear that the woman succumbed from the wounds suffered in the attack. Gerald was positive that if anyone would get his description correct, it would be her. He also thought that, if he became a suspect, she would have picked him from a lineup without pause. Thankfully for Gerald, that was not in the cards. During the attack on this woman, she was looking at him closely as his knife was plunging into her and doing serious internal damage, albeit far too slowly for Gerald's liking. At several points, it actually unnerved him. She was looking at him, through him, maybe looking for a soul which he knew she would never discover. It was at this precise moment when he decided, "Using a knife isn't for me". He remembered a brief statement his father always made, "Work smart, not hard".

The flashing commences again. It is far brighter than any of the others I'd seen this evening. The vertical and horizontal lines are

repeatedly colliding with a fluctuating circle that keeps shattering like glass and reforming as the lines continuously strike. The bottles are deflecting at a frantic pace, and the combination is bothersome to my eyes. The sounds are familiar as well: crackling electricity fills the air. A new twist develops. I actually smell smoke which reminds me of a rubbish fire. Within a moment or two, the mirror and bottle display gradually slow down. It is trying to form a shape which fully manifests itself in short order: it is a breathing and living entity in front of me. It is clearly depicting the ominous form of - the Zodiac..

This latest, eerie trip about to commence has me standing at the intersection of Mason and Geary Streets. This spot is one block west from Union Square in San Francisco. I'm looking around and speculating what the fuck was going to happen this time. I sense Gerald approaching from behind me and hear him mutter, "Gotta get in this fucking cab". For the life of me, I don't know if he was telling me to get inside the cab or if he was just talking to himself. I do what I may or may not have been instructed to do as Gerald hops into the front passenger seat, to the dismay of the cab driver. I quickly settled into the back seat, shimmying a bit toward the center, as a way to avoid car sickness. Would I get car sick in a vision? I have no goddamn clue, but I do so anyway. While I sit looking forward, I notice the dashboard clearly indicating the name of this Yellow Cab Co. driver as Paul Stine.

Gerald seems equally agitated and excited. I have a feeling that it's not too long after the events of his recent knife attack. My assumption is soon rewarded by the mirror: the date is October 11th, 1969. The actions of this man are now national news. The hunt is on for the Zodiac Killer.

Quickly, Gerald orders Mr. Stine to take him to Washington and Maple Streets in Presidio Heights. As I sit and observe my surroundings, I noticed Gerald looking in his wallet which is confusing because I can see from my vantage point that it's empty. I'm thinking a new shit storm is about to happen, and, within seconds, my instincts are again proven correct. It was at this moment which, I believe, was roughly 10 p.m. that I hear Gerald hollering at the driver. He is loudly complaining that the driver drove past the requested destination and, because of that, he was not going to pay the fare.

Mr. Stine matter-of-factly requested Gerald to relax; he would just turn the cab around and the fee on the meter would be backtracked. As the vehicle came to a stop, Gerald calmly reached out with his left hand and shot the driver point blank in the head with a 9 mm. I am now seeing this vision somehow from the front of the car, I am not sure when my perspective changed, but, by now, you know these visions have a mind of their own.

I noticed that Gerald remained in the vehicle for an uncomfortably long time considering the fact he was being watched. Prior to making his escape, Gerald removed the driver's car keys and wallet. He also tore away a large section of the driver's bloodstained shirt tail, which I found confounding. It was well past time to get away, but he made sure to wipe down the passenger side door and the steering wheel. He did miss some prints that were discovered by the police, but they were never connected to him. The prints he left were on the driver's side armrest from when he was making an attempt to position the driver in a sitting position, for reasons only known to Gerald. It was a fruitless endeavor, because the dead guy would not cooperate. Gerald does not know why it was important for him to reposition the driver, or why he left the car running as well as the meter. At the time, his panic must have made him take actions that were not in his best interests.

After Gerald finally came to his senses and realized he needed to get the hell out of this area, he walked at a fast pace away, and I followed from a distance of about ten yards. Our walk led us in the direction of Presidio one block to the north. As we got a couple blocks from the scene, Gerald made another precarious move. He stepped into a stairway leading to the front yard of a home on the north side of the street. His facial expression and body language show he is desperate to conceal himself, and my theory is kindly confirmed by the mirror. The sound of sirens seems to be growing louder from every direction, and Gerald actually appears terrified and desperate to take cover in any way possible.

Just as he draws near the door, Gerald sees an officer in a patrol car responding to the suspected robbery and possible murder of a cab driver. The officer makes clear and concentrated visual observation of him. Gerald's now thinking, "Well, looks like the jig is up". However, just as the officer begins to pull over to question him, he takes his eyes off Gerald and looks toward his radio. Within that instant, the officer suddenly drives away with lights flashing and sirens blaring. Gerald, as relieved as he is to see the officer vacate the area, seems disappointed in some way. The reason for his angst is because he had made the decision, just seconds after being looked over by the officer, that if he'd had to enter the home for cover, he was going to kill everyone inside and go out in a blaze of glory. He figured, "If my story is gonna end, It will have been a hell of a way for it to go." His crowning moment would have been to use the blood of his victims to draw his zodiac symbol on their wall. "Woulda been a great movie," he thought. As he turns from the house and walks briskly away with the sirens still blaring, although fading, he briefly contemplates what actor would have played him. It did not take long. Peter Fonda would be perfect, not necessarily because of his similar appearance, but more so the attitude he carries.

I soon notice that I'm becoming aware of my actual surroundings again and I'm detecting the others in the bar. The transition back to the bar was slower than what I had experienced before. Gerald's incredible vision was over but it hesitated on returning me to the present time. At last, I took a big slug from my beer which thrilled Gerald to no end. He asked, "How you like them apples?" After a short respite, I asked if I might ask him some questions since he was the infamous "Zodiac" and his story and the investigation was a worldwide news mystery comparable to the location of Jimmy Hoffa's body and the identity of Jack the Ripper. I looked at the clock again, and this time I was not surprised to see that I'd only been in this place for not even one hour. I was thinking that I was one of a handful of living people in the entire world that knew the identity of the Zodiac. The only other people on the planet that knew his identity were either in this room or dead. It was as thrilling as it was scary, and I wrestled with the thought if he was just going to let an outsider, like myself, learn his secret and then just waltz on out the door. I took a slug of beer and pushed that terrifying thought aside...

As I sat on my stool gathering my thoughts, Gerald loudly announced, "You're drinking! 'Bout fucking time. This guy drinks like a queer".

Wheels chimed in, using her typical abrasive tone, saying, "Just let the asshole enjoy his beer., He'll drink his second before he leaves. I'll bet anyone here that this panty waste will finish two beers before he leaves". I was too deep in thought to take offense to Gerald and Wheel's less than complimentary comments about me. I was now feeling like Mike Wallace from my favorite show, "60 Minutes", and it was 'lil old me (the queer and the panty waste) getting the interview of the century. Like the visions and ESP moments, I remember the interview clearly.

THE INTERVIEW OF THE CENTURY...

I took a deep breath, processed my thoughts for a moment, and began the interview that any television network star would kill for. I'm going to put my questions to the one and only Zodiac. and for the first time this evening, I'm thrilled. For the reader to follow this interview, I'm putting my questions in bold to make this give-and-take a little easier to follow.

"During these visions, there were some really strange things happening — aside from the visions themselves — like the fact that during all of the visions I've experienced, hardly any time has passed, oh, and the fact that I can read or hear thoughts but cannot hear a whisper ..."

"First of all, slow the fuck down, and, second of all, no idea".

"Ok, duly noted. I will try to ask my questions in a more organized manner. Why are the owners' pictures not on the wall? I'm assuming, from what I've seen in the visions, that you would qualify to be included in the photographs" (nervous chuckle)?

"Tradition. That is what the previous owner instructed me to do. I'm the third owner of this facility, or to be more accurate, the third owner of the mirror. Yes, all three owners would qualify easily if we had been patrons rather than owners".

"Who are the first two owners?"

"None of your fucking business".

"Why is Scott not on the wall?"

"Wow, cuz he's a minor, you dumb fuck. I'm sure the mirror will invite him next year."

Do you call all your customers names like "dumb fuck"? I would not think it's good for business.

Not acknowledging my last question, he continues, "Maybe you and Scott will stand side by side with Wheels, and if you're lucky", adding with a wink, "Wheels will give you guys a hand job afterwards".

Wheels steam rolls into the conversation, exclaiming for all to hear, "Hey, you ain't my pimp Gerald. If they're good boys, I'll take care of them". Shuddering, I jumped right back to the questions before this line of conversation could proceed any further.

"What do you mean the mirror will invite Scott? How does an object invite anyone anywhere? You are the owner; aren't you the person that sends the invites or sets the date for the picture day?"

"I don't invite anyone. The mirror draws the guests here like a magnet, and, when it does, I just grab my trusty camera and click a picture."

After some confusion, the interview continues, **"Why on earth do you keep hinting that I will be back? This is my first and last time in this place, no offense".**

"Oh, don't get your panties in a bunch, I'm just busting your balls a bit. I like to get a rise out of people; it's how I have fun. After all, as they say, the best things in life are free". He said this with a disturbing smirk and a renewed vigorous rubbing of his fucking mug.

"Well, since we're not getting anywhere here, can you tell me why you stopped killing?"

"Well", (pausing for an uncomfortably long time, appearing to choose the right words for his answer), he continued, "The attack with the knife really unsettled me, to say the least. I had been enjoying myself thoroughly up to that point. The knife really slowed things down and left me exhausted and vulnerable to capture. It's just not easy to stab a person. Lotta damn hard work and extremely personal. As you can tell by now, I'm not the kind of person that enjoys close physical contact. The woman managed to turn around as I was stabbing her, and she was looking at me as if she was looking for something within me. For a little while, I was concerned that I didn't have what she was looking for. It was really disturbing, for lack of a better word, and it drove me to not only kill her, but to destroy her. A few days after that attack, I figured I'd had my fun and had not been caught, so why fuck with fate, you know? I figured I'd just fuck with the pigs and media for a spell, which, I gotta say, was fun.

"The cabbie murder was purely impulsive. I think that I may have been more surprised than the cab driver. Well, maybe not...But I made a lasting impression on him...(small chuckle).

"It all came down to luck, because I later learned that the police dispatcher apparently screwed-up. She told the patrol officer that had been giving me the once-over to be on the lookout for a black male suspect".

(Gerald now goes into a laughing fit that lasts for several uncomfortable minutes).

Wheels bursts into my historic mock interview with her cackling laugh, saying "Gerald being confused with a black guy is hilarious, I've seen his dick…"

Gerald harshly interjects, "You've never seen my dick, you two dollar whore" to which Leah actually appeared hurt.

She responded with, "No need to get mean, asshole".

Gerald resumes his answer by claiming his last two attacks were getting out of hand and honestly the results would have been bad for him. The first two attacks went flawlessly; the last two attacks were potentially disastrous. "I came to the conclusion that the murders were entertaining but the letters were far more satisfying and the risk factor greatly reduced. Torturing the police and teasing the media was total excitement, and I kept that up very carefully for a few years". It sure didn't hurt that the cops and the media were inundated with fake letters. They didn't know what was real and what was not. It was like taking candy from a blind cripple.

"I don't think that's the right version of that saying", I responded.

Baxter abruptly pops in with, "Man, you gotta tell him the cool part of the cabbie murder, you know what I mean?"

"Ok, I can't let that nugget go by. What was the cool part of that murder?"

"Well, thanks for dragging this out, Baxter. Anyway, as you know from what I've said and the visions you've witnessed, soon after the college couple I had attacked under the tree with a knife, it was my intention to stop. I was just going to have fun with letters and ciphers when I impulsively decided to kill the cab driver. However, the nugget that Baxter referred to was the fact that I was on my way to kill another couple when I hopped in the cab".

"I thought you were going to stop?"

"I know. Apparently I had unknowingly staked out this couple and, at some point, I overheard them speaking of going to meet in very secluded portion of Presidio park that evening".

Interrupting his story, I ask, "How do you unknowingly stake someone out?"

"Trust me, I have no goddamn idea. Anyway, I was following them and listening to their conversations. At some point early on, I realized they were handing me the perfect opportunity. It reminded me of my first attack with that young couple that went so flawlessly". He puts the damn mug down that he'd been rubbing for the entire time I'd been at the bar and appears to become lost in thought; he just stood there transfixed.

"And?"

He snapped out of whatever mental place he was in and continued, "I had overheard this couple setting up a date at Baker Beach, which is in Presidio Park, with the hope of skinny dipping if things got private enough for them. The scenario was a perfect way to end my attacks cleanly on a nice secluded beach. Instead, I just fucked it up even more. If not for gross incompetence by that dispatcher, I'd have been captured. I think the officer's name that spotted me was Fouke, but I could be mistaken. It was something like that. About a month after the cabbie attack, he came forward and admitted he likely let me walk right past him. I had to admire him for that. It's not easy to confess an error of such magnitude, and he didn't try to skirt the blame by mentioning the dispatcher's call.

"So, the cabbie was collateral damage and not the intended target. Wrong place and wrong time, but I guess you could say that about all my victims. Somewhere out there are two people that have no idea how fucking lucky they are. I often think about if they had their chance to skinny dip, but I'll never know now thanks to that cabbie".

"Wow, that didn't manifest itself in my visions at all. Do you know why?"

"The mirror picks what visions are shared and what are not; no rhyme, no reason."

"Why did I not see visions of the ciphers or letters?"

"Not violent or important enough for the mirror, I suppose."

"Ok, that is another issue. What is it with the mirror and the flashes? How does it work?"

"I'm afraid that is a whole other subject, my pathetically dawdling, drinking friend. Maybe some other time I'll answer that."

The last answer agitated me; however, I soon felt a sense of relief because his answer meant I was going to live after this interview. I took a sip of beer and kept my train of thought moving. Hoping to mix things up a bit, I asked, "You have been connected to other murders. What about those?"

"Yes, the press has me responsible for hundreds of unsolved murders, and even connected to murders committed by Charles Manson and Ted Bundy, which was fucking hilarious. The fingerprints gathered at the last murder cleared the two of them of that attack.

"I also exaggerated my totals with the pigs as well as the media, I just wanted to fuck with them. That was, without a doubt, the best part. But to cut to the chase, the only crimes I committed are the ones you've seen."

"Have you ever been a cop or a soldier? As I recall, the police had a theory that you may have had a police or military background, especially after the first attack. Shooting the girl with a pistol as she fled could not have been easy. I believe the police referred to that as a pretty good shot group, or some similar term."

"I have not been in the military, nor have I been with the police, but I can understand why they would have that view. My father was a cop in the town of Killingly (gesturing outward with his hands), Connecticut where we are sitting right now. He taught me how to fire a handgun. I'm a good shot, and the five I put into the first young lady sure proves it."

"I know we touched on the letters and the ciphers. What were their purpose?"

"Misdirection. As I said before, mainly to fuck with the cops and media, but it was also simple self-preservation. I wanted them working on things that had nothing to do with me. The ciphers I sent really fucked them up, that was probably my greatest ruse to throw them off my scent. I'm proud of that. I have always had an interest in code; everyone needs to have a hobby, am I right? (creepy smirk). They only solved one cipher and they will never solve the others".

"Why will they never solve them? Maybe, someday, a code breaker or computer will solve it…"

"It's pure genius. The following three ciphers are gibberish, complete crap. The first cipher was written to be solved, but with great difficulty; that was the worm on the hook. It dangled the promise of my identity, and I knew they'd go to any length to solve the following ciphers. This is where it got really fun. I assigned each code to a number and rolled several die. I laugh when I speculate how many hours they put into solving those ciphers" (oddly, he didn't laugh, but his look of pride was very evident).

"Why was each weapon different? What was the purpose of that?"

"Well, when you come right down to it, the purpose was to take measures to avoid capture. However, if you'd like, I could elaborate."

"By all means, proceed."

At that moment, Mr. Trivia loudly exclaims that he needs a commercial break to hit the men's room.

Gerald's retort is simply, "Fuck you. I ain't stopping for you".

"Guess I can wait", Mr. Trivia meekly responds.

Gerald continued, "I own many weapons because my father had left me his collection in his will. I had the handgun from the first attack with me, and it was my intention to use it again in the attack under the tree. However, I had just purchased a 10" knife with a wooden handle that inspired me, at the last moment, to do some hands on work and mix things up a bit. It was a last second decision which I would soon regret. As you know, from the vision and this silly interview, it's not easy to stab someone to death. You hit all kinds of bone and ligaments. It is a real pain in the ass to kill someone with a knife. The guy hung on while playing dead like a chicken shit as I was busy brutalizing the young lady. I barely made it to the victim's car to write my message for the pigs, because I was worn-out from the stabbing".

"So, you knew the college boy smart ass was playing dead?"

"Hell, I got him right in the lung, I could hear the air whistling out. I just figured, with that wound and the time it would take to transport him to a hospital, he'd be long dead. The fact is that I was fucking tired. Also, to be honest, he was such a know-it-all prick, I wanted him to suffer."

"What about your claims of bombs and shooting children on school buses?"

"Just another ruse to have fun and confuse the cops. The possibility of killing kids got their attention, and I am sure it scattered their resources even further. I actually followed a bus shortly after my declaration, and it had an adult in the back. I have no doubt it was a police officer. I had them chasing their tails, and it was a joy to witness. Also, it would be too damn easy to kill children in any manner. Plus, it takes a special kind of twisted fucking evil to resort to that".

"About five or six months after the Stine murder, I remember there was a pregnant woman who claimed you kidnapped her and her infant daughter and drove them around for a couple hours, and they escaped?"

"Holy shit, yes. That was fucking hilarious, I've not thought of that in quite some time. If this event happened, ok". (Gerald starts laughing to such an extent his eyes are watering.) "Ok, ok, let me try again" (uncontrollably laughing again).

The others join the laughter, and the sound is soon dominated by Leah's cackling and the following coughing fit...

After several minutes, Gerald finally recovers and continues his response, "I just love the mental image of this. I go through all this trouble of kidnapping a very far-along pregnant woman and her young baby just to have them toddle off into the woods and escape...". (He's laughing again).

"What did you think about the various facial descriptions provided by the surviving victims? Anyone come close, in your opinion?"

"Somewhat close, but they were vague enough to match a million other men. Hell, the annoying college boy described my height as being between 5'8" to 6', and that was coming from a guy that was always on the ground, so his perspective was off. A few weeks after the drawings came out, I was actually standing next to a poster in a public building that had my supposed picture displayed, and nobody blinked. I don't think my mother would have recognized that drawing as portraying me.

"I guess, if you want to break them down, we'll get that piece of shit male from the second attack out of the way first. I believe his last name is Mageau, but that does not matter. The only thing he got right was that I'm white. He barely saw me from a side angle and he was too busy cowering like a goddamn faggot from the pistol shots. That prick should thank me for his 15 minutes of fame".

"Backtracking just a moment or two, does your mother or any other family member know about your hobby?"

"Nobody in my family ever knew about this chapter in my life, and just so we're clear, the next time you bring up my mother, you'll find yourself at the hospital getting this mug removed from your ass. Is that clear?"

"Crystal clear. What about the cop that saw you leaving the last attack of the cab driver? If I recall from the vision, his name was Paul Stine?"

"Yes, that was his name. The cop really eyeballed me, and his description was close, but vague, as well. I was stunned by the weak description and contemplated if they taught facial features in the Academy. I guess I should thank my parents for my ordinary looks". Continuing on, "The officer did get my height closer than the others and he was fairly close to my weight, as well. At that age, I was always 175 pounds on the dot, but had a large frame that made me look bigger. In addition, I was wearing glasses as a disguise. I don't even use reading glasses. He got the color of my clothes right. However, if I remember, the material was not accurate. If he had followed his instincts and stopped me, he'd be the new host of the 'Tonight Show'".

"Did the officer get anything else wrong, other than being vague?"

"I think he said I was barrel chested? Not sure where that came from. The guy even said I had grey hair in the back. Fuck, I'm barely gray now. That pissed me off (laughing). Oh shit, he also said I had a crew-cut. I don't know why some of these witnesses were saying that. Look at my fucking hair. Would you cut this? Hell no…"

"The young woman from the third attack gave a description before she died. I remember reading that in the paper. What did you think?"

"This woman got a great look at me, and when I'd heard she had not died during the attack, I got very nervous and thought again what a significant mistake it was to use the damn knife! I was planning to head east to Connecticut, but prior to leaving, I'd heard she died. To my great relief, her description prior to dying was incomplete, and had she survived or gained some strength back before passing, she may have been able to nail down my looks a bit more, but I'm just speculating here. Also, if I had a scar of some sort on my face, arms or hands? Maybe a tattoo? Maybe a description would have been more effective, but I'm just a plain looking guy with really nice hair, and I guess it's pretty obvious that people suck at describing faces or body types. Maybe these witnesses could have pulled me from a lineup, but describing a person's looks is not an easy skill to perform. Thankfully."

"What did you think of the description by the last young man that you failed to kill with the knife?"

"Same vague descriptions as the others. He did get the hair color correct, but I was wearing glasses that clipped on, not goggles. He also said I was heavy which, has never been true a day in my life. I don't know how he thought that; he looked right at me like he was studying my features, but I didn't care. I truly believed he'd be meeting St. Peter very soon. How he survived, I have no goddamn idea. The only reason I can think of how he survived is that God himself found him to be an annoying pain in the ass.

Also, he reported that I had greasy hair. That was surprising, as well. Maybe his terror played tricks with his mind. He said that I had a drawl in his report, which was kinda right; however, my accent is so slight that people pay it no mind or even notice it. Oh, another important fact on the description he gave, I soon learned that the guy was blind as a bat. Maybe his eyes were seeing things that were not really there? I'm not sure about that, just spit-balling here".

"Have you ever had any other close calls? Been investigated or questioned?"

"The only close call I had with the police was when I was walking away from the cab driver incident."

"I noticed you said incident and not murder".

"Po-tah-to - po-tay-to".

"Ok, last question. Do you have any regrets? You killed young people that may have done something important with their lives and you destroyed families. The young lady that first comes to mind is the young lady from the first attack, on her first date; she seemed so innocent. Surely that must keep you awake at night?"

"I sleep like a baby. Zero regrets. Think about all the visions you've seen tonight. Everyone in this room sleeps soundly. I guess that would make us sociopaths because we lack empathy, but I don't like that title. I prefer..."

"What do you prefer?"

"I'm thinking, Jesus Christ, give me a fucking minute, I guess I'm a free-spirit. That sounds much better".

After my deluge of questions, he inquired, "You know, there is a big question you've not asked yet. It's time buddy."

I knew the question, I knew damn well what he was referring to..."You mean, why am I seeing these flashes from the mirror and being the recipient of all its charms?" My answer was meant to keep the charade of this mock interview proceeding; however, I really hoped he would not share the answer with me.

"That would be it. That is the most important goddamn question you've asked tonight!. Everyone in this bar could tell you were bothered by the flashing from the mirror the moment you arrived. I'm not exactly sure how the damn thing works, and trust me, we have spent many late evenings trying to figure out this damn mystery (gesturing toward the mirror with his hands) without success".

I glance around the room and see that everyone in the bar has moved their seats closer to Gerald and me, and they're listening intently. Wheels rolls closer than the others but says nothing, which is in itself a minor miracle. Without missing a beat, Gerald continues, "We've developed some theories about who the mirror affects and the possible meaning of the bottles. As near as we can tell, the mirror allows like-minded people to see the horrible things they've done in their past. I don't mean like cheating on your spouse or your taxes. It's the type of sins you've witnessed tonight. The bottles act as interference, almost like a... (he pauses, again searching for the right word, then continues once he finds the applicable phrase)... blocker which pushes a tragic occurrence to the subconscious. This ability to push or suppress awful memories helps your mind live with your sins to maintain your sanity. If people didn't have the ability to block horrible memories like ours, the asylums would be overflowing". Getting a bit excited, Gerald adds, "Not only does the mirror let a person see their hidden sins but also the sins of others, again, like you've witnessed tonight".

I snapped a response quickly and defended my honor with venom, "What the hell are you insinuating, like-minded people? I'm not a sick, twisted, fucking killer like you freaks are". I was past being really pissed off, not to mention scared to death about the idea of insulting murderers...I took a glance at the clock and saw I'd only been there for an hour and a half, and most of that time was this stupid damn interview I had insisted on. I could not figure out what the hell was happening. I had never taken a life, and the very idea of it was loathsome...or was it?

Slightly exasperated, Gerald continued, "The bottles interfere with the memory of the person looking into the mirror, not the others for some damn reason. We've already seen what you've done, and it's about time that you do as well."

Gerald turned toward the mirror with his back to me and began moving the bottles (aka blockers) that were between me and the mirror.

As Gerald continued his work, he said, "It is time to see your past in an unobstructed new light. I'm allowing you the clarity to see what you've done in the past." With his back still turned, he now presented an offer, "I'm giving you an opportunity to get up and leave before I step aside". This statement was surprising because, on the surface, it seemed to be an act of kindness; however, it came across as a challenge to my manhood, which I'm sure was intentional.

I sat steadfast on my stool, responding meekly, "I may have some regrets, but I am not a monster like you and your customers", although the statement came across flat. For a fleeting moment, I contemplate the intelligence of insulting people that have tortured and murdered innocent bystanders. I sat up, thinking hard, what could I have possibly done to warrant being mixed up with this group? I had not killed anyone with a gun, knife or baseball bat. I had never raped, molested, or chopped off the penis of a child. Hell, I never cheated on my wife...It began to dawn on me with a now spinning head that Gerald had been telling me constantly that I was "where I belong", and when I'd disagree, it sounded more like I was trying to convince myself. But, my God, I've never killed anyone, blockers be damned!

As Gerald finished rearranging the bottles, he still had his back to me. He repeated the offer by asking in a far more put-out voice, "Do you want me to turn around and step away from the space in front of the mirror or not?" I realized my prior responses were not really answers; they were more of a long-winded, nervous series of comments. I could see more frequent flashes of red. They were the familiar flashes that I'd been seeing from my peripheral vision since I'd arrived.

For the first time since I'd witnessed his story, Baxter approached me and said, "There is no shame in leaving," which was seconded by Wheels with a simple head nod of agreement. I glanced around the room and noticed that everyone seemed to be of the same mind. Gerald, observing my hesitation, simply stated that everyone had demons, and I should see mine.

Leah chimed in with, "Asshole, it's his call".

Gerald's response was, "Fair nuff. What's your decision?, I ain't got all damn day".

Again, Wheels added, "Yeah, Gerald, I forgot you go to the Mensa meetings this time of night". It was a barb, but nobody laughed. I could tell this group enjoyed tweaking Gerald, but only to a certain point.

Ken approached me, put his hand on my shoulder, and said with a smile that was in itself a horror to see, "You have a family. Leave now. If I had this opportunity, I'd run from this dump like my ass was on fire".

Gerald interjected, "Dump! This place is not a dump!"

Leah drawing closer to Gerald's boiling point, added her two cents, "Oh, Gerald, please. This place would make a honky-tonk bar look like The Ritz".

The room returned its gaze toward me and the conversation at hand. I took the biggest breath I'd ever taken and clearly said, "I've got nothing to hide; step aside".

I heard Wheels say, "Shit, I guess he is as dumb as he looks".

Upon hearing Wheel's comment and taking stock of what I'd seen that night, I swiftly came to my senses. Leaving was the right decision. I cried out, "Wait!" It was too late. Gerald had already stepped aside...

The flashes started. They were all white and these flashes hurt the eyes.

I vaguely heard Baxter remarking, "The flashes will hurt more than before cuz you are inside the flash, if that make any sense to ya". It would make sense later, but at the time it didn't, nor did I care. It was soon obvious that Baxter was right. The flashing is intense but different.

The vertical and horizontal lines were not present, nor the oddly moving circle. The bottles were not deflecting as the interference had been removed.

This is simply an unveiling. My mind raced. I'm not a monster, am I?

CHAPTER 9

Yours Truly

"So it is more useful to watch a man in times of peril, and in adversity to discern what kind of man he is; for then at last words of truth are drawn from the depths of his heart, and the mask is torn off, reality remains."

— Titus Lucretius Carus

I was behind the wheel of one of my favorite cars, my first car to be exact. It was a 1975, light green Monte Carlo that I had inherited from my grandfather. The feeling about this particular trip seemed vaguely familiar to my latest road trip to The Last Call. An ESP moment informed me that I was on my way to visit my mother. At the point in my life, when this terrible evening occurred, she was, to her great dismay, residing at a retirement home. It was difficult driving as it was snowing like hell and the gusting wind only added to the difficulty. I clearly recalled thinking about why I didn't just wait a few days and visit when the weather was better. The conditions were worse than the storm that took me to my present location. This retirement home was very remote, and the roads were extremely perilous. I would imagine these roads were dangerous even under normal conditions for drivers unfamiliar with the terrain. One particular section of this road that I was cautiously driving on featured a wicked curve on one side and a large concrete abutment for a dam on the other side. The location had caused many accidents throughout the years. In addition, there was a steep, sheer ledge face on the side opposite the bridge abutment that was always seeping water downward onto the road. So when the rain was heavy, the road flooded, causing hydroplaning, or if the weather was cold enough, the water froze, turning the road into a hockey rink. I would eventually learn that the locals were very cautious on this curve; however, those individuals (usually young or intoxicated) that did not know about this dangerous section of road tended to ignore the signs. These travelers kept the local ambulance drivers and morticians very busy, with the annual uptick during the holidays notwithstanding. I took this curve slowly, as I'm typically a cautious driver and I could not see very far in this dreadful weather.

SANTA GAVE THE WRONG GUY COAL FOR CHRISTMAS...

I would also learn that the locals had aptly named this section of road "Santa's revenge". If I may digress just a little bit, and by now I'm sure you know I will, the following information I'm about to share was obtained from research. The visions or the ESP moments didn't contribute to my knowledge of this particular portion of road. I took it upon myself to learn the eerie history at the public library shortly after my experience on this strange evening. I was very curious and the name of this portion of road nagged in my mind for some time.

Apparently, 40 some odd years ago, a family of four (husband and wife, son and daughter) were heading to a Christmas party where a very special guest was expected: Jolly Saint Nicholas himself was going to make a starring appearance. The two children were both very young, and I forget if it was the boy or the girl who was older, but that doesn't really matter; the children's ages were 4 and 6.

Anyway, the father was going to drive his prized 1933 Pierce Arrow to the event to impress his friends and family despite the dicey weather conditions on this particular evening. The fact that he was well intoxicated from the work party he had attended earlier that afternoon added to a recipe for disaster.

Just moments before the family approached this dangerous portion of road, a gentleman dressed as Kris Kringle had stepped out of his vehicle, which had broken down on the dangerous section of road. I can only imagine that he was not a very jolly Santa.

Police reports indicated Saint Nick exited his vehicle to investigate what might be the problem under the smoking hood, but failed to first check for oncoming vehicles. As Mr. Kringle stepped out, he was immediately struck by the Pierce Arrow vehicle traveling at a high rate of speed. He was struck solidly and killed instantly. This is where the story goes from unfortunate to just horrifying.

It was noted in the police report and diagrams, but not reported in the media, that the gentleman dressed as Santa Claus, and later identified as Mr. David Johnson, had been decapitated in the accident. Seeing Santa magically appear in front of him, the inebriated driver applied the brakes, causing the very large vehicle to swerve just enough to strike Santa's vehicle (or sleigh). The timing of the brakes being applied, the gentle swerve of the vehicle's front end drift, and the immediate collision, resulted in the vehicle stopping instantaneously. The report goes onto state that Mr. Johnson's cranium was lodged solidly on the vehicle's hood ornament. The ornament on this vehicle was known as an "Archer", which is found on most Pierce Arrow models. Apparently, from what I could gather, the head and upper portion of the bow of the "Archer" went through the right orbital socket and entered Santa's brain, thereby bringing him the mercifully quick death. With the skull being locked onto the hood ornament via the eye socket, similar to a barb on a fishing hook latching onto the thick lip of a fish, and the vehicle's momentum stopping on a dime, Jolly old Saint Nick's head remained on the car. The body, however, was dislodged at impact and was jettisoned about 15 yards into the woods.

So, imagine the visual the police saw when they arrived on the scene. Santa's head mounted on the hood ornament and a headless body dressed as St. Nick dangled from a low tree branch in the woods. The driver and his wife died in the accident, as well as the young boy. There is a photograph in the police report that fully displays Santa's head on the hood along with the upper extremities of the parents and the boy. It almost looked like they were having a meeting on the hood. The girl survived because of the position she was in when the collision occurred. Her primary impact was with the passenger seat in front of her, not the windshield that her parents and brother had the misfortune of traveling through at well north of 60 miles per hour. The report summarized that, if Mr. Johnson (Santa) had not been there, the family would have likely not fared much better, as it was traveling too fast for the weather conditions directly into a dangerous curve.

Due to its tragic holiday connection, it was an accident that made national headlines (maybe not Santa's head being mounted on the hood of the car). Having Santa get run down a few days before Christmas was a ghoulish media dream come true.

Almost to the day a year later, another tragedy struck just feet from the scene of Santa losing his head (too early?). A young couple traveling under very similar and slippery conditions. The vehicle approached the turn too fast and spun out on ice, striking an oak tree. The young man driving and his lady friend were killed in the accident. It is local folklore that the young lady was thrown from the car and was hanging from the identical branch as the grisly Santa corpse; however, my investigation has not turned up any such supporting evidence. You gotta admit, it does make for a gruesome local tall tale.

After these terrible accidents occurred in the equivalent area close to a year apart, all accidents in this deadly area, and there have been many, have been referred to as "Santa's revenge." Fortunately, no more Santas have run into engine issues on this portion of road since that night.

Now, back to the night in question. As much as I loved my mother, she would inevitably drive me fucking crazy within minutes of my arrival. I would always attempt to visit her with the best of intentions and realize beforehand that she was elderly and suffered from many mental ailments. Most of her problems were related to senile dementia and a plethora of physical issues. The vast amount of her physical ailments were caused by smoking cigarettes. This is not surprising after a lifetime of smoking multiple packs a day. It was a tremendous challenge to maintain a good frame of mind during my visits. It would not take long for me to just nod my head at whatever crazy scenario her brain traveled to. Soon, she'd get into an especially ugly place in her mind, and I'd get pissed off and take my leave. Even in her poor mental state, she still maintained her skill in dishing out guilt as only a mother can.

MEANWHILE, BACK TO THE CURRENT VISION, I PROMISE...

I was traveling toward my mother's residence with the snow blowing left to right. The gusts were blowing my big, powerful Monte Carlo all over the road. I struggled to see the road in front of me; a sign that I almost missed warned of a sharp curve approaching. I soon detected what looked like tail lights a bit further up the road to my left. As I approached the source of these lights, I could see it was a large, dark blue or black panel van that had the name of a church youth group on the side. I believe it was a Baptist church name, but that is neither here nor there.

Anyway, upon exiting my vehicle with the intention of helping, if possible, I carefully trudged through the snow, ice, and bitter wind. I was very concerned about another vehicle coming along, taking the curve too fast, and taking us all out. As I approached the van, I noticed, to my amazement, that it was precariously balanced on the edge of a concrete barrier. The large vehicle had sustained heavy damage to the front end and the passenger side which I could barely see due to the weather. The van had obviously struck this barrier at full speed to be in such a very precarious position. I was already very cold, the wind was biting, and I was trying to contemplate my limited options. I considered leaving to call for help or to remain and do what I could. Since I was not sure who would be open in this awful weather, and how long the emergency services would take to arrive, I carefully approached the driver's side door to see what condition everyone was in and how many were in the vehicle. I continued to constantly check for oncoming traffic, hoping that if anyone did come along, that they would be careful.

Approaching the van's driver's side door, I noticed the driver was a young woman. It was not easy to determine her age, at first glance, as she was covered in blood. Nonetheless, I could tell she was a young woman, and she appeared to be starting to come around from what looked like a nasty head wound. The young lady was wearing a seatbelt; however her head must have still struck the steering wheel pretty hard. She was beginning to mumble, and all I could make out was the word "chills" which she repeated a few times before passing out again. I first thought she was cold due to the windows being broken. However, as I cautiously peered into the back of the van, toward the passenger seats, I saw several children but could not ascertain exactly how many. I then figured out she was trying to say "children", but she was unable to finish the complete word. The driver soon came around again and seemed to gain a bit more lucidity, but not much. She managed to mumble while crying that she had been driving for several hours. She was really lost and could not find the highway due to the abysmal weather. The driver had no idea where they were. The children became impatient, as children do when stuck in a car for several hours. The commotion by the children caused the woman to look behind her, taking her eyes off the road at the worst moment possible. She had approached this curve far too fast, slamming the brakes far too late, thereby causing her vehicle to fishtail on a sheet of ice headlong into the barrier. The woman was trying to look at me as she was speaking, but the blood was running down into her eyes, making it difficult. Most alarmingly, she could not see the extremely dangerous situation she and her passengers were currently in. The van was precariously balanced on a concrete ledge with one side being the safety of solid ground and the other side looming ominously over the partially frozen reservoir.

At that point, not knowing what the hell I was going to do, I backed away carefully after requesting the young lady not to panic, telling her we had to make sure the children kept calm. I reinforcing that it was urgent that the children remain in their seats so as to not shift the weight from the van's dangerous position. It concerned me that the young lady appeared to not grasp a single word I said, because she was looking through me, not at me. I carefully stepped away from the van and took a deep breath. I glanced at my surroundings and again looked toward the road for possible headlights approaching, but failed to see any. I then noticed a solid tree branch a few feet from me. It was approximately 14 feet long and partially leaning against a tree. I went and lifted the piece of wood, carefully checking how solid it was. Soon satisfied of its strength, I placed the branch under the rear fender and, with a great hoist, I managed to tilt the van just enough to tip the vehicle into the abyss below. It struck the water and the thin ice, remaining buoyant for an uncomfortably long time; however, in reality, it was no more than 30 seconds. The church van eventually slipped under the water and produced an amazing amount of bubbles which in a short time vanished. At no point did I decide to do what I did; it was just done.

I stepped back to the road to look for vehicles and, not seeing any, I returned to my car and drove away safely. Somehow early on, I felt as though

I helped. I have no idea why I would think that. Maybe a self-imposed coping mechanism? To this day, I am not proud of what I did, but I do not regret it, either, and, like Gerald, I too sleep like a baby. It is my belief that I was put there at that time and place for a reason. I'm sure most of you are thinking, "Yes, asshole, you could have helped save them". Oh well. As I've heard, opinions are like assholes. Everyone has one.

Anyway, that was about the extent of thought I put into my evening as I drove through the storm on my way home following another frustrating visit with my mother. Upon my safe return home, I was in time to tuck my younger child into bed and I answered his usual questions about monsters in the closet and under the bed. I told him, as gently as I could, that the monsters have gone home to tuck-in their baby monsters, which meant he was safe. I gave him a kiss and went to bed. The irony was not lost on me.

About a week after the incident, while sitting down and enjoying a hearty Sunday breakfast which consisted of a stack of blueberry pancakes smothered in blueberry sauce, I came across an interesting article in the local paper. Most people would have been terrified to realize what they had done, but I read the page three article with undefinable interest. In the article, it stated that a vehicle, which had been missing for several days, was found in the reservoir approximately 25 feet under water. The large church van had been well over 50 miles off course at the time of the accident. Also, the article reported that seven children and one young adult female who was driving had died from drowning in this accident. The incident and subsequent investigation concluded that this tragic accident was due to extreme weather, as well as the driver not being familiar with the dangerously serpentine local roads.

I briefly contemplated, were the bottles, or blockers, as Gerald called them, already pushing this terrible deed I'd performed deep into my subconscious? Was it something simpler than that? Was I just a fucking sociopath, a person without a conscience, empathy, remorse, guilt, or shame? Knowing that conscience is an aptitude and the faculty that helps a person make a moral intuition or judgement, I questioned, "Was it this part of the brain that I was lacking?" Even after considering the possibilities, I determined that I was ok with not knowing these particular answers. All I had was a dim perspective, as if reading that my taxes were going to go up by .001%. In summary, I'd say extreme indifference would be the right term for my actions that night.

In just a few months after my night with the church van, I had completely forgotten about that night - until I arrived at The Last Call. It was at that terrible place that my eyes were opened with the help of that damn mirror. The truly sad part in this is that, even being made aware of this terrible thing I did many years ago, I still don't give a damn about that group of people that I tipped over the edge to their watery deaths. I guess my son is right: there is indeed a monster in our house, but it does not dwell under the bed. It drinks beer and watches the football Giants every Sunday in our living room.

Just before rising from my stool at the bar to head home, I looked at my second bottle of beer that I had barely started and drained it like it was water. I'm not really paying attention, but I do hear Leah loudly exclaim, "Told you bitches he'd finish his second beer", followed by her melodious cackling and accompanying hacking cough.

I placed the bottle down and walked out of the bar, at the same time announcing that I'd see them next week.

EPILOGUE

What became of…

"Behavior is the mirror in which everyone shows their image."

— Johann Wolfgang Von Goethe

The epilogue and the prologue were written at the point of my decision to release the stories I had written many years ago. I would like to take the time to tell you how Leah, Gerald and Ken met their demise, and so will conclude this book with what I will refer to as the "What became of …" portion of the book. Lastly, there are a few other interesting minor characters in this story that I thought the reader of this evening's events might appreciate learning about.

Leah Rose

Also known affectionately as "Wheels", she was a regular frequenter at The Last Call for another year or so after my first visit. As abrasive as she was, I took a liking to her brutal blend of childlike honesty, elderly, crass behaviour, and the odd way she would stick by me when the other cronies were busting my balls for one reason or another. As her disability combined with her diabetes and heavy smoking took its toll, her visits soon decreased to only the occasional visit. The gang went to visit her a couple times when she had to be hospitalized, but her bouts of coughing, followed by the accompanying phlegm made further visits difficult to manage. I know that sounds shallow, but when you combine that with the sight of her stump frequently popping out of her hospital gown, it was just too much for the men to bear. Occasionally, she'd realize that we were, well... grossed out and she'd call us pantywaists or some other equally derogatory name. Somehow, that would make us feel better. Thankfully for her and our collective guilty conscience at not visiting her, she didn't last long. I hope you, the reader, will be happy to hear that Wheels did make it to the picture day, and I stood right beside her. Scott was on the other side just as Gerald had so irritably, although correctly, predicted. Leah Rose smiled from ear to ear, and I gotta say, I saw some of the sparkle in her eyes that had so long ago vanished.

Freddy Flynn - (aka Double F)

During my many conversations with Wheels before she became too ill, the conversation would always begin or end with a story about Double F. Although I'd never met Freddy, I did find his story extremely interesting.

It was soon obvious that this man was a "love-em or hate-em" type of man. It was the side of a transaction you had with him that would determine what side you were on. He could be a Saint one minute while doling out his humorous southern quips, and the next minute, you could be an unexpected organ donor. It was his unique way of speaking that kept his friends and foes off balance. Wheels divulged everything from his shady business deals to his family history. If I had the time (which I don't) or the wherewithal (which I don't), I'd write a book on his family history. Since my time is short, I'll give you the highlights.

The family history begins during the American Civil War, which coincided with a very large amount of Irish immigrants landing on North American shores.

This is where Freddy's great grandfather came into play. His name was Jeremiah Flynn, and like many Irish, he was not opposed to slavery. The Irish didn't want blacks in the paid workplace taking the scarce available jobs for unskilled labor. Many concessions to the Irish were made by The Army of the Potomac (The north) to keep them on their side. Despite these concessions, there were still many Irish immigrants that would fight and die for the southern cause.

It was during this time of growing mistrust within the United States that an Army captain named Thomas Francis Meagher became the Brigadier General of an All-Irish Brigade.

Meagher's story begins at his birth in Ireland, where he grew into an active member of the Young Ireland movement. His involvement in this group was despite his father's pleading. His father's concerns were soon realized when Meagher was exiled to a British Penal colony in Australia for being labeled a traitor to the crown, along with several additional trumped up charges.

Young and very impressionable, Jeremiah would learn during a speech given by this Irish stalwart Meagher that he had escaped Australia and made his way to the United States. Jeremiah was impressed by this young and charismatic Irish leader who had an eloquent way with words and was a well-known activist on behalf of the Irish cause. Jeremiah energetically decided he would follow this man into the gates of hell if asked.

Meagher planned to raise an all-Irish brigade and believed, if he was able to accomplish this, the Northern Army would make him its commander. His assumption was soon proven correct as President Lincoln appointed him the post he desired. It was Meagher's hope that the Irish Division in the Union Army would put Irish citizens on the world stage.

Jeremiah, indeed, followed Meagher into hell as he fought in the Army of the Potomac's biggest battles, such as the battle at Antietam and the Battle at Fredericksburg, where a soldier was known to write: "Irish blood and Irish bones cover that terrible field today and we are slaughtered like sheep".

It would get worse at the Battle of Gettysburg: over 300 of the remaining 500 Irish soldiers died on the field of battle.

It was shortly after Gettysburg that many consider the turning point of the war. It turned out to be the turning point for the All-Irish army, as well. The federal government instituted a National Conscription Act which required every unmarried male between the ages of 21 and 45 to enlist for the draft. A loophole was carved out at the time of the conscription act allowing a man to hire a replacement or pay a $300.00 fee to avoid service. This ability to avoid military service clearly favored the wealthy and left the vast majority of the Irish immigrants exposed to military service. Combining this unequal treatment with the Irish immigrants' lack of opposition to slavery led to a five day riot in New York City in July of 1863. Black people and sympathetic white people were attacked, and black businesses were destroyed, as well as many black homes. Eventually, Federal troops arrived and quelled the hostility.

This riot, for all intent and purpose, ended the all-Irish participation in the Civil War. The Irish Brigade was soon disbanded, and their charismatic leader, General Meagher, would perish in a mysterious drowning a few years later. This General would soon be largely forgotten with the passage of time.

The Flynn family would remain in the south after the war, unlike the majority of the Irish that returned to the north.

This was the beginning of the Flynn's Irish heritage as southern rednecks.

Soon after the war, Jeremiah met a lovely Irish girl named Nora Malone, and together they would have 14 children. The last child was a boy named Killian, which in Gaelic means "war" or "strife". The parents thought it applicable, since the young lad would have 13 older siblings to tangle with in a three room house.

Killian led a surprisingly uneventful life; however, it was he who really embraced the southern way of life, including hating everyone that was not a southern white person and his love of southern cooking. He would always say, "If you ain't a southern white man, you ain't shit". The biggest influence Killian would have on young Fergus would be his preaching that he should be his own boss. He would inform Freddy that his bosses at the mill were incredibly stupid. In his opinion, if he'd been a smarter man, he would have worked for himself.

Killian would say that his boss dished out so much work that he was, "Busy as a one legged cat in a sandbox". He'd also complain when raises were due, saying, "The company squeezed their quarter so tight, the eagle would scream".

One of Freddy's fondest memories was listening to his parents bantering back and forth with some silly arguments while using some quips they had devised to entertain the family:

Mom: "My God, your father is so slow, he doesn't know whether to check his ass or scratch his watch..."

Dad: "Hell, will you ever stop nagging? You'd start an argument in an empty house..."

Mom: Looking at her husband with mock disappointment, "You woulda thought I could have married a better looking man. You're so ugly, you missed the ugly stick, but got whacked by the forest..."

Dad: "You don't think I could have done better? Your mother is so skinny, you can't even see her shadow..."

Mom: "If your father were an inch taller, he'd be round..."

Freddy told Leah that his father always let his mom deliver the last barb. The entire family would be thoroughly entertained from the humorous faux arguments.

As Fergus reached his middle-teenage years, he felt that it was time to leave home and fend for himself. He left his home with very little money and no plan on how to make any. Fergus correctly figured that he had some sense, and between that and his parent's gift of gab, money opportunities would present themselves in due time. He knew if he headed north, he'd make a killing, cuz his father had told him many times that "Yankees do not have the sense God gave a goose".

He soon found himself in the streets of Baltimore planning all manner of scams. It was his intent not to go after the wealthy because they would cry the loudest when they lost their money, drawing the attention of the police. He figured that common, hard-working people didn't mean much to the police or the local politicians. That line of thinking was, for the most part, correct.

Prior to putting his plan in motion, he felt it imperative to change his first name. He figured that "Ferguson" was too ethnic sounding, and "Fergie", as his closest friends were calling him, was not a name that would strike fear into the hearts of other players in the streets.

He wanted a name that would roll off the tongue and also blend into the community. It would not take long to find the name he desired. A local Polish girl who he met at a restaurant on the Baltimore pier had immediately begun calling him Freddy, saying in her thick accent, "I just love the name Freddy". Once he heard the name, he immediately realized the name "Freddy Flynn" was perfect.

Once his new name was chosen and his plans set in motion, it didn't take him long to become heavily involved with the Baltimore underworld. He soon had many illegal methods of making money and a couple legit businesses for money laundering purposes. It was his belief that covering many avenues would protect him if the police got wind of one or more of his scams. If the price was right, he'd do a hit, but that was rare for him. Not because he had some morals by any means, it just was not in his business model. It was his hope to be a big player, but not big enough to draw the attention of the police. The police always knew about Freddy, but there were always bigger fish to fry. This was his common sense approach, which he steadfastly adhered to. I'm sure he would've said, in his unique way, "If common sense was lard, most people wouldn't be able to grease a pan". As far as his plans to stay in the shadows, you might say, "Mission accomplished."

Freddy Flynn was his own boss, and, for that, his father would be proud.

On the day Freddy met Leah, he was sitting in his booth sipping coffee and reading his paper. He noticed a stunningly beautiful young woman — red hair, legs a mile long, and perfect breasts. She reminded him of those female figures on the WWII airplanes. She was so beautiful she looked as if she were drawn.

I remember one time, as she was telling me this story, Ken interrupted and laughingly said, "Every time she tells this story, she becomes more beautiful.

Leah vigorously responded, "My God, that's coming from a man that when he breathes-in his dick disappears," causing Ken to return to his slumped-over defeated position over his beer. He had a slight grin. He knew the shot delivered by Wheels was a good one, and if it had been delivered elsewhere, he'd be laughing his ass off.

When the laughter died down, Wheels would conclude her story...

She went on to say that, after the first awkward meeting at his booth, the two of them would have many conversations in the diner when things got slow. "Freddy always told me that he'd be able to get me into some serious and fast money cuz I was, 'Finer than frog hair split eight ways!'"

By this stage in the story, like clockwork, Baxter would stand-up, fart loudly, and sit back down.

Wheels, looking mildly agitated and rolling her eyes, continued her story. She had known that Freddy worked in some shady businesses and assumed he meant that she'd be a prostitute. Sadly, it was accurate, but you already know that from the visions.

Baxter stood up again, looked to be trying to fart for a moment, then said, "Nope, got nothing to add," and sat back down.

"You gonna let me tell this story or not?" Leah hollered.

Using his best fake southern accent, Baxter said, "Oh, by all means, please do continue Ms. Rose".

Taking a deep breath, she continued. "All in all, I think he meant to help me. It's not his fault I got hooked on drugs and screwed up my life". The animosity toward men that she harbored in the visions no longer seemed apparent, and, if I didn't know any better, I'd say she was more comfortable with men than women.

Without fail, the story would end with her saying, "Freddy died fucking one of his gold-digging girlfriends". The story would end inevitably when she'd request a beer in a not-so-ladylike manner.

Ken

The man with the beautiful, toothless smile met his untimely demise while working on his beloved tractor. It was about a year or so after Wheel's unfortunate demise.

He had set up the vehicle on four jerry-rigged jacks to lift the vehicle to gain better access under the tractor. As you may recall, the carport was outside, and, although it was covered, the ground was always wet. While working on the wet grass in the carport, one of the jacks slipped, and he was crushed to death by the full weight of his vehicle. I have no doubt that, as quick as his death was, it was equally as agonizing.

Summing up Ken's life, the only redeeming traits about him were his work ethic and his garage. I did learn that his funeral was very well attended, which surprised me greatly. I will, however, bet that there was not a dentist to be found.

Gerald

The bartender, Gerald, who we now know as the Zodiac, had unforeseen depths. On the surface, he was unimpressive at best. If you get past the first impression, he's not what you'd expect. The man is highly intelligent, eluding a national manhunt, and had the wherewithal to leave fake clues, causing the police and media to put their focus on red herrings. He was a leader of a very dangerous group of people and one of the few individuals trusted with the role of "Keeper of the mirror". All these attributes are what made him one of the most famous serial killers of all time. I think he'd be the first to say that luck had a big part of his success, as well.

The Zodiac was head-long into a deep decline when I first entered his establishment. I would soon learn the extent of his health issues after a few more visits. From what I'd learned, most of his health concerns revolved around the vast amount of alcohol he was consuming. It was a vicious cycle. He was drinking away his profits, which in turn increased his depression, causing him to drink further to drown his sorrows. Well, that's my uneducated theory, anyway.

It was a year or two after Leah had wheeled herself into the sunset that Gerald's drinking escalated to where he began suffering from frequent blackouts. The end came for Gerald when, one evening, a gentleman entered the bar for a quick respite. The flashing didn't affect him, which meant the guy was normal, for lack of a better term. It's not known whether or not he knew this, but Gerald, in his deeply inebriated state, began to tell the newcomer the story of the mirror and that he was the infamous Zodiac and what we all had in common. The customer took the information well, which likely saved his life. He sat politely and listened to the story as if it were from a senile grandparent or a drunken lunatic, the latter of which was very close to the truth. I approached this man once Gerald finally shut the hell up to deliver a beer to another patron. I simply stated to the newcomer, "Last week he thought he was former president Nixon". The man politely laughed and said he understood Gerald's condition, but it sure was an amusing story. I said, "Oh, come again next week; he'll be the Queen of England" to which we shared another good chuckle, and the rest of the regulars breathed easier. After all, "Who in their right minds would believe a story from a drunk about killers hanging out in a bar with a magic mirror?"

Very soon afterward, the gentleman took his leave with a happy wave because we had paid for his two beers (even drunk off his ass, Gerald made him drink the two beer minimum). Knowing we were all at risk with Gerald's behavior, we waited for him to pass out. Then we drew straws. I still find it amusing that a room full of killers resorted to the drawing of straws. It was agreed that the loser would arrange an accident for Gerald that evening. It was distressing for two reasons. One, someone was going to commit a murder which, no matter how well planned, still carries risks. Two, what would happen to the bar and its all-knowing, evil-detecting mirror?

We drew the straws, and fuck if you know it, I won, or lost, depending on how you look at it, I guess.

The simple plan that I followed to the letter was for me to take Gerald home in his latest drunken stupor. I find it strange that the only guilt I've ever really felt was the fact that our plan for Gerald was being conducted with him passed out not two feet from our spot at the bar. Anyway, I drove Gerald's vehicle with him in a near coma in the passenger seat (which I found humorously ironic). I wanted to loudly exclaim, "Look who's driving now, bitch", but I didn't. As we entered his driveway and drew close the garage, I put the vehicle in park, climbed out to lift the garage door, and returned to drive the vehicle into the garage. I then turned the ignition off. It was time to put our plans into action.

I didn't wipe my prints because Gerald had been driven home before, and different prints would not be suspicious. We had a lengthy debate on this aspect of our plan, but to cut to the chase, we felt that if the steering wheel was completely clean of any prints, the cops would have reason to suspect foul play.

I exited the vehicle, went around to the other side, and pushed Gerald over to the driver's side. Surprisingly, he woke just long enough to help me move him over, then passed out again. I placed his hands on the wheel but didn't care when they fell down. The important matter was that the hands would drop normally from the wheel into a natural position on his lap.

I closed the passenger door and stood for a moment to contemplate if I'd overlooked something or forgotten part of the plan. Realizing I'd done well, I reached into the open driver's side window and turned the ignition on, re-starting the vehicle. I closed the garage door and waited for Baxter to pick me up at the agreed upon time. It only took a few minutes to return to the bar's parking lot. We entered the bar again to have a nightcap and to toast the man we knew as the one and only Zodiac. After our toast, we took bets on how long it would take for our friend to be found. Once the bets were taken, we locked up for Gerald. After all, we're not savages.

The winner of our bet ended up being Baxter. He chose 20 days, being the closest to the actual time of three weeks. Gerald's body was found when a neighbor had entered his garage to borrow his lawnmower. I deliberate to this day how long it would have taken if Gerald's neighbor had his own mower.

The local police and homicide detectives ran a cursory investigation and concluded, as we had hoped, that, in his condition, he most likely committed suicide due to his failing business. We were all interviewed by the police as we knew we would be, but the police bought our explanations as there was no plausible motive or signs of foul play.

Jess

On that first day Jess met Leah Rose in the hospital, Jess was roughly 60 years old.

The mirror didn't reveal much about her past. But it did offer extensive information for the time period in which she was a part of Wheel's life.

Jess was a portly woman that stood no taller than 5'1" or so. She weighed well over 200 pounds and had the appearance of a dowdy English matron. She had shoulder-length, straight, dishwater-blonde hair, a large wide nose, and a mouth that was filled with what I'd call layered brown teeth. The mirror made it clear that her eyes revealed her true, menacing character. They were penetrating and always seemed to be looking through you and rarely at you. If that were not enough to be drawn to her eyes, there was a large mole on the corner of her left eye which was so ugly, you couldn't help but look. Her arms and legs were very short and thick. I would summarize her looks as that of a human English bulldog.

Aside from her piercing eyes and her oddly layered teeth, she was far from physically intimidating. What she did have in spades were connections to a wide variety of men to do her bidding.

Legend has it that she obtained most of her henchmen in an interesting manner. When Jess heard of a single mother who had a very strong son with a tendency toward violence, she would help that mother financially without requesting the woman to prostitute herself, thus indirectly obtaining the loyalty of the woman's son. What didn't hurt, also, was that she'd pay that young man very well and, more often than not, would pay for bail when needed. This earned the unquestioned loyalty of these men. She was a woman not to be trifled with.

It was a few years after Wheels had been working for Jess in her agency when the Jackal began to slow down and loosened her grip on her business. In any city, a person running this type of business that shows a weakness will soon be "out of business", or worse, out of a life.

Jess getting rubbed out

The mirror did provide an ESP moment regarding the evening in question, Jess had traveled to her family's home for Thanksgiving dinner, as she did every year. Once the meal was consumed, the family retired to the living room to watch the football game and to let their stomachs settle before returning for dessert. They sat in their chairs with belts loosened, watching the game, when, suddenly, every window exploded inward from a massive hail of bullets. After what seemed like forever, but was only a moment, the bullets stopped, and Jess looked around to take stock of the situation. She could see, easily, that many family members were hit, and a few appeared to be dead. As she tried to make sense of the situation, the front and back doors were smashed inward. Several masked men came in from both directions toting shotguns. It was immediately obvious to Jess who was in charge. As the ringleader entered through the doorway, the gun-fire smoke gave him the appearance of being supernatural, and it looked as if he were walking in slow motion. This man was very tall, but that may have been due to the fact that Jess was lying on the floor as he entered.

She also noticed that the intruder had a thick body, thick legs, thick shoulders, and thick arms, as well. He handled the shotgun like it was a child's toy. As he drew closer through the haze, he shot every person in his path, whether they showed signs of life or not. Once he reached her, he simply said, "Happy Thanksgiving", and promptly shot her in the head. Each of the killers that had entered the house took a dessert from the dining room table upon their departure.

Detective Uliasz

This Detective was of Polish heritage, and before you struggle with his name, it is pronounced as - "u-lee-iss". He would always introduce himself as "Name is Detective Uliasz, last name Uliasz, first name, Detective".

In his 30 year career, he expeditiously climbed the law enforcement career ladder using his critical thinking skills and his attention to detail to reach, ultimately, homicide detective. It was his writing skills and ability to communicate at the appropriate level of the listener that set him apart from his fellow officers. Also, his ability to write a report was legendary. It was said by his Captain of over 20 years that "Detective Uliasz writes a great report, says everything required and, when I've finished perusing it, I feel thoroughly entertained."

During his distinguished career, he'd had many successful cases and received several medals and accommodations.

It was at the very end of his career when he had his run-ins with Leah Rose. He was close to retirement and to say the thrill of the chase was missing in his life would be an understatement. This was evident to his fellow officers because he would mention retirement in Florida within every conversation. If that were not enough to clue you in about his motivation, his savvy report writing was a thing of the past. Simply put, he was tired and he just didn't give a shit anymore.

Cancel Retirement

Detective Uliasz and his wife were very close to their retirements and their pending move to Florida when his best friend and fellow detective passed away. The death was quite the story, according to all the papers. The seasoned detective died in the line of duty while in pursuit of a dangerous armed felon. The mirror knew better and gave me the true story.

Let's start with what was correct in the story; it won't take long: The detective's name, age, years in the force, and cause of death. That didn't take long did it? Detective Johnson had just entered a small mom-and-pop convenience store for some beer after his shift. As this newspaper-enshrined hero waited his turn in line, he observed a young man display his goods to an elderly woman. Responding to the situation, he attempted to apprehend the flasher in the store. The young man, not being overly burdened with extra weight, such as pants or underwear, easily avoided the near-retirement-age detective, running out the front entrance. The chase of this dangerous felon lasted less than a city block, where the detective fell to his death.

Serving as a pallbearer at Detective Johnson's funeral service, Detective Uliasz misstepped on a portion of the sidewalk where the seams didn't line up properly. The stumble took place as the casket was just a few yards away from the hearse. He was unable to recover and began to fall to the ground. With the sudden shift in weight, the other pallbearers lost their balance and their grip as well. While Detective Uliasz attempted to maintain his hold on the casket, the others let go of the casket rails. It fell downward, and the corner of the casket landed with its full weight on the detective's head. He died instantly.

Once the ambulance arrived and took the detective away, it was promptly decided that the military style funeral would continue since hundreds of officers and their families were in attendance and waiting at the grave site. In addition to the large turnout of police officers attending, the funeral was widely attended by many political leaders, judges, and union representatives. The only deviation from the original schedule of events at this funeral was an extra round of rifle salutes requested by the widow to honor the tragic death of Detective Uliasz. Needless to say, an already sad occasion was elevated to an extremely somber event.

Just a few days later, Detective Uliasz's funeral would take place, and, since his death was of such an odd manner, it was thought best by his family to keep it limited to just themselves and close friends.

The detective's son, keeping in mind the extremely odd and tragic manner of his father's death, kept his speech short and amusing, saying, "My father would want it this way".

He began, "My name is Joe Uliasz. As you know, my father and Detective Johnson were very close friends. I can recall numerous picnics with our families, and it would be inevitable that Detective Johnson and my father would get into something competitive. It might be whiffle-ball, bocce, lawn darts; you name it, they played it. The loser of the event would get an all-day, humorous razzing. What I fondly recall was that, when the two of them would start to argue about whose family was better at something, both families would make themselves scarce" (light laughter from the immediate families). As the short eulogy was headed toward closure, the detective's son attempted one last bit of humor when he mentioned that his father and Detective Johnson had a long standing bet on who would meet St. Peter first. "Dad would be upset that Detective Johnson got the drop on him". The joke, whether appropriate or not, resulted in subdued and stifled laughter. As the speaker was working toward his conclusion, he stated, "Friendship is measured by sharing your life and facing all of life's surprises together. These two men had a great friendship". Finally, concluding his eulogy with another shot of humor, whether it was proper or not, "I can picture my father showing up at the gates of heaven, welcomed by Detective Johnson, who immediately forgoes pleasantries and belts out another challenge, "Wanna bet whose wife remarries first?"

Baxter made a comeback, Scott, Mr. Trivia as well as yours truly continued to have interesting stories after my first evening visiting The Last Call. As I'm sure you understand, the stories I've told are only up to the evening of my first visit. Anything these people did afterward is locked in the mirror and the hearts of like-minded souls.

If the Big C permits, I will follow-up with information on Baxter, Scott and Mr. Trivia, as well as our updated theories and an amazing discovery about the mirror. I'm also happy to announce that we have a new female patron that our mirror has brought to The Last Call. Wheels would be so proud.

See you on the other side.

ACKNOWLEDGMENTS

My wife - for not laughing at me when I told her I'd be writing a book, and proofreading

My son - for being a scout and a great kid

Shelly Love - for sharing her knowledge of hot wiring a motor vehicle.

Blake Bugay - for his assistance with car related information.

Bill Uliasz - for being with me while driving home during a winter storm at the moment the book idea struck.

Tom Sommerfield - for discussing information relating to psychological aspects of the human mind.

My disturbed imagination.

And last but not least...

Zodiac (if you're out there, give me a call, preferably long distance)